The Lady of the Mount

By

Frederic Stewart Isham

THE LADY OF THE MOUNT

CHAPTER I

A CHANCE ENCOUNTER

"Don't you know, boy, you ought not to get in my way?"

The tide was at its ebb; the boats stranded afar, and the lad addressed had started, with a fish—his wage—in one hand, to walk to shore, when, passing into the shadow of the rampart of the Governor's Mount, from the opposite direction a white horse swung suddenly around a corner of the stone masonry and bore directly upon him. He had but time to step aside; as it was, the animal grazed his shoulder, and the boy, about to give utterance to a natural remonstrance, lifted his eyes to the offender. The words were not forthcoming; surprised, he gazed at a tiny girl, of about eleven, perched fairy-like on the broad back of the heavy steed.

"Don't you know you ought not to get in my way?" she repeated imperiously.

The boy, tall, dark, unkempt as a young savage, shifted awkwardly; his black eyes, restless enough ordinarily, expressed a sudden shyness in the presence of this unexpected and dainty creature.

"I—didn't see you," he half stammered.

"Well, you should have!" And again the little lady frowned, shook her disordered golden curls disapprovingly and gazed at him, a look of censure in her brown eyes. "But perhaps you don't know who I am," she went on with a lift of the patrician doll-like features. "I don't think you do, or you wouldn't stand there like a booby, without taking off your hat." More embarrassed, he removed a worn cap while she continued to regard him with the reverse of approval. "I am the Comtesse Elise," she observed; "the daughter of the Governor of the Mount."

"Oh!" said the boy, and his glance shifted to the most important and insistent feature of the landscape.

Carrying its clustered burden of houses and palaces, a great rock reared itself from the monotony of the bare and blinding sands. Now an oasis in the desert, ere night was over he knew the in-rushing waters would convert it into an island; claim it for the sea! A strange kingdom, yet a mighty one, it belonged alternately to the land and to the ocean. With the sky, however, it enjoyed perpetual affiliation, for the heavens were ever wooing it; now winding pretty ribbons of light about its air-drawn castles; then kissing it with the tender, soft red glow of celestial fervor.

"Yes; I live right on top among the clouds, in a castle, with dungeons underneath, where my father puts the bad people who don't like the nobles and King Louis XVI. But where," categorically, "do you live?"

His gaze turned from the points and turrets and the clouds she spoke of—that seemed to linger about the lofty summit—to the mainland, perhaps a mile distant.

"There!" he said, and specifically indicated a dark fringe, like a cloud on the lowlands.

"In the woods! How odd!" She looked at him with faint interest. "And don't the bears bother you? Once when I wanted to see what the woods were like, my nurse told me they were filled with terrible bears who would eat up little girls. I don't have a nurse any more," irrelevantly, "only a governess who came from the court of Versailles, and Beppo. Do you know Beppo?"

"No."

"I don't like him," she confided. "He is always listening. But why do you live in the woods?"

"Because!" The reason failed him.

"And didn't you ever live anywhere else?"

A shadow crossed the dark young face. "Once," he said.

"I suppose the bears know you," she speculated, "and that is the reason they let you alone. Or, perhaps, they are like the wolf in the fairy-tale. Did you ever hear of the kind-hearted wolf?"

He shook his head.

"My nurse used to tell it to me. Well, once there was a boy who was an orphan and everybody hated him. So he went to live in the forest and there he met a wolf. 'Where are you going, little boy?' said the wolf. 'Nowhere,' said the boy; 'I have no home.' 'No home!' said the kind-hearted wolf; 'then come with me, and you shall share my cave.' Isn't that a nice story?"

He looked at her in a puzzled manner. "I don't know," he began, when she tossed her head.

"What a stupid boy!" she exclaimed severely. A moment she studied him tentatively through her curls, from the vantage point of her elevated seat. "That's a big fish," she remarked, after the pause.

"Do you want it?" he asked quickly, his face brightening.

"You can give it to Beppo when he comes," she said, drawing herself up loftily. "He'll be here soon. I've run away from him!" A sudden smile replaced her brief assumption of dignity. "He'll be so angry! He's fat and ugly," more confidentially. "And he's so amusing when he's vexed! But how much do you ask for the fish?"

"I didn't mean—to sell it!"

"Why not?"

"I—don't sell fish."

"Don't sell fish!" She looked at the clothes, frayed and worn, the bare muscular throat, the sunburned legs. "You meant to give it to me?"

"Yes."

The girl laughed. "What a funny boy!"

His cheek flushed; from beneath the matted hair, the disconcerted black eyes met the mocking brown ones.

"Of course I can't take it for nothing," she explained, "and it is very absurd of you to expect it."

"Then," with sudden stubbornness, "I will keep it!"

Her glance grew more severe. "Most people speak to me as 'my Lady.' You seem to have forgotten. Or perhaps you have been listening to some of those silly persons who talk about everybody being born equal. I've heard my father, the Governor, speak of them and how he has put some of them in his dungeons. You'd better not talk that way, or he may shut you up in some terrible dark hole beneath the castle."

"I'm not afraid!" The black eyes shone.

"Then you must be a very wicked boy. It would serve you right if I was to tell."

"You can!"

"Then I won't! Besides, I'm not a telltale!" She tossed her curls and went on. "I've heard my father say these people who want to be called 'gentilhomme' and 'monsieur' are low and ignorant; they can't even read and write."

Again the red hue mantled the boy's cheek. "I don't believe you can!" she exclaimed shrewdly and clapped her hands. "Can you now?" He did not answer. "'Monsieur'! 'Gentilhomme'!" she repeated.

He stepped closer, his face dark; but whatever reply he might have made was interrupted by the sound of a horse's hoofs and the abrupt appearance, from the direction the child had come, of a fat, irascible-looking man of middle age, dressed in livery.

"Oh, here you are, my Lady!" His tone was far from amiable; as he spoke he pulled up his horse with a vicious jerk. "A pretty chase you've led me!"

She regarded him indifferently. "If you will stop at the inn, Beppo—"

The man's irate glance fell. "Who is this?"

"A boy who doesn't want to sell his fish," said the girl merrily.

"Oh!" The man's look expressed a quick recognition. "A fine day's work is this—to bandy words with—" Abruptly he raised his whip. "What do you mean, sirrah, by stopping my Lady?"

A fierce gleam in the lad's eyes belied the smile on his lips. "Don't beat me, good Beppo!" he said in a mocking voice, and stood, alert, lithe, like a tiger ready to spring. The man hesitated; his arm dropped to his side. "The very spot!" he said, looking around him.

A moment the boy waited, then turned on his heel and, without a word, walked away. Soon an angle in the sea-wall, girdling the Mount, hid him from view.

"Why didn't you strike him?" Quietly the child regarded the man. "Were you afraid?" Beppo's answering look was not one of affection for his charge. "Who is he?"

"An idle vagabond."

"What is his name?"

"I don't know."

"Don't you?"

A queer expression sprang into his eyes. "One can't remember every peasant brat," he returned evasively.

She considered him silently; then: "Why did you say: 'The very spot'?" she asked.

"Did I? I don't remember. But it's time we were getting back. Come, my Lady!" And Beppo struck his horse smartly.

CHAPTER II

AN ECHO OF THE PAST

Immovable on its granite base, the great rock, or "Mount," as it had been called for centuries, stood some distance from the shore in a vast bay on the northwestern coast of France. To the right, a sweep of sward and marsh stretched seaward, until lost in the distance; to the left, lay the dense Desaurac forest, from which an arm of land, thickly wooded, reached out in seeming endeavor to divide the large bay into two smaller basins. But the ocean, jealous of territory already conquered, twice in twenty-four hours rose to beat heavily on this dark promontory, and, in the angry hiss of the waters, was a reminder of a persistent purpose. Here and there, through the ages, had the shore-line of the bay, as well as the neighboring curvatures of the coast, yielded to the assaults of the sea; the Mount alone, solidly indifferent to blandishment or attack, maintained an unvarying aspect.

For centuries a monastery and fortress of the monks, at the time of Louis XVI the Mount had become a stronghold of the government, strongly ruled by one of its most inexorable nobles. Since his appointment many years before to the post, my lord, the Governor of the rock, had ever been regarded as a man who conceded nothing to the people and pursued only the set tenure of his way. During the long period of his reign he committed but one indiscretion; generally regarded as a man confirmed in apathy for the gentler sex, he suddenly, when already past middle age, wedded. Speculation concerning a step so unlooked for was naturally rife.

In hovel and hut was it whispered the bride Claire, only daughter of the Comtesse de la Mart, had wept at the altar, but that her mother had appeared complacent, as well she might; for the Governor of the Mount and the surrounding country was both rich and powerful; his ships swept far and wide, even to the Orient, while the number of métayers, or petty farmers that paid him tribute, constituted a large community. Other gossips, bending over peat fires within mud walls, affirmed—beneath their breath, lest the spies of the well-hated lord of the North might hear them!—that the more popular, though impoverished Seigneur Desaurac had been the favored suitor with the young woman herself, but that the family of the bride had found him undesirable. The Desaurac fortune, once large, had so waned that little remained save the rich, though heavily encumbered lands, and, in the heart of the forest, a time-worn, crumbling castle.

Thus it came to pass the marriage of the lady to the Governor was celebrated in the jeweled Gothic church crowning a medley of palaces, chapels and monastery on the Mount; that the rejected Seigneur Desaurac, gazing across the strip of water—for the tide was at its full—separating the rocky fortress from the land, shrugged his shoulders angrily and contemptuously, and that not many moons later, as if to show disdain of position and title, took to his home an orphaned peasant lass. That a simple church ceremony had preceded this step was both affirmed and denied; hearsay described a marriage at a neighboring village; more malicious gossip discredited it. A man of rank! A woman of the soil! Feudal custom forbade belief that the proper sort of nuptial knot had been tied.

Be this as it may, for a time the sturdy, dark brown young woman presided over the Seigneur's fortunes with exemplary care and patience. She found them in a chaotic condition; lands had either been allowed to run to waste, or were cultivated by peasants that so long had forgotten to pay the métayage, or owner's due, they had come to regard the acres as their own— a delusion this practical helpmate would speedily have dispelled, save that the Seigneur himself pleaded for them and would not permit of the "poor people" being disturbed. Whereupon she made the best of an anomalous situation, and all concerned might have continued to live satisfactorily enough unto themselves, when unfortunately an abrupt break occurred in the chain of circumstances. In presenting the Seigneur with a child, half-peasant, half-lord, the mother gave up her own life for his posterity.

At first, thereafter, the Seigneur remained a recluse; when, however, a year or two had gone by, the peasants—who had settled in greater numbers thereabouts, even to the verge of the forest—noticed that he gradually emerged from his solitude, ventured into the world at large, and occasionally was seen in the vicinity of the Mount. This predilection for lonely walks clearly led to his undoing; one morning he was found stabbed in the back, on the beach at the foot of the Mount.

Carried home, he related how he had been set upon by a band of miscreants, which later, coming to the Governor's ears, led to an attempt to locate the assailants among the rocky isles to the northwest, haunts of privateersmen, rogues and those reformers who already were beginning to undermine the peace of Louis XVI's northern provinces. In the pursuit of these gentry, the Governor showed himself in earnest. Perhaps his own sorrow at the rather sudden death of his lady, occurring about this time, and leaving him, a morose widower, with a child, a little girl, led him to more relentless activities; perhaps the character of the crime—a noble stabbed!— incensed him.

Certainly he revenged himself to the full; not only raked the rocks for runagates, but dragged peasants, inclined to sullenness, from their huts; clapped some in dungeons and hanged the rest. In the popular mind his name became synonymous with cruelty, but, on his high throne, he continued to exercise his autocratic prerogative and cared not what the people thought.

Meanwhile, the Seigneur Desaurac, recovering, became a prey to greater restlessness; no sooner was he able to get about, than, accompanied by a faithful servant, Sanchez, he left the neighborhood, and, for a number of years, led a migratory existence in continental capitals. The revolt of the colonies in America and the news of the contemplated departure of the brave Lafayette for the seat of hostilities, offered, at least, a pretext to break the fetters of a purposeless life. At once, he placed his sword at Lafayette's disposal, and packed himself and servitor—a fellow of dog-like fidelity—across the ocean. There, at the seat of war's alarms, in the great conflict waged in the name of liberty, he met a soldier's end, far from the fief of his ancestors. Sanchez, the man, buried him, and, having dutifully performed this last task, walked away from the grave and out of the army.

During this while, the son by the peasant woman, intrusted to an old fishwife who had been allowed to usurp a patch of his father's lands, received scanty care and attention, even when the stipulated fees for his maintenance had continued to come; but when, at the Seigneur's death, they ceased, any slight solicitude on the caretaker's part soured to acrimony. An offspring of dubious parentage, she begrudged him his bread; kept him from her own precious brood, and taught them to address him as "brat," "pauper," or by terms even more forcible. Thus set upon, frequently he fought; but like young wolves, hunting in packs, they worried him to the earth, and, when he continued to struggle, beat him to unconsciousness, if not submission.

One day, after such an experience at the hands of those who had partaken of the Seigneur's liberality, the boy, all bruised and aching, fled to the woods, and, with the instinct of an animal to hide, buried himself in its deepest recesses. Night came; encompassed by strange sounds, unknown terrors, he crept to the verge of the forest, and lying there, looked out across the distance toward the scattered habitations, visible through the gloom. One tiny yellow dot of light which he located held his glance. Should he return? That small stone hut, squalid as it was, had been his only remembered home. But the thought of the reception that awaited him there made him hesitate; the stars coming out, seemed to lend courage to his resolution, and, with his face yet turned toward the low long strip of land, sprinkled with the faint, receding points of light, he fell asleep.

The earliest shafts of morn, however, awaking him, sent him quickly back into the dark forest, where all day he kept to the most shadowy screens and covers, fearing he should be followed, and, perhaps, captured. But the second night was like the first, the next like the second, and the days continued to pass with no signs of pursuit. Pinched by hunger, certain of the berries and roots he ate poisoned him, until in time he profited by his sufferings and learned to discriminate in his choice of the frugal fare about him. Not that his appetite was ever satisfied, even when he extended his explorations to the beach at night, digging in the sand with his fingers for cockles, or prowling about the rocks for mussels.

Yet, despite all, he hugged to his breast a compensating sense of liberty; the biting tooth of autumn was preferable to the stripes and tongue-lashings of the old life; and, if now frugal repasts were the rule, hunger had often been his lot in the past. So he assimilated with his surroundings; learned not to fear the animals, and they, to know him; indeed, they seemed to recognize him by that sharp unsated glint of the eye as one of their kind. When the days grew bleaker and the nights colder, he took refuge in a corner within the gray walls of the moss-grown castle of his ancestors, the old Seigneurs. No cheerful place, above all at night, when the spirits of the dead seem to walk abroad, and sobs, moans, and fierce voices fill the air! Then, creeping closer to the fire he had started in the giant hearth, wide-eyed he would listen, only at length through sheer weariness to fall asleep. Nevertheless, it was a shelter, and here, throughout the winter, the boy remained.

Here, too, Sanchez, the Seigneur's old servant, returning months later from long wanderings to the vicinity of the Mount—for no especial reason, save the desire once more to see the place—had found him. And at the sight the man frowned.

In the later days, the Seigneur Desaurac had become somewhat unmindful, if not forgetful, of his own flesh and blood. It may be that the absorbing character of the large and chivalrous motives that animated him left little disposition or leisure for private concerns; at any rate, he seemed seldom to have thought, much less spoken of, that "hostage of fortune" he had left behind; an absent-mindedness that in no wise surprised the servant— which, indeed, met the man's full, unspoken approval! The Seigneur, his master, was a nobleman of untarnished ancestry, to be followed and served; the son—Sanchez had never forgiven the mother her low-born extraction. He was, himself, a peasant!

CHAPTER III

A SUDDEN RESOLUTION

After his chance encounter with my lady, the Governor's daughter, and Beppo, her attendant, the boy walked quickly from the Mount to the forest. His eyes were still bright; his cheeks yet burned, but occasionally the shadow of a smile played about his mouth, and he threw up his head fiercely. At the verge of the wood he looked back, stood for a moment with the reflection of light on his face, then plunged into the shadows of the sylvan labyrinth. Near the east door of the castle, which presently he reached, he stopped for an armful of faggots, and, bending under his load, passed through an entrance, seared and battered, across a great roofless space and up a flight of steps to a room that had once been the kitchen of the vast establishment. As he entered, a man, thin, wizened, though active looking, turned around.

"So you've got back?" he said in a grumbling tone.

"Yes," answered the boy good-naturedly, casting the wood to the flagging near the flame and brushing his coat with his hand; "the storm kept us out last night, Sanchez."

"It'll keep you out for good some day," remarked the man. "You'll be drowned, if you don't have a care."

"Better that than being hanged!" returned the lad lightly.

The other's response, beneath his breath, was lost, as he drew his stool closer to the pot above the blaze, removed the lid and peered within. Apparently his survey was not satisfactory, for he replaced the cover, clasped his fingers over his knees and half closed his eyes.

"Where's the fish?"

The boy, thoughtfully regarding the flames, started; when he had left the child and Beppo, unconsciously he had dropped it, but this he did not now explain. "I didn't bring one."

"Didn't bring one?"

"No," said the boy, flushing slightly.

"And not a bone or scrap in the larder! Niggardly fishermen! A small enough wage—for going to sea and helping them—"

"Oh, I could have had what I wanted. And they are not niggardly! Only—I forgot."

"Forgot!" The man lifted his hands, but any further evidence of surprise or expostulation was interrupted by a sudden ebullition in the pot.

Left to his thoughts, the boy stepped to the window; for some time stood motionless, gazing through a forest rift at the end of which uprose the top of an Aladdin-like structure, by an optical illusion become a part of that locality; a conjuror's castle in the wood!

"The Mount looks near to-night, Sanchez!"

"Near?" The man took from its hook the pot and set it on the table. "Not too near to suit the Governor, perhaps!"

"And why should it suit him?" drawing a stool to the table and sitting down.

"Because he must be so fond of looking at the forest."

"And does that—please him?"

"How could it fail to? Isn't it a nice wood? Oh, yes, I'll warrant you he finds it to his liking. And all the lands about the forest that used to belong to the old Seigneurs, and which the peasants have taken—waste lands they have tilled—he must think them very fine to look at, now! And what a hubbub there would be, if the lazy peasants had to pay their métayage, and fire-tax and road-tax—and all the other taxes—the way the other peasants do—to him—"

"What do you mean?"

"Nothing!" The man's jaw closed like a steel trap. "The porridge is burned."

And with no further word the meal proceeded. The man, first to finish, lighted his pipe, moved again to the fire, and, maintaining a taciturnity that had become more or less habitual, stolidly devoted himself to the solace of the weed and the companionship of his own reflections. Once or twice the boy seemed about to speak and did not; finally, however, he leaned forward, a more resolute light in his sparkling black eyes.

"You never learned to read, Sanchez?"

At the unexpected question, the smoke puffed suddenly from the man's lips. "Not I."

"Nor write?"

The man made a rough gesture. "Nor sail to the moon!" he returned derisively. "Read? Rubbish! Write? What for? Does it bring more fish to your nets?"

"Who—could show me how to read and write?"

"You?" Sanchez stared.

"Why not?"

"Books are the tools of the devil!" declared Sanchez shortly. "There was a black man here to-day with a paper—a 'writ,' I think he called it—or a 'service' of some kind—anyhow, it must have been in Latin," violently, "for such gibberish, I never heard and—"

The boy rose. "People who can't read and write are low and ignorant!"

"Eh? What's come over you?"

"My father was a gentleman."

"Your father!—yes—"

"And a Seigneur!—"

"A Seigneur truly!"

"And I mean to be one!" said the boy suddenly, closing his fists.

"Oh, oh! So that's it?" derisively. "You! A Seigneur? Whose mother—"

"Who could teach me?" Determined, but with a trace of color on his brown cheek, the boy looked down.

"Who?" The man began to recover from his surprise. "That's not so easy to tell. But if you must know—well, there's Gabriel Gabarie, for one, a poet of the people. He might do it—although there's talk of cutting off his head—"

"What for?"

"For knowing how to write."

The lad reached for his hat.

"Where are you going?"

"To the poet's."

"At this late hour! You are in a hurry!"

"If what you say is true, there's no time to lose."

"Well, if you find him writing verses about liberty and equality, don't interrupt him, or you'll lose your head," shouted the man.

But when the sound of the boy's footsteps had ceased, Sanchez's expression changed; more bent, more worn, he got up and walked slowly to and fro. "A fine Seigneur!" The moldering walls seemed to echo the words. "A fine Seigneur!" he muttered, and again sat brooding by the fire.

In the gathering dusk the lad strode briskly on. A squirrel barked to the right; he did not look around. A partridge drummed to the left; usually alert to wood sound or life, to-night he did not heed it. But, fairly out of the forest and making his way with the same air of resolution across the sands toward the lowland beyond, his attention, on a sudden, became forcibly diverted. He had but half completed the distance from the place where he had left the wood to the objective point in the curvature of the shore, when to the left through the gloom, a great vehicle, drawn by six horses, could be seen rapidly approaching. From the imposing equipage gleamed many lamps; the moon, which ere this had begun to assert its place in the heavens, made bright the shining harness and shone on the polished surface of the golden car. Wondering, the boy paused.

"What is that?"

The person addressed, a fisherman belated, bending to the burden on his shoulders, stopped, and, breathing hard, looked around and watched the approaching vehicle intently.

"The Governor's carriage!" he said. "Haven't you ever heard of the Governor's carriage?"

"No."

"That's because he hasn't used it lately; but in her ladyship's day—"

"Her ladyship?"

"The Governor's lady—he bought it for her. But she soon got tired of it—or perhaps didn't like the way the people looked at her!" roughly. "Mon dieu! perhaps they did scowl a little—for it didn't please them, I can tell you!—the sight of all that gold squeezed from the taxes!"

"Where is he going now?"

"Nowhere himself—he never goes far from the Mount. But the Lady Elise, his daughter—some one in the village was saying she was going to Paris—"

"Paris!" The lad repeated the word quickly. "What for?"

"What do all the great lords and nobles send their children there for? To get educated—married, and—to learn the tricks of the court! Bah!" With a coarse laugh the man turned; stooping beneath his load, he moved grumblingly on.

The boy, however, did not stir; as in a dream he looked first at the Mount, a dark triangle against the sky, then at the carriage. Nearer the latter drew, was about to dash by, when suddenly the driver, on his high seat, uttered an exclamation and at the same time tugged hard at the reins. The vehicle took a quick turn, lurched dangerously in its top-heavy pomp, and, almost upsetting, came to a standstill nearly opposite the boy.

"Careless dog!" a shrill voice screamed from the inside. "What are you doing?"

"The lises, your Excellency!" The driver's voice was thick; as he spoke he swayed uncertainly.

"Lises—quicksands—"

"There, your Excellency," indicating a gleaming place right in their path; a small bright spot that looked as if it might have been polished, while elsewhere on the surrounding sands tiny rippling parallels caressed the eye with streaks of black and silver. "I saw it in time!"

"In time!" angrily. "Imbecile! Didn't you know it was there?"

"Of course, your Excellency! Only I had misjudged a little, and—" The man's manner showed he was frightened.

"Falsehoods! You have been drinking! Don't answer. You shall hear of this later. Drive around the spot."

"Yes, your Excellency," was the now sober and subdued answer.

Ere he obeyed, however, the carriage door, from which the Governor had been leaning, swung open. "Wait!" he called out impatiently, and tried to close it, but the catch—probably from long disuse—would not hold, and, before the liveried servant perched on the lofty carriage behind had fully perceived the fact and had recovered himself sufficiently to think of his duties, the boy on the beach had sprung forward.

"Slam it!" commanded an irate voice.

The lad complied, and as he did so, peered eagerly into the capacious depths of the vehicle.

"The boy with the fish!" exclaimed at the same time a girlish treble within.

"Eh?" my lord turned sharply.

"An impudent lad who stopped the Lady Elise!" exclaimed the fat man— surely Beppo—on the front seat.

"Stopped the Lady Elise!" The Governor repeated the words slowly; an ominous pause was followed by an abrupt movement on the part of the child.

"He did not stop me; it was I who nearly ran over him, and it was my fault. Beppo does not tell the truth—he's a wicked man!—and I'm glad I'm not going to see him any more! And the boy wasn't impudent; at least until Beppo offered to strike him, and then, Beppo didn't! Beppo," derisively, "was afraid!"

"My lady," Beppo's voice was soft and unctuous, "construes forbearance for fear."

"Step nearer, boy!"

Partly blinded by the lamps, the lad obeyed; was cognizant of a piercing scrutiny; two hard, steely eyes that seemed to read his inmost thoughts; a face, indistinguishable but compelling; beyond, something white—a girl's dress—that moved and fluttered!

"Who is he?"

"A poor boy who lives in the woods, papa!"

But Beppo bent forward and whispered, his words too low for the lad to catch. Whatever his information, the Governor started; the questioning glance on an instant brightened, and his head was thrust forward close to the boy's. A chill seemed to pass over the lad, yet he did not quail.

"Good-by, boy!" said the child, and, leaning from the window, smiled down at him.

He tried to answer, when a hand pulled her in somewhat over-suddenly.

"Drive on!" Again the shrill tones cut the air. "Drive on, I tell you! Diable! What are you standing here for!"

A whip lashed the air and the horses leaped forward. The back wheels of the vehicle almost struck the lad, but, motionless, he continued staring after it. Farther it drew away, and, as he remained thus he discerned, or fancied he discerned, a girl's face at the back—a ribbon that waved for a moment in the moonlight, and then was gone.

Eight years elapsed before next he saw her.

CHAPTER IV

A DANCE ON THE BEACH

The great vernal equinox of April 178-, was the cause of certain unusual movements of the tide, which made old mariners and coast-fishermen shake their heads and gaze seaward, out of all reckoning. At times, after a tempest, on this strange coast, the waters would rise in a manner and at an hour out of the ordinary, and then among the dwellers on the shore, there were those who prognosticated dire unhappiness, telling how the sea had once devoured two villages overnight, and how, beneath the sands, were homes intact, with the people yet in their beds.

Concerned with a disordered social system and men in and out of dungeons, the Governor had little time and less inclination to note the caprices of the tide or the vagaries of the strand. The people! The menacing and mercurial ebb and flow of their moods! The maintenance of autocratic power on the land, and, a more difficult task, on the sea—these were matters of greater import than the phenomena of nature whose purposes man is powerless to shape or curb. My lady, his daughter, however, who had just returned from seven years' schooling at a convent and one year at court where the Queen, Marie Antoinette, set the fashion of gaiety, found in the conduct of their great neighbor, the ocean, a source of both entertainment and instruction for her guests, a merry company transported from Versailles.

"Is it not a sight well worth seeing after your tranquil Seine, my Lords?" she would say with a wave of her white hand toward the restless sea. "Here, perched in mid air like eagles, you have watched the 'grand tide,' as we call it, come in—like no other tide—faster than a horse can gallop! Where else could you witness the like?"

"Nowhere. And when it goes out—"

"It goes out so far, you can no longer see it; only a vast beach that reaches to the horizon, and—"

"Must be very dangerous?"

"For a few days, perhaps; later, not at all, when the petites tides are the rule, and can be depended on. Then are the sands, except for one or two places very well-known, as safe as your gardens at Versailles. But remain, and—you shall see."

Which they did—finding the place to their liking—or their hostess; for the Governor, who cared not for guests, but must needs entertain them for reasons of state, left them as much as might be to his daughter. She, brimming with the ardor and effervescence of eighteen years, accepted these responsibilities gladly; pending that period she had referred to, turned the monks' great refectory into a ball-room, and then, when the gales had swept away, proposed the sands themselves as a scene for diversion both for her guests and the people. This, despite the demur of his Excellency, her father.

"Is it wise," he had asked, "to court the attention of the people?"

"Oh, I am not afraid!" she had answered. "And they are going to dance, too!"

"They!" He frowned.

"Why not? It is the Queen's own idea. 'Let the people dance,' she has said, 'and they will keep out of mischief.' Besides," with a prouder poise of the bright head, "why shouldn't they see, and—like me?"

"They like nothing except themselves, and," dryly, "to attempt to evade their just obligations."

"Can you blame them?" She made a light gesture. "Obligations, mon père, are so tiresome!"

"Well, well," hastily, "have your own way!" Although he spoke rather shortly, on the whole he was not displeased with his daughter; her betrothal with the Marquis de Beauvillers, a nobleman of large estates,—arranged while she was yet a child!—promised a brilliant marriage and in a measure offered to his Excellency some compensation for that old and long-cherished disappointment—the birth of a girl when his ambition had looked so strongly for an heir to his name as well as to his estate.

And so my lady and her guests danced and made merry on the sands below, and the people came out from the mainland, or down from the houses in the town at the base of the rock, to watch. A varied assemblage of gaunt-looking men and bent, low-browed women, for the most part they stood sullen and silent; though exchanging meaning glances now and then as if to say: "Do you note all this ostentation—all this glitter and display? Yes; and some day—" Upon brooding brows, in deep-set eyes, on furrowed faces a question and an answer seemed to gleam and pass. Endowed with natural optimism and a vivacity somewhat heedless, my lady appeared unconscious of all this latent enmity until an unlooked-for incident, justifying in a measure the Governor's demur, broke in upon the evening's festivities and claimed her attention.

On the beach, lighted by torches, a dainty minuet was proceeding gaily, when through the throng of onlookers, a young man with dark head set on a frame tall and powerful, worked his way carefully to a point where he was afforded at least a restricted view of the animated spectacle. Absorbed each in his or her way in the scene before them, no one noticed him, and, with hat drawn over his brow, and standing in the shadow of the towering head-dresses of several peasant women, he seemed content to attract as little attention to himself as possible. His look, at first quick and alert, that of a man taking stock of his surroundings, suddenly became intent and piercing, as, passing in survey over the lowly spectators to the glittering company, it centered itself on the young mistress of festivities.

In costume white and shining, the Lady Elise moved through the graceful numbers, her slender supple figure now poised, now swaying, from head to foot responsive to the rhythm of that "pastime of little steps." Her lips, too, were busy, but such was the witchery of her motion—all fire and life!—the silk-stockinged cavaliers whom she thus regaled with wit, mockery, or jest, could, for the most part, respond only with admiring glances or weakly protesting words.

"That pretty fellow, her partner," with a contemptuous accent on the adjective, "is the Marquis de Beauvillers, a kinsman of the King!" said one of the women in the throng.

"Ma foi! They're well matched. A dancing doll for a popinjay!"

The young man behind the head-dresses, now nodding viciously, moved nearer the front. Dressed in the rough though not unpicturesque fashion of the northern fisherman, a touch of color in his apparel lent to his bearing a note of romance the bold expression of his swarthy face did not belie. For a few moments he watched the girl; the changing eyes and lips, shadowed by hair that shone and flashed like bright burnished gold; then catching her gaze, the black eyes gleamed. An instant their eyes lingered; hers startled, puzzled.

"Where have I seen him?" My lady, in turning, paused to swing over her shoulders a glance.

"Whom?" asked her companion in the dance—a fair, handsome nobleman of slim figure and elegant bearing.

"That's just what I can't tell you," she answered, sweeping a courtesy that fitted the rhythm of the music. "Only a face I should remember!"

"Should?" The Marquis' look followed hers.

But the subject of their conversation, as if divining the trend of their talk, had drawn back.

"Oh, he is gone now," she answered.

"A malcontent, perhaps! One meets them nowadays."

"No, no! He did not look—"

"Some poor fellow, then, your beauty has entrapped?" he insinuated. "Humble admirer!"

"Then I would remember him!" she laughed as the dance came to an end.

Now in a tented pavilion, servants, richly garbed in festal costume, passed among the guests, circulating trays, bright with golden dishes and goblets, stamped with the ancient insignia of the Mount, and once the property of the affluent monks, early rulers of the place. Other attendants followed, bearing light delicacies, confections and marvelous frosted towers and structures from the castle kitchen.

"The patron saint in sugar!" Merry exclamations greeted these examples of skill and cunning. "Are we to devour the saint?"

"Ah, no; he is only to look at!"

"But the Mount in cake—?"

"You may cut into that—though beware!—not so deep as the dungeons!"

"A piece of the cloister!"

"A bit of the abbey!"

"And you, Elise?"

The girl reached gaily. "A little of the froth of the sea!"

Meanwhile, not far distant, a barrel had been broached and wine was being circulated among the people. There, master of ceremonies, Beppo dispensed advice with the beverage, his grumbling talk heard above the light laughter and chatter of the lords and ladies.

"Drink to his Excellency!" As he spoke, the Governor's man, from the elevated stand upon which he stood, gazed arrogantly around him. "Clods! Sponges that sop without a word of thanks! Who only think of your stomachs! Drink to the Governor, I say!"

"To the Governor!" exclaimed a few, but it might have been noticed they were men from the town, directly beneath the shadow of his Excellency's castle, and now close within reach of the fat factotum's arm.

"Once more! Had I the ordering of wine, the barrels would all be empty ones, but her ladyship would be generous, and—"

Beppo broke abruptly off, his wandering glance, on a sudden, arrested.

"Hein!" he exclaimed, with eyes protruding.

A moment he stammered a few words of surprise and incredulity, the while he continued to search eagerly—but now in vain! The object of his startled attention, illumined, for an instant, on the outskirts of the throng, by the glare of a torch, was no more to be descried. As questioning the reality of a fleeting impression, his gaze fixed itself again near the edge of flickering lights; shifted uncertainly to the pavilion where servants from the Mount hurried to and fro; then back to the people around him. His jaw which had dropped grew suddenly firm.

"Clear a space for the dance!" he called out in tones impatient, excited. "It is her ladyship's command—so see you step blithely! And you fellows there, with the tambourin and hautbois, come forward!"

Two men, clad in sheepskin and carrying rude instruments, obediently advanced, and at once, in marked contrast to the recent tinkling measures of the orchestra, a wild, half-barbaric concord rang out.

But the Governor's man, having thus far executed the orders he had received, did not linger to see whether or not his own injunction, "to step blithely," was observed; some concern, remote from gaillarde, gavotte or bourrée of the people, caused him hastily to dismount from his stand and make his way from the throng. As he started at a rapid pace across the sands, his eyes, now shining with anticipation, looked back.

"What could have brought him here? Him!" he repeated. "Ah, my fine fellow, this should prove a lucky stroke for me!" And quickening his step, until he almost ran, Beppo hurried toward the tower gate of the Mount.

CHAPTER V

AN INTERRUPTION

"They seem not to appreciate your fête champêtre, my Lady!" At the verge of the group of peasant dancers, the Lady Elise and the Marquis de Beauvillers, who had left the other guests to the enjoyment of fresh culinary surprises, paused to survey a scene, intended, yet failing, to be festal. For whether these people were too sodden to avail themselves of the opportunity for merrymaking, or liked not the notion of tripping together at Beppo's command, their movements, which should have been free and untrammeled as the vigorous swing of the music, were characterized only by painful monotony and lagging. In the half-gloom they came together like shadows; separated aimlessly and cast misshapen silhouettes—caricatures of frolicking peasants—on the broad surface of the sands beyond. These bobbing, black spots my lady disapprovingly regarded.

"They seem not in the mood, truly!" tapping her foot on the beach.

"Here—and elsewhere!" he laughed.

But the Governor's daughter made an impatient movement; memories of the dance, as she had often seen it, when she was a child at the Mount, recurred to her. "They seem to have forgotten!" Her eyes flashed. "I should like to show them."

"You? My Lady!"

She did not answer; pressing her red lips, she glanced sharply around. "Stupid people! Half of them are only looking on! When they can dance, they won't, and—" She gave a slight start, for near her, almost at her elbow, stood the young seaman she had observed only a short time before, when the minuet was in progress. His dark eyes were bent on her and she surprised on his face an expression half derisory, half quizzical. Her look changed to one of displeasure.

"You are not dancing?" severely.

"No, my Lady." Too late, perhaps, he regretted his temerity—that too unveiled and open regard.

"Why not?" more imperiously.

"I—" he began and stopped.

"You can dance?"

"A little, perhaps—"

"As well as they?" looking at the people.

"Wooden fantoccini!" said the man, a flicker of bold amusement returning to his face.

"Fantoccini?" spoke the girl impatiently. "What know you of them?"

"We Breton seamen sail far, on occasion."

"Far enough to gain in assurance!" cried my lady, with golden head high, surveying him disdainfully through half-closed, sweeping lashes. "But you shall prove your right."

"Right?" asked the fellow, his eyes fixed intently upon her.

"The right of one who does not dance—to criticize those who do!" she said pointedly, and made, on the sudden, an imperious gesture.

He gave a start of surprise; audacious though he was, he looked as if he would draw back. "What? With you, my Lady?"

A gleam of satisfaction, a little cold and scornful, shone from the girl's eyes at this evidence of his discomfiture. "Unless," she added maliciously, "you fear you—can not?"

"Fear?" His look shot around; a moment he seemed to hesitate; then a more reckless expression swept suddenly over his dark features and he sprang to her side.

"At your Ladyship's command!"

My lady's white chin lifted. The presumptuous fellow knew the dance of the Mount—danced it well, no doubt!—else why such ease and assurance? Her lids veiled a look of disappointment; she was half-minded curtly to dismiss him, when a few words of low remonstrance and the sight of my lord's face decided her. She drew aside her skirts swiftly; flashed back at the nobleman a smile, capricious and wilful.

 The presumptuous fellow knew the dance of the Mount

The presumptuous fellow knew the dance of the Mount

"They," indicating the peasants, "must have an example, my Lord!" she exclaimed, and stood, with eyes sparkling, waiting the instant to catch up the rhythm.

But the Marquis, not finding the reason sufficient to warrant such condescension, gazed with mute protest and disapproval on the two figures, so ill-assorted: my lady, in robe of satin, fastened with tassels of silver—the sleeves, wide and short, trimmed at the elbow with fine lace of Brussels and drawn up at the shoulder with glistening knots of diamonds; the other, clad in the rough raiment of a seaman! The nice, critical sense of the Marquis suffered from this spectacle of the incongruous; his eyes, seeking in vain those of the Governor's daughter, turned and rested querulously on the heavy-browed peasants, most of whom, drawing nearer, viewed the scene with stolid indifference. In the gaze of only a few did that first stupid expression suffer any change; then it varied to one of vague wonder, half-apathetic inquiry!

"Is he mad?" whispered a clod of this class to a neighbor.

"Not so loud!" breathed the other in a low tone.

"But he," regarding with dull awe the young fisherman, "doesn't care! Look! What foolhardiness! He's going to dance with her!"

"Witchcraft! That's what I call it!"

"Hush!"

My lady extended the tips of her fingers. "Attack well!" runs the old Gallic injunction to dancers; the partner she had chosen apparently understood its significance. A lithe muscular hand closed on the small one; whirled my lady swiftly; half back again. It took away her breath a little, so forcible and unceremonious that beginning! Then, obeying the mad rhythm of the movement, she yielded to the infectious measure. An arm quickly encircled her waist; swept the slender form here,—there. Never had she had partner so vigorous, yet graceful. One who understood so well this song of the soil; its wild symbolism; the ancient music of the hardy Scandinavians who first brought the dance to these shores.

More stirring, the melodies resounded—faster—faster. In a rapid turn, the golden hair just brushed the dark, glowing face. He bent lower; as if she had been but a peasant maid, the bold eyes looked now down into hers; nay, more—in their depths she might fancy almost a warmer sparkle—of mute admiration! And her face, on a sudden, changed; grew cold.

"Certes, your Ladyship sets them an example!" murmured the audacious fellow. "Though, pardi!—one not easy to imitate!"

She threw back her head, proudly, imperiously; the brown eyes gleamed, and certain sharp words of reproof were about to spring from her lips, when abruptly, above the sound of the music, a trumpet call, afar, rang out. My lady—not sorry perhaps of the pretext—at once stopped.

"I thank your Ladyship," said the man and bowed low.

But the Governor's daughter seemed, or affected, not to hear, regarding the other dancers, who likewise had come to a standstill—the two musicians looking up from instruments now silent. A moment yet the young fisherman lingered; seemed about once more to voice his acknowledgments, but, catching the dull eye of a peasant, stepped back instead.

"Sapristi! They might, at least, have waited until the end of the dance!" he muttered, and, with a final look over his shoulder and a low laugh, disappeared in the crowd.

"Where are the enemy?" It was the Marquis who spoke—in accents he strove to make light and thereby conceal, perhaps, possible annoyance. Coming forward, he looked around toward the point whence the sound had proceeded. "If I mistake not," a note of inquiry in his tone, "it means—a call to arms!"

My lady bit her lips; her eyes still gleamed with the bright cold light of a topaz. "Why—a call to arms?" she asked somewhat petulantly, raising her hand to her hair, a little disarranged in the dance.

"Perhaps, as a part of the military discipline?" murmured the Marquis dubiously. "See!" With sudden interest, he indicated a part of the Mount that had been black against the star-spangled sky, now showing sickly points of light. "It does mean something! They are coming down!"

And even as the Marquis spoke, a clatter of hoofs on the stone pavement leading from the Mount to the sand ushered a horseman into view. He was followed by another and yet another, until in somewhat desultory fashion, owing to the tortuous difficulties of the narrow way that had separated them above, an array of mounted men was gathered at the base of the rock. But only for a moment; a few words from one of their number, evidently in command, and they dispersed; some to ride around the Mount to the left, others to the right.

"Perhaps Elise will enlighten us?" Of one accord her guests now crowded around the girl.

"Does the Governor intend to take us prisoners?"

"You imply it is necessary to do that—to keep you?" answered my lady.

"Then why—"

Her expression, as perplexed as theirs, answered.

"Beppo!" She waved her hand.

The Governor's servitor, who was passing, with an anxious, inquiring look upon his face, glanced around.

"Beppo!" she repeated, and beckoned again.

The man approached. "Your Ladyship wishes to speak with me?" he asked in a voice he endeavored to make unconcerned.

"I do." In her manner the old antipathy she had felt toward him as a child again became manifest. "What do the soldiers want? Why have they come down?"

His eyes shifted. "I—my Lady—" he stammered.

The little foot struck the strand. "Why don't you answer? You heard my question?"

"I am sorry, my Lady—" Again he hesitated: "Le Seigneur Noir has been seen on the beach!"

"Le Seigneur Noir?" she repeated.

"Yes, my Lady. He was caught sight of among the peasants, at the time the barrels were opened, in accordance with your Ladyship's command. I assure your Ladyship," with growing eagerness, "there can be no mistake, as—"

"Who," interrupted my lady sharply, "is this Black Seigneur?"

Beppo's manner changed. "A man," he said solemnly, "his Excellency, the Governor, has long been most anxious to capture."

The girl's eyes flashed with impatience, and then she began to laugh. "Saw you ever, my Lords and Ladies, his equal for equivocation? You put to him the question direct, and he answers—"

The loud report of a carbine from the other side of the Mount, followed by a desultory volley, interrupted her. The laughter died on her lips; the color left her cheek.

"What—" The startled look in her eyes completed the sentence.

Beppo rubbed his hands softly. "His Excellency takes no chances!" he murmured.

CHAPTER VI

A MESSENGER FOR MY LADY

"So you failed to capture him, Monsieur le Commandant?"

The speaker, the Marquis de Beauvillers, leaned more comfortably back in his chair in the small, rather barely furnished barracks' sitting-room in which he found himself later that night and languidly surveyed the florid, irate countenance of the man in uniform before him.

"No, Monsieur le Marquis," said the latter, endeavoring to conceal any evidence of mortification or ill humor in the presence of a visitor so distinguished; "we didn't. But," as if to turn the conversation, with a gesture toward a well-laden table, "I should feel honored if—"

"Thank you, no! After our repast on the beach—however, stand on no ceremony yourself. Nay, I insist—"

"If Monsieur le Marquis insists!—" The commandant drew up his chair; then, reaching for a bottle, poured out a glass of wine, which he offered his guest.

"No, no!" said the Marquis. "But as I remarked before, stand on no ceremony!" And daintily opening a snuff-box, he watched his host with an expression half-amused, half-ironical.

That person ate and drank with little relish; the wine—so he said—had spoiled; and the dishes were without flavor; it was fortunate Monsieur le Marquis had no appetite—

Whereupon the Marquis smiled; but, considering the circumstances, in his own mind excused the commandant, who had only just come from the Governor's palace, and who, after the interview that undoubtedly had ensued, could hardly be expected to find the pâté palatable, or the wine to his liking. This, despite the complaisance of the young nobleman whom the commandant had encountered, while descending from the Governor's abode, and who, adapting his step to the other's had accompanied the officer back to his quarters, and graciously accepted an invitation to enter.

"Well, you know the old saying," the Marquis closed the box with a snap, "'There's many a slip'—but how," airily brushing with his handkerchief imaginary particles from a long lace cuff, "did he get away?"

"He had got away before we were down on the beach. It was a wild-goose chase, at best. And so I told his Excellency, the Governor—"

"A thankless task, no doubt! But the shots we heard—"

"An imbecile soldier saw a shadow; fired at it, and—"

"The others followed suit?" laughed the visitor.

"Exactly!" The commandant's face grew red; fiercely he pulled at his mustache. "What can one expect, when they make soldiers out of every dunderpate that comes along?"

"True!" assented the Marquis. "But this fellow, this Black Seigneur—why is the Governor so anxious to lay hands on him? Who is he, and what has he done? I confess," languidly, "to a mild curiosity."

"He's a privateersman and an outlaw, and has done enough to hang himself a dozen times—"

"When you capture him!" interposed the visitor lightly. A moment he studied the massive oak beams of the ceiling. "Why do they call him the Black Seigneur? An odd sobriquet!"

"His father was a Seigneur—the last of the fief of Desaurac. The Seigneurs have all been fair men for generations, while this fellow—"

"Then he has noble blood in him?" The Marquis showed surprise. "Where is the fief?"

"The woods on the shore mark the beginning of it "

"But—I don't understand. The father was a Seigneur; the son—"

Bluntly the commandant explained; the son was a natural child; the mother, a common peasant woman whom the former Seigneur had taken to his house—

"I see!" The young nobleman tapped his knee. "And that being the case—"

"Under the terms of the ancient grant, there being no legal heir, the lands were confiscated to the crown. His Excellency, however, had already bought many of the incumbrances against the property, and, in view of this, and his services to the King, the fief, declared forfeited by the courts, was subsequently granted and deeded, without condition, to the Governor."

"To the Governor!" repeated the Marquis.

"Who at once began a rare clearing-out; forcing the peasants who for years had not been paying métayage, to meet this just requirement, or—move away!"

"And did not some of them object?"

"They did; but his Excellency found means. The most troublesome were arrested and taken to the Mount, where they have had time to reflect—his Excellency believes in no half-way measures with peasants."

"A rich principality, no doubt!" half to himself spoke the Marquis.

"I have heard," blurted the commandant, "he's going to give it to the Lady Elise; restore the old castle and turn the grounds surrounding it into a noble park."

The visitor frowned, as if little liking the introduction of the lady's name into the conversation. "And what did the Black Seigneur do then," he asked coldly, "when he found his lands gone?"

"Claimed it was a plot!—that his mother was an honest woman, though neither the priest who performed the ceremony nor the marriage records could be found. He even resisted at first—refused to be turned out—and, skulking about the forest with his gun, kept the deputies at bay. But they surrounded him at last; drove him to the castle, and would have captured him, only he escaped that night, and took to the high seas, where he has been making trouble ever since!"

"Trouble?"

"He has seriously hampered his Excellency's commerce; interfered with his ships, and crippled his trade with the Orient."

"But—the Governor has many boats, many men. Why have they failed to capture him?"

"For a number of reasons. In the first place he is one of the most skilful pilots on the coast; when hard pressed, he does not hesitate to use even the Isles des Rochers as a place of refuge."

"The Isles des Rochers?" queried the nobleman.

"A chevaux-de-frise on the sea, my Lord!" continued the commandant; "where fifty barren isles are fortified by a thousand rocks; frothing fangs when the tide is low; sharp teeth that lie in wait to bite when the smiling lips of the treacherous waters have closed above! There, the Governor's ships have followed him on several occasions, and—few of them have come back!"

"But surely there must be times when he can not depend on that retreat?"

"There are, my Lord. His principal harbor and resort is a little isle farther north—English, they call it—that offers refuge at any time to miscreants from France. There may they lie peacefully, as in a cradle; or go ashore with impunity, an they like. Oh, he is safe enough there. Home for French exiles, they designate the place. Exiles! Bah! It was there he first found means to get his ship—sharing his profits, no doubt, with the islander who built her. There, too, he mustered his crew—savage peasants who had been turned off the lands of the old Seigneur; fisher-folk who had become outlaws rather than pay to the Governor just dues from the sea; men fled from the banalité of the mill, of the oven, of the wine-press—"

"Still must he be a redoubtable fellow, to have done what he did to-night; to have dared mingle with the people, under the Governor's very guns!"

"The people! He has nothing to fear from them. An ignorant, low, disloyal lot! They look upon this fellow as a hero. He has played his cards well; sends money to the lazy, worthless ones, under pretext that they are poor, over-taxed, over-burdened. In his company is one Gabriel Gabarie, a poet of the people, as he is styled, who keeps in touch with those stirring trouble in Paris. Perhaps they hope for an insurrection there, and then—"

"An insurrection?" The Marquis' delicate features expressed ironical protest; he dismissed the possibility with an airy wave of the hand. "One should never anticipate trouble, Monsieur le Commandant," he said lightly and rose. "Good night."

"Good night, Monsieur le Marquis," returned the officer with due deference, and accompanied his noble visitor to the door.

At first, without the barracks, the Marquis walked easily on, but soon the steepness of the narrow road, becoming more marked as it approached the commanding structures at the top of the Mount, caused his gait gradually to slacken; then he paused altogether, at an upper platform.

From where he stood, by day could be seen, almost directly beneath, the tiny habitations of men clinging like limpets to the precipitous sides of the rocks at the base; now was visible only a void, an abysm, out of which swam the sea; so far below, a boat looked no larger than a gull on its silver surface; so immense, the dancing waves seemed receding to a limit beyond the reach of the heavens.

"You found him?" A girl's clear voice broke suddenly upon him. He wheeled.

"Elise! You!"

"Yes! why not? You found him? The commandant?"

"At your command, but—"

"And learned all?"

"All he could tell."

"It is reported at the castle that the man escaped!" quickly.

"It is true. But," in a voice of languid surprise, "I believe you are glad—"

"No, no!" She shook her head. "Only," a smile curved her lips, "Beppo will be so disappointed! Now," seating herself lightly on the low wall of the giant rampart, "tell me all you have learned about this Black Seigneur."

The Marquis, considered; with certain reservations obeyed. At the conclusion of his narrative, she spoke no word and he turned to her inquiringly. Her brows were knit; her eyes down-bent. A moment he regarded her in silence; then she looked up at him suddenly.

"I wonder," she said, her face bathed in the moonlight, "if—if it was this Black Seigneur I danced with?"

"The Black Seigneur!" My lord started; frowned. "Nonsense! What an absurd fancy! He would not have dared!"

"True," said the girl quickly. "You are right, my Lord. It is absurd. He would not have dared."

CHAPTER VII

A DISTANT MENACE

But guests come and guests go; pastimes draw to a close, and the hour arrives when the curtain falls on the masque. The friends of my lady, however reluctantly, were obliged at last to forgo further holiday-making, depart from the Mount, and return to the court. An imposing cavalcade, gleaming in crimson and gold, they wended down the dark rock; laughing ladies, pranked-out cavaliers who waved their perfumed hands with farewell kisses to the grim stronghold in the desert, late their palace of pleasure, and to the young mistress thereof.

"Good-by, Elise!" The Marquis was last to go.

"Good-by."

He took her hand; held it to his lips. On the whole, he was not ill-pleased. His wooing had apparently prospered; for, although the marriage had been long arranged, my lady's beauty and capriciousness had fanned in him the desire to appear a successful suitor for her heart as well as her hand. If sometimes she laughed and thus failed to receive his delicate gallantries in the mood in which they were tendered, the Marquis' vanity only allowed him to conclude that a woman does not laugh if she is displeased. It was enough that she found him diverting; he served her; they were friends and had danced and ridden through the spring days in amicable fashion.

"Good-by," he repeated. "When are you coming to court again? The Queen is sure to ask. I understand her Majesty is planning all manner of brilliant entertainments, yet Versailles—without you, Elise!"

"Me?" arching her finely penciled brows. "Oh, I'm thinking of staying here, becoming a nun, and restoring the Mount to its old religious prestige."

"Then I'll come back a monk," he returned in the same tone.

"If you come back at all!" provokingly. "There, go! The others will soon be out of sight!"

"I, too—alas, Elise!"

He touched his horse; rode on, but soon looked back to where, against a great, grim wall, stood a figure all in white gleaming in the sunshine. The Marquis stopped; drew from his breast a deep red rose, and, gazing upward, gracefully kissed the glowing token. Beneath the aureole of golden hair my lady's proud face rewarded him with a faint smile, and something—a tiny handkerchief—fluttered like a dove above the frowning, time-worn rock. At that, with the eloquent gesture of a troubadour, he threw his arm backward, as if to launch the impress on the rose to the crimson lips of the girl, and then, plying his spurs, galloped off.

And as he went at a pace, headlong if not dangerous and fitting the exigencies of the moment, my lord smiled. Truly had he presented a perfect, dainty and gallant figure for any woman's eyes, and the Lady Elise, he fancied, was not the least discerning of her sex. And had he seen the girl, when an unkind angle of the wall hid him from sight, his own nice estimate of the situation would have suffered no change. The Mount, which formerly had resounded to the life and merriment of the people from the court, on a sudden to her looked cold, barren, empty.

"Heigh-ho!" she murmured, stretching her arms toward that point where he—they—had vanished. "I shall die of ennui, I am sure!" And thoughtfully retraced her steps to her own room.

But she did not long stay there; by way of makeshift for gaiety, substituted activity. The Mount, full of early recollections and treasure-house mystery, furnished an incentive for exploration, and for several days she devoted herself to its study; now pausing for an instant's contemplation of a sculptured thing of beauty, then before some closed door that held her, as at the threshold of a Bluebeard's forbidden chamber.

One day, such a door stood open and her curiosity became cured. She had passed beneath a machicolated gateway, and climbing a stairway that began in a watch-tower, found herself unexpectedly on a great platform. Here several men, unkempt, pale, like creatures from another world, were walking to and fro; but at sight of her, an order was issued and they vanished through a trap—all save one, a misshapen dwarf who remained to shut the iron door, adjust the fastening and turn a ponderous key. For a moment she stood staring.

"Why did you do that?" she asked angrily.

"The Governor's orders," said the man, bowing hideously. "They are to see no one."

"Then let them up at once! Do you hear? At once!"

And as he began to unlock the door, walked off. After that, her interest in the rock waned; the Mount seemed but a prison; she, herself, desired only to escape from it.

"Have my saddle put on Saladin," she said to Beppo the next day, toward the end of a long afternoon.

"Very well, my Lady. Who accompanies your Ladyship?"

"No one!" With slight emphasis. "I ride alone."

Beppo discretely suppressed his surprise. "Is your Ladyship going far? If so, I beg to remind that to-night is the change of the moon, and the 'grand,' not the 'little' tide may be coming in."

"I was already aware of it, and shall keep between the Mount and the shore. Have my horse sent to the upper gate," she added, and soon afterward rode down.

The town was astir, and many looked after her as she passed; not kindly, but with the varying expressions she had of late begun to notice. Again was she cognizant of that feeling of secret antagonism, even from these people whose houses clung to the very foundations of her own abode, and her lips set tightly. Why did they hate her? What right had they to hate her? A sensation, almost of relief, came over her, when passing through the massive, feudal gate, she found herself on the beach.

Still and languorous was the day; not a breath stirred above the tiny ripples of the sand; a calm, almost unnatural, seemed to wrap the world in its embrace. The girl breathed deeper, feeling the closeness of the air; her impatient eyes looked around; scanned the shore; to the left, low and flat— to the right, marked by the dark fringe of a forest. Which way should she go? Irrcsolutcly shc turncd in the direction of the wood.

Saladin, her horse, seemed in unusually fine fettle, and the distance separating her from the land was soon covered; but still she continued to follow the shore, swinging around and out toward a point some distance seaward. Not until she had reached that extreme projection of land, where the wooing green crept out from the forest as far as it might, did she draw rein. Saladin stopped, albeit with protest, tossing his great head.

"You might as well make an end of that, sir!" said the girl, and, springing from the saddle, deftly secured him. Then turning her back toward the Mount, a shadowy pyramid in the distance, she seated herself in the grass with her eyes to the woods.

Not long, however, did my lady remain thus; soon rising, she walked toward the shadowy depths. At the verge she paused; her brows grew thoughtful; what was it the woods recalled? Suddenly, she remembered—a boy she had met the night she left for school so long ago, had told her he lived in them. She recalled, too, as a child, how the woman, Marie, who had been maid to her mother, had tried to frighten her about that sequestered domain, with tales of fierce wild animals and unearthly creatures, visible and invisible, that roamed within.

She had no fear now, though faint rustlings and a pulsation of sound held her listening. Then, through the leafy interstice, a gleaming and flashing, as if some one were throwing jewels to the earth, lured her on to the cause of the seeming enchantment—a tiny waterfall!

The moment passed; still she lingered. Around the Mount's high top, her own home, only transcendent silence reigned; here was she surrounded by babbling voices and all manner of merry creatures—lively little squirrels; winged insects, romping in the twilight shade; a portly and well-satisfied appearing green monster who regarded her amicably from a niche of green. A butterfly, poised and waving its wings, held her a long time—until she was suddenly aroused by the wood growing darker. Raising her eyes, she saw through the green foliage overhead that the bright sky had become sunless. At the same time a rumbling detonation, faint, far-off, broke in upon the whisperings and tinklings of that wood nook. Getting up, she stood for a moment listening; then walked away.

Near the verge of the sand, Saladin greeted her with impatience, tossing his head toward the darkening heavens. Nor did he wait until she was fairly seated before starting back at a rapid gait along the shore. But the girl offered no protest; her face showed only enjoyment. A little wild he might be at times, as became one of rugged ancestry, but never vicious, only headstrong! And she didn't mind that—

Already had he begun to slack that first thundering pace when something white—a veil, perhaps, dropped from the cavalcade of lords and ladies some days before on the land and wafted to the beach—fluttered like a live thing suddenly before him. In his tense mood, Saladin, affrighted, sprang to one side; then wheeling outright, madly took the bit in his teeth. Perforce his mistress resigned herself, sitting straight and sure, with little hands hard and firm at the reins. Saladin was behaving very badly, but—at least he was superb, worth conquering, if—

A brief thrill of apprehension seized her as, again drawing near the point of land, he showed no signs of yielding; resisted all her attempts to turn, to direct him to it. With nostrils thrust forward and breathing strong, he continued to choose his own course; to whirl her on; past the promontory; around into the great bay beyond—now a vast expanse, or desert of sand, broken only, about half-way across, by the small isle of Casque. Toward this rocky formation, a pygmy to the great Mount from which it lay concealed by the intervening projection of land, the horse rushed.

On, on! In vain she still endeavored to stop him; thinking uneasily of stories the fishermen told of this neighboring coast; of the sands that often shifted here, setting pitfalls for the unwary. She saw the sky grow yet darker, noted the nearer flashings of light, and heard the louder rumblings that followed. Then presently another danger she had long been conscious of, on a sudden became real.

She saw, or thought she saw, a faint streak, like a silver line drawn across the sky where the yellow sands touched the sombrous horizon. And Saladin seemed to observe it, too; to detect in it cause for wonder; reason for hesitation. At any rate, that headlong speed now showed signs of diminishing; he clipped and tossed the sand less vigorously, and looked around at his mistress with wild, uneasy eyes. Again she spoke to him; pulled with all her strength at the reins, and, at once, he stopped.

None too soon! Great drops of rain had begun to fall, but the girl did not notice them. The white line alone riveted her attention! It seemed to grow broader; to acquire an intangible movement of its own; at the same time to give out a sound—a strange, low droning that filled the air. Heard for the first time, a stranger at the Mount would have found it inexplicable; to the Governor's daughter, the menacing cadence left no room for doubt as to its origin.

The girl's cheek paled; her gaze swung in the opposite direction, toward the point of land, now so distant. Could they reach it? She did not believe they could; indeed, the "grand" tide coming up behind on the verge of the storm, faster than any horse could gallop, would overtake them midway. And Saladin seemed to know it also; beneath her, he trembled. Yet must they try, she thought, and had tightened the reins to turn, when looking ahead once more, she discerned a break in the forbidding cliffs of the little island of Casque, and, back of the fissure, a shining spot which marked a tiny cove.

A moment she hesitated; what should she do? Ride toward the isle and the white danger, or toward the point of mainland and from it? Either alternative was a desperate one, but the isle lay much nearer; and quickly, the brown eyes gleaming with sudden courage, she decided; touched her horse and pressed him forward.

But fast as she went the "grand" tide came faster; struck with a loud, menacing sound the seaward side of the isle and swung hungrily around.

My lady cast over her shoulder a quick glance; the cove, however, was near; only a line of small rocks, jutting from the sand, separated her from it. If they could but pass, she thought; they had passed, she told herself joyfully, when of a sudden the horse stumbled; fell. Thrown violently from his back, a moment was she cognizant of a deafening roar; a riotous advance of foam; above, a hundred birds that screamed distractedly; then all these sounds mingled; darkness succeeded, and she remembered no more.

CHAPTER VIII

THE OLD WATCH-TOWER

A wall! A window—a prison-like interior! As her eyes opened, the Governor's daughter strove confusedly to decipher her surroundings. The wall seemed real; the narrow window, too, high above, framing, against a darkening background, a slant of fine rain! Again she closed her eyes, only to be conscious of a gentle languor; a heaviness like that of half-sleep; of bodily heat, and also a little bodily pain. For an indefinite period, really a moment or two, she resigned herself to that dreamy torpor; then, with an effort, lifted her lashes once more.

As she gazed before her, something bright seemed leaping back and forth; a flame—that played on the wall; revealing the joints between the stones of massive masonry; casting shadows, but to wipe them out; paling near a small window, the only aperture apparent in the cell-like place. Turning from the flickerings, her glance quickly sought their source—a fire in a hearth, before which she lay—or half-sat, propped against a stone.

But why? The spot was strange; in her ears sounded a buzzing, like the murmur of a waterfall. She remembered now; she had lingered before one— in the woods; and Saladin had run away, madly, across the sands, until— my lady raised her hand to her brow; abruptly let it fall. In the shadow on the other side of the hearth some one moved; some one who had been watching her and who now stepped out into the light.

"Are you better?" said a voice.

She stared. On the bold, swarthy features of a young man now standing and looking down at her, the light flared and gleamed; the open shirt revealed a muscular throat; the down-turned black eyes were steady, solicitous. His appearance was unexpected, yet not quite strange; she had seen him before, but, in the general surprise and perplexity of the moment, did not ask herself where. The interval between what she last remembered on the beach—the rush and swirl of water—and what she woke to, absorbed the hazy workings of her mind.

The young man stopped; stirred the fire, and after a pause, apparently to give her time to collect her thoughts, repeated his question: "Are you better, now?"

"Oh, yes," she said, with an effort, half sitting up. And then irrelevantly, with rather a wild glance about her: "Isn't—isn't it storming outside?"

"A little—not much—" A smile crossed the dark features.

"I remember," she added, as if forcing herself to speak, "it had just begun to, on the beach, when it—the 'grand' tide—" The words died away; mechanically she lifted her hand, brushed back the shining waves of hair.

"Why think of it now?" he interposed gently.

"But," uncertainly she smoothed her skirt; it was damp and warm; "I suppose this is the island of Casque?"

"Yes."

"And this place?"

"The old watch-tower."

"But how—" Then she noticed that his hands, long, brown and well-formed, were cut and bruised; bore many jagged marks as from a fierce struggle. "How did you hurt your hands?"

He thrust them into his pockets.

"Was it from the rocks—and the waves? How did I get here?"

"Oh, I was standing on the cliff," he answered carelessly, "and—saw your horse running away!"

"You did? And then—came down?"

"What else was there to do?" he said simply.

Her gaze returned to the fire. "But the tide was rushing in—rushing! it was right upon me!"

 "But the tide--it was right upon me!"

"But the tide—it was right upon me!"

She looked again toward the pockets into which his hands were thrust; observed his shirt, torn at the shoulder; then arose unsteadily. "I know—it was not so easy!" she said. "It was brave of you—"

"Your Ladyship is no coward!" he interrupted, a sparkle in his eyes. "When you turned the horse toward the tide, I was watching; hoping you would dare, and you did!"

About to reply, she became once more aware she was still very dizzy from the fall on the sand; the shapely figure swayed and she put out her hand with a gesture of helplessness. At the same time, the man reached forward quickly and caught her. A moment was she conscious of a firm grasp; a dark, anxious gaze bent upon her; then, slid gently back to the stone seat.

A brief interval, and gradually she began to see again more distinctly—a man's face, not far from hers; a face that drew back as her own look cleared. At a respectful distance he now stood, his bearing at once erect and buoyant, and more curiously she regarded him. A distinct type, here pride and intelligence stamped themselves strongly on the dark, handsome features; courage and daring were written on the bold, self-reliant brow. And with this realization of something distinctive, compelling, in his personality, came another.

"I have seen you—spoken with you before! On the beach—the night of the dance!"

The young man turned. "Your Ladyship so far honored me—as to dance with me!" he said, in his eyes a touch of that brightness that had caused her to regard him imperiously, as he had swung her to the measure of the music, on the occasion in question.

"Started to!" She corrected him, straightening suddenly at the recollection of that evening, when humility and modesty were virtues conspicuously wanting in his demeanor.

"Your Ladyship is right," he said quietly. "An alarm from the Mount interrupted."

She glanced at him quickly. His eyes met hers with a look of unconcern.

"Are you—a fisherman?" she asked abruptly.

"On occasions."

"And when you are not one—what are you then?"

"At times—a hunter."

"Ah!" Her eye lingered on something bright on the ledge beneath the window. "And that is the reason you have—pistols?"

"Exactly, my Lady!"

She continued to regard the weapons, of finest workmanship, inlaid with a metal that gleamed dully, like gold, in the light from the fire. His glance followed hers; she was about to speak, when quickly he interrupted.

"Has your Ladyship thought how she is going to get back to the Mount?"

My lady's questioning, along the line of personal inquiry, ceased; the Governor's daughter looked a little blank. "No—that is, haven't you a boat?"

"Not here."

"Then you walked over?"

He neither affirmed, nor denied.

"And the tide will not be out for hours!" Her look showed consternation; she glanced toward the opening in the wall. "Isn't it becoming dark now?"

"Yes, my Lady."

"Of course, it was almost sundown when— But I must return at once! Don't you understand?"

He regarded her silently; the beautiful, impatient eyes; the slim, white fingers that tapped restlessly, one against another. "I will do what I can!" he said at last slowly.

"But what?" she demanded. "What can you do?"

He did not answer; my lady made a gesture.

"How ridiculous! A prisoner on an island!"

"There may be a way," he began.

"My horse?" she said quickly. "What became of him?"

"He was swept away by the tide!"

Into the proud eyes came a softer light—of regret, pain.

"Your Ladyship should remember it might have been worse," he added, in tones intended to reassure her. "After all, it was only a horse—"

"Only a horse!" she exclaimed indignantly. "But, I suppose you can't understand—caring for a horse!"

"I can understand caring for a ship!" he answered quickly, a flash of amusement, hardly concealed, in his bold, dark eyes.

"A ship!" scornfully; "dead wood and iron."

"Live wood and iron! Beautiful as—" The simile failed him; he looked at my lady. "Something to be depended on, with a hand to the wheel, and an eye keen for mad dancings and curvetings."

"I might appreciate them better," she interrupted dryly, with delicate brows uplifted, "an they brought me nearer to the Mount. That, and not idle opinions," in accents that conveyed surprise at the temerity of one in his position to express them, "is of most moment!"

He accepted the reproof with a readiness that further surprised her. "Your Ladyship is right," he said. "I will see what may be done. The storm has passed. There is yet daylight, and"—an expression, almost preoccupied, came to his features—"a boat may be sighted."

"To be sure!" At the prospect, all other considerations passed from my lady's mind. "A boat may be sighted! Why did you not think of it before? Come! Too much time has already been lost." And she rose.

"One moment!" His voice was quiet; respectful; although, she fancied, constrained. "I had better go alone. The way to the cliff is rough, and—"

"I shall not mind that!"

"Besides, your clothes—"

"Are dry!"

"No!" She flushed at the abrupt contradiction. "I mean, I don't see how they could be!" he went on hurriedly, "and," his tone assumed a certain obduracy, "I assure your Ladyship, it will be best."

"Best?" She looked at him more sharply. "Is that your only reason?"

"Why?" A trace of embarrassment, for an instant, crossed his dark features. "What other reason, my Lady?"

"That I know not!" quickly, assured her words had struck home. "Only I am certain there is one!"

"Then, if your Ladyship must know," he spoke slowly. "I did not wish to alarm you. But this is a rough coast, with—many rough people about—smugglers, privateersmen—"

"Whom you, perhaps, are expecting?" she cried suddenly.

"I!" with a careless laugh. "A fisherman! Your Ladyship is imaginative—" he began, when a sudden, hasty footstep clinked on the stones without; a hand caught at the fastenings of the door; flung it open.

"I thought I should find you here, Seigneur!" exclaimed a voice. "Since—"

The young man made a movement and the speaker stopped; caught sight of my lady, just beyond, in the fading light. And at the picture—her figure behind that other one—the fine, patrician features, framed by the disordered golden hair, the widely opened eyes, bright, expectant, the intruder started back.

"The Governor's daughter! You, Seigneur!" he stammered, and, raising his hand, involuntarily crossed himself.

<h1 style="text-align:center">CHAPTER IX</h1>

<h2 style="text-align:center">A DISCOVERY</h2>

"Why did you do that?" It was Lady Elise who now spoke, lifting her head haughtily to regard the new-comer, as she stepped toward him. "Cross yourself, I mean?"

"This good fellow, my Lady, is surprised to see you here, and small wonder he forgets his manners!" said the young man coolly, speaking for the other. "But he is honest enough—and—intends no disrespect!"

"None whatever!" muttered the intruder, a thin, wizened, yet still active-looking person.

My lady did not reply; her gaze, in which suspicion had become conviction, again met the young man's, whose black eyes now gleamed with a sudden, challenging light.

"With your permission, my Lady, I will speak with this fellow," he said, and abruptly strode from the tower; walked a short distance away, followed by the man, when he stopped.

"Certes, your tongue betrayed you that time, Sanchez!" he said confronting the other.

The man made a rough gesture. "C'est vrai!" regretfully. "But when I saw you two together I thought I had seen a—" He stopped. "She is so like—"

"Nay; I don't blame you; the sight was certainly unexpected! I had thought to come down and prepare you, but—'tis done!"

"And I knew what it meant." The old servant looked over his shoulder toward the tower.

"Call it magic!" with a short laugh.

"Diablerie!" muttered the other.

"Well, have your way! Why," abruptly, "did you not meet me here last night at high tide, as we had planned?"

"The priest came not in time; fearing he was watched, waited until night to leave his hiding-place at Verranch."

"And after missing me last night, you thought to find me here to-day?"

"I knew you were most anxious to see him; that upon him depended your chance to undo some of his Excellency, the Governor's, knavery! And, then, to find you here with the daughter of the man who has wrought you so much wrong; robbed you of your lands—your right to your name!" A cloud shadowed the listener's bold brow. "I know not how it came about, Seigneur, but be assured, no good can come of it!"

From where she stood, at the distance to the tower, the Governor's daughter saw now the two men descend; she perceived, also, at a turn in the path, coming up slowly, as one whose years had begun to tell upon him, another figure, clad in black; a priest. This last person and the Black Seigneur accosted each other; stopped, while the other man, who had crossed himself at sight of her, drew aside. At length, somewhat abruptly, they separated, the priest and Sanchez going down the hill and the young man starting to walk up. Then quickly leaving the ancient, circular structure for observation, she stepped toward the cliff, not far to the right; and in an attitude of as great unconcern as she could summon, waited.

Below the ocean beat around the rock, and her eyes seemed to have rested an interminable period on the dark surface of the water, when at length she heard him; near at hand; directly behind. Still she did not stir; he, too, by the silence, stood motionless. How long? The little foot moved restlessly; why did he not speak? She knew he was looking at her—the Governor's daughter who had inadvertently looked into a forbidden chamber; was possessed of dangerous knowledge.

Again she made a movement. When was he going to speak? It was intolerable that he should stand there, studying, deducing! That she, accustomed to command; to be served; to have her way at court and Mount, should now be judged, passed upon, disposed of, by—whom? Quickly she looked around; the flashing brown eyes met the steady black ones.

"Well?"

"The man will take you back." His manner was quiet; composed; implied a full cognizance of what she knew, and an absence of any further desire to attempt to disguise the truth.

"Back! Where?" She could not conceal her surprise.

"To the Mount."

For the moment she did not speak; she had not known what to expect— certainly not that.

"Why not?" A smile, slightly forced, crossed his face. "Does your Ladyship think I make war on women? Only, before your Ladyship departs, it will be necessary for you to agree to a little condition."

"Condition?" She drew her breath quickly.

"That you will say nothing to incriminate him. He is an old servant of mine; has broken none of the laws of the land," with a somewhat contemptuous accent, "works his bit of ground; pays métayage, and a tax on all the fish he brings in. Only in a certain matter to-day has he served me."

"You mean I must say nothing about meeting him? You?"

"For his sake!"

"And your own!"

"Mine?" He made a careless gesture. "I should not presume! For myself I should exact, or expect, from your Ladyship no promise. To-night I shall be far away. But this good fellow remains behind; should be allowed to continue his peaceful, lowly occupation. I would not have anything happen to him on my account."

"And if I refuse to promise?" she asked haughtily. "To enter into any covenant with—you!"

"But you will not!" he said steadily. "Your Ladyship, for her own sake, should not force the alternative."

"Alternative?"

"Why speak of it?"

"What is the alternative?" she demanded.

"If your Ladyship refuses to promise, it will be necessary for the man to return alone."

"You mean," in spite of herself, she gave a start, "you would make me—a prisoner?"

"It should not be necessary."

"But you would not dare!" indignantly.

"Not dare! Your Ladyship forgets—"

"True!" with a scornful glance. After a pause: "But suppose I did promise? Are you not reposing a good deal of confidence in me?"

"Not too much!"

"I presume," disdainfully, "I should feel flattered in being trusted by—" She did not finish the sentence.

But the young man apparently had not heard. "I'll take the chance on your own words," he added unexpectedly.

"My words?"

"That you are no telltale."

The girl started. "Telltale?" she repeated.

"You once told me you were not!"

"I—told you!" She stared at him.

"Told me you were no telltale," he repeated. "And—when Beppo lied, you told the truth—about a ragged vagabond of a boy."

"Beppo!" The look in her eyes deepened; cleared. "I remember now," she said slowly. "You were the boy with the fish, who said he lived in the woods. I met you while riding, and again that night, as a child, leaving for Paris; but I did not know, then, you would become—"

The young man's face changed. "An outlaw!" he said coolly.

"Yes; an outlaw," she repeated firmly. Angered by his unflinching gaze, she went on: "Who dares not fly the flag of his king! Who dares not come openly into any honest port!"

She ended, her brown eyes flashing. His own darkened; but he only remarked coldly; "My Lady, at any rate, dares much!"

"Oh, I've no doubt you don't care to hear—"

"From you!" He looked at her oddly, from the golden hair to the small, dainty foot. "From your Ladyship!" he repeated, as if amused. An instant he regarded her silently, intently; but his voice when at length he again spoke was cool and slightly mocking: "My Lady speaks, of course, from the standpoint of her own world—a very pretty world! A park of plaisance, wherein, I can vouch for it, my Lady dances very prettily."

She started; a flush of resentment glowed and faded on her cheek; a question his words suggested trembled on her lips.

"Why did you come to the beach that night of the dance? How dared you, knowing that if—"

"Why?" His eyes lost their ironical light. "Why?" he repeated; then laughed with sudden recklessness. "I wished to see your Ladyship."

"Me?" She shrank back.

"You!" he repeated, his gaze fastened on the startled, proud face. "Though I looked not forward to a dance—with your Ladyship!" The black eyes glowed. "Pardi! It was worth the risk." A moment he waited; then his manner changed. "I will leave your Ladyship now," he said quietly. "You will have opportunity to consider"—she did not answer—"whether you will give me your promise, or not," he added, and, wheeling abruptly, walked away.

Some time later, in the fast-gathering darkness, from the cove a small boat put out, with Sanchez, gloomy and sullen, in the stern; at the bow, the Governor's daughter. As the isle receded and the point of land loomed bigger before them, the girl gazed straight ahead; but the man looked back: to the sands of the little cove, a pale simitar in the dragon-like mouth of the rock; toward the tower, near which he fancied he could see a figure, turned from them—seaward—where, far out, a ship might just be discerned, a dim outline on the horizon.

CHAPTER X

THE CLOISTER IN THE AIR

Irrespective of environment, the cloister of the Mount would have been a delight to the eye, but, upheld in mid air, with the sky so near and the sands so far below, it seemed more an inspiration of fancy than a work of hand. Dainty, delicate, its rose-colored columns of granite appeared too thin for tangible weight; the tympan's sculptured designs, fanciful as the carvings in some palace of a poet's dreams. Despite, however, this first impression of evanescence, it carried a charm against the ravages of time, and ethereal though it was, had rested like a crown on the grim head of the rock through the ages.

Once a place for quiet meditation, the cloister had, through a whirligig of change, become the favorite resort of the Governor, for déjeûner, or after-dinner dram, and, on occasions, for the transaction of much profane though necessary labor pertaining to his office and private concerns. He busied himself there now; or had been busying himself, but paused to look up from the large book before him, whose pages were inscribed with items and figures. His finger, following the mental computation, remained stationary. Fouage—tax upon fires; banvin—duties on wine; vingtain—the lord's right to his share of the produce; minage—his due from each mine or half setier of coin—consideration of these usually all-important matters seemed for the moment to have been forgotten.

He leaned back, and as he sat thus, the light and shadow playing on him, the dark, steely eyes looked the more sunken, the hard, cynical lips beneath the white mustache, the more cruel, the spare figure the more alert and ready, as if to grapple with some hidden danger.

"J'arrive en ce pays

De Basse Normandie—"

At one of the apertures looking out to the barren waste of sand stood the Lady Elise; the words of the old Norman chant she was singing in desultory fashion rang softly, oddly, in that spot, where black-clad brethren for centuries had been wont to tread. Mechanically the Governor listened, but the voice soon ceased abruptly and again, after the manner of one of orderly habits, he bent over the big book; once more the curving finger slid up and down, and parsimony, the vice of the aged, had begun to shine from his pinched features, when a footstep rang on the marble pavement.

"Your Excellency sent for me?" The commandant stood respectfully near.

The Governor closed the book with deliberation; lifted his eyes. "The prisoners that were taken last night are safely housed?"

"Housed? Yes, your Excellency! But we have little room. The upper cells are all occupied; the dungeons, fairly full! Even the In-pace and Les Deux Jumeaux have been pressed into service."

"Hum!" The long hand tapped restlessly a moment; the cold eyes gleamed, then shot an inquiring look. "There are no new particulars about last night's encounter with this—Black Seigneur?"

"None, your Excellency, except," the commandant drew a paper from his breast pocket, "I have here in writing the detailed account of the officer in charge of your Excellency's boat, who was wounded himself in the encounter."

"Read it."

The commandant obeyed. "'Our schooner, belonging to his Excellency, the Governor, was returning last night to the Mount with troops—reinforcements for the garrison from St. Dalard—when it happened quite by accident near a ship, maneuvering at a respectful distance from the island of Casque. The night was dark and cloudy, but our men got a look at her and suspecting who she was and knowing her armament, against our will, we felt obliged to bear away. She, having no reason to think us other than a fishing schooner, or that we were freighted with troops instead of cod, did not follow and we had passed out of sight, and were rounding the island when we ran into two small sail-boats that had just set out from there.'"

"To join the ship of this outlaw!" interposed the Governor. "Go on!" shortly.

"'We hailed; their answer was unsatisfactory; we ordered them to halt, whereupon they tried to sail away. We followed and overtaking them, commanded them to surrender. Their leader, who was the Black Seigneur himself, refused, and we attacked'—"

"Bien! 'We attacked!' But what then? Eh, what then?"

"'With fury they responded; in spite of their inferiority of numbers tried to board us. Bravely our men repulsed them; yet still they persisted; led by their captain, the Black Seigneur, had gained the deck when a chance shot struck him. As he fell back, the others tried to escape; one boat was sunk'—"

"And the other, bearing their leader, got away!" interrupted the Governor harshly.

"In the confusion—yes, your Excellency."

The Governor waved his hand impatiently.

"'By this time the ship of the Black Seigneur had drawn nearer and our men put about and made for the Mount with a number of prisoners. Several shots were sent after us, but we managed to reach port.'"

"The officer in charge of the troops thinks this fellow, their leader, was wounded severely—fatally perhaps?"

"He thinks it most probable, your Excellency."

For some time the Governor, with frowning brows, sipped silently from a glass of liquor at his elbow, and, stiff, motionless, the commandant waited; close at hand, a dove plumed itself on the roof of the cloister walk; beyond, the girl again began to sing fitfully.

Out of the corner of his eye the commandant dared look at her, leaning now against the wall, the clear-cut, white features outlined against an illimitable blue background.

"Les amours—"

Involuntarily he started to raise a hand to his warlike mustache, when abruptly was his wandering attention recalled. "The man ashore I spoke to you about, has been taken into custody?"

"Yes, your Excellency; and is now at the barracks."

"Send him here. One moment—" The commandant paused, vaguely conscious the girl had moved away from the wall. "You spoke of there being a lack of room—these new prisoners must be confined in the dungeons; if necessary, crowd more of the others in the upper cells, and—there is still the Devil's Cage."

"The Devil's Cage?" Through the rose-tinted columns, above the Governor's head, the commandant could discern the figure of the Lady Elise, who had approached and now was gazing inquiringly at them. "Your Excellency would use that? One can neither lie down in it, nor sit in it, upright?"

"Well," the cold eyes flashed, "it is not intended for upright people! But the man you were ordered to arrest!" with sudden sharpness; "the man from the shore! Send him to me!"

"At once, your Excellency!" And responding promptly to his superior's mood, the commandant saluted briskly, and retired.

"What man?" The drapery of her gown drawn back, the Lady Elise stood poised on the court's low coping between the fairy-like pillars.

"No one you know, my dear."

"Which means—it is none of my concern?"

"Not at all." His voice was now perfunctory; and his expression, as he surveyed her, slightly questioning. "You are looking somewhat pale to-day?"

"Am I?" carelessly. "I—I feel very well." As she spoke, she went to him and leaned over the back of his chair. "Mon père, won't you do something for me?"

"What?"

"Promise first." With her hand on his shoulder.

He reached up; the long, cold fingers stroked the shapely, warm ones. "One should never leap into the dark with a promise," he answered. "Especially to a woman."

"Not even when that woman is one's own daughter?" she asked, sliding to the arm of the chair.

He regarded the bright face now thoughtful; the lips, usually laughing, set sensitively. "Is it another trip to the court, or do you wish to turn this stern old Mount again into a palace of pleasure? To invite once more the Paris lords and ladies—the King, himself, perhaps? It would not be the first time a monarch has been entertained at the Mount—or a Marquis, either, eh? Shall we ask the Marquis?"

She made an impatient movement. "I want you to promise to break up the terrible iron cage, and—"

"Tut!" Jocosely he pinched the fair cheek. "A girl's thoughts should be of the court and the cavaliers."

She turned away her head. "You treat me like a child," she said with a flash in her eyes.

"No, no! Like a woman," he laughed. "But the Marquis—perhaps he could not come here; perhaps he is too much concerned with the gaieties of Paris!" Her figure straightened; she was about to walk away, when—

"You ride this afternoon?" he asked.

"I had not thought of it."

"If you do I desire that some one accompany you." Her face changed; she looked at him quickly, and half turned. "Remember Saladin as well, and—keep closer to the Mount in the future."

"Poor Saladin!" she breathed, with averted glance.

"He got his deserts!" answered the Governor harshly. "An ugly trick that of his—to bolt and leave you stranded at the extreme point of the mainland where the bay swings around!"

"The 'grand' tide—it came in so fast—and made so much noise—"

"It frightened him! Well, fortunate it was, indeed, you were not on his back; that you had already reached the point, and had had time to dismount! An unpleasant experience, nevertheless—with the water separating you from the Mount, and a great curve of land to be walked before you could arrive at a human habitation!"

"I—it wasn't a very comfortable feeling," she acknowledged, flushing.

"And if the fisherman hadn't subsequently seen you and taken you across in his little boat, you would have been more uncomfortable later. You rewarded him well, I trust?"

"He—wouldn't take anything."

"And you neglected to inquire his name?"

"I—did not think."

"You were so glad to get back?" remarked the Governor, regarding her closely. "What sort of man was he?" abruptly.

"Old."

"And—"

"That—is all I remember."

"Hum! Not very lucid. No doubt you were too overwrought, my dear, to be in an observant mood." His voice sank absently; his fingers sought among the papers, and, as his glance fell, the girl walked away. Again she leaned on the parapet, and once more regarded the barren waste below—the figures of the cockle-seekers, mere specks, the shadow of the Mount, stamped on the sand, with the saint, a shapeless form, holding up a tapering black line—a sword—at the apex.

"She is keeping back something. What?" Above an official-looking document the Governor watched her, his lips compressed, his eyes keen; then shrugged his shoulders and resumed his occupation. The death-like hush of an aërial region surrounded them; the halcyon peace of a seemingly chimerical cloister; until suddenly broken by an indubitable clangor—harsh, hard!—of a door, opening; shutting. The Governor lifted his head in annoyance; the dove on the roof of the cloister-walk flew away, and a short, fat man, breathing hard, appeared.

"Pardon, your Excellency! But the drafts! They seem sometimes to sweep up from the very dungeons themselves, and—"

"Well?"

Beppo cut short excuse, or explanation. "A prisoner is waiting without. The man, Sanchez, from the shore! Monsieur le Commandant, who brought him, told me to inform you."

The Governor considered a moment with down-bent brows. "You may show him in, but first," he glanced up with a frown, "I have a question to put to you."

"Your Excellency?"

"This morning you thought fit to apprise me," Beppo looked uncomfortable, "in view of the events of last night—that you saw yesterday this fellow, Sanchez, setting out in a sail-boat, accompanied by a priest—a fact that might have been of great service to me, had I been aware of it in season!" The Governor paused to allow the full weight of his disapproval to be felt. "At what hour did you see them start out?"

"About dusk, the time of the 'grand' tide," was the crestfallen answer. "I was following the shore, feeling anxious on account of the Lady Elise, who, I knew, had gone in the direction of the forest, when I saw them, some distance out, but not too far to recognize this fellow's boat and in it two men, one of them in the black robes of a priest. I attached no importance to the incident until—"

The Governor interrupted. "You may send the prisoner in," he said shortly. "No—wait!" Toward the spot where the girl had been standing the Governor glanced quickly, but that post of observation was now vacant, and his Excellency more deliberately looked around; caught no sight of her. "You may send him in here," he said, "alone. I will speak with the prisoner in private."

CHAPTER XI

THE GOVERNOR IS SURPRISED

But the Lady Elise had not gone. Passing from the cloister through the great arched doorway leading to the high-roofed refectory, she had stopped at the sight of a number of people gathered near the entrance. At first she had merely glanced at them; then started, as, in the somewhat dim light prevailing there, her eyes became fixed upon one of their number.

Obviously a prisoner, he stood in the center of the group, with head down-bent, a hard, indifferent expression on his countenance. Amazed, the girl was about to step forward to address him—or the commandant—when Beppo appeared from the cloister, walked toward the officer, and, in a low ill-humored tone, said something she could not hear. Whatever it was, the commandant caused him to repeat it; made a gesture to the soldiers, who drew back, and spoke himself to the prisoner.

The latter did not reply nor raise his eyes, and the commandant laid a heavy hand on his shoulder, whereupon the prisoner moved forward mechanically, through the doorway.

"You are sure his Excellency said 'alone'?" asked the commandant.

"As sure as I have ears," answered Beppo. "But her ladyship—see! She is walking after him."

Beppo shrugged his shoulders. "She always does what she pleases; no orders apply to her."

In the shadow of the cloister roof, at a corner where the double row of pillars met, the girl paused; looked out through the columns, her hand at her breast. The Governor was unconcernedly writing; not even when the prisoner stepped forward did he turn from his occupation; at his leisure dotted an "i" and crossed a "t"; sprinkled sand lightly over the paper; waited a moment; then tapped the fine particles from the letter. For his part, the prisoner displayed equal patience, standing in an attitude of stolid endurance.

"Your name is Sanchez?" At length the Governor seemed to notice the other's presence.

"Yes."

"And you formerly served the Seigneur Desaurac? Followed him to America?"

"As your Excellency knows." The servant's tone was veiled defiance.

A trace of pink sprang to the Governor's brow, though the eyes he lifted were impassive. "You will answer 'yes' or 'no'!" He reached for a stick of wax, held it up to the tiny flame of a lamp; watched the red drops fall. "When you returned, it was to live in the forest with—a nameless brat?"

"My master's son!"

"By a peasant woman, his—"

"Wife!"

The Governor smiled; applying a seal, pressed it hard. "The courts found differently," he observed in a mild, even voice, as speaking to himself and extolling the cause of justice.

"The courts! Because the priest who married them had been driven from Brittany! Because he could not be found then! Because—" The man's indignation had got the better of his taciturnity, but he did not finish the sentence.

"Either," said the Governor quietly, "you are one of those simple-minded people who, misguided by loyalty, cherish illusions, or you are a scheming rogue. No matter which, unfortunately," in crisp tones, "it is necessary to take time to deal with you."

"At your Excellency's service!" And the man folded his arms but, again turning to his table, the Governor apparently found some detail of employment there of paramount importance; once more kept the prisoner waiting.

The silence lengthened; in the dim light of the walk noiselessly the girl drew nearer; unseen, reached the old abbot's great granite chair with its sheltering back to the court and close to the Governor's table. Into the capacious depths of this chilly throne, where once the high and holy dignitary of the church had been accustomed to recline while brethren laved his feet from the tiny stone lavatorium before it, she half sank, her cheek against one of its cold sides; in an attitude of expectation breathlessly waited. Why was it so still? Why did not her father speak? She could hear his pen scratch, scratch!

They were again speaking; more eagerly she bent forward; listened to the hard, metallic voice of the Governor.

"You left the castle at once when the decree of the court, ordering it vacated, was posted in the forest?"

"My master told me to, pretending he was going, but—"

"Remained to resist; to kill." The Governor's tones, without being raised, were sharper. "And when, after the crime against these instruments of justice, he escaped to the high seas, why did you not go with him?"

"He wouldn't have it."

"Thinking you would be more useful here? A spy?"

"He said he would be held an outlaw; a price put on him, and—he dismissed me from his service."

"Dismissed you? An excellent jest! But," with sudden incisiveness, "what about the priest, eh? What about the priest?"

The man straightened. "What priest?" he said in a dogged tone.

"You are accused of harboring and abetting an unfrocked fellow who has long been wanted by the government, a scamp of revolutionary tendencies; you are accused of having taken him to sea," the prisoner started, "to some rendezvous—a distant isle—to meet some one; to wait for a ship; to be smuggled away—?"

The man did not reply; with head sunk slightly, seemed lost in thought.

"Speak—answer!"

"Who accuses me?"

From the stone chair the girl sprang; looked out. Her face white, excited, peering beneath the delicate spandrils and stone roses, seemed to come as an answer.

"Have I not told you—" began the Governor sternly, when—

"Bah!" burst from the prisoner violently. "Why should I deny what your Excellency so well knows? I told my master not to trust her; that she would play him false; and that once out of his hands—"

"Her? Whom do you mean?" The Governor's eyes followed the man's; stopped. "Elise!"

"I think," her eyes very bright, the girl walked quickly toward them, "I think this man means me."

"Elise!" the Governor repeated.

"Forgive me, mon père; I didn't intend to listen, but I couldn't help it—because—"

"How long," said the Governor, "have you been there?"

"Ever since—he came in. I suppose," proudly turning to the man, "it is useless to say that I did not play this double rôle of which you accuse me, and that I did keep, in every particular, the promise I made—"

"Oh, yes; you could say it, my Lady!" with sneering emphasis.

"But you reserve to yourself the right not to believe me? That is what you mean?" The man's stubborn, vindictive look answered. "Then I will deny nothing to you; nothing! You may think what you will."

His face half-covered by his hand, the Governor gazed at them; the girl, straight, slender, inflexibly poised; the prisoner eying her with dark, unvarying glance.

"Dieu!" he muttered. "What is this?" and concern gave way to a new feeling. Her concern for something—somebody—held him. A promise! "You can step back a few moments, my man!" to Sanchez. "A little farther—to the parapet! I'll let you know when you're wanted." And the prisoner obeyed, moving slowly away to the wall, where he stood out of ear-shot, his back to them. "You spoke of a promise?" the Governor turned to his daughter. "To whom?"

A suggestion of color swept her face, though she answered at once without hesitation: "To the Black Seigneur."

The slight form of the Governor stirred as to the shock of a battery.

"There is no harm in telling now," hurriedly she went on. "He saved me from the 'grand' tide—for I was on Saladin's back when he bolted and ran. I had not dismounted, though I allowed you to infer so, and he had carried me almost to the island of Casque when we heard and saw the water coming in. The nearest place was the island—not the point of the mainland, as I felt obliged to lead you to think, and we started for it; we might have reached the cove, had not Saladin stumbled and thrown me. The last I remembered the water came rushing around, and when I awoke, I was in a watch-tower, with him—the Black Seigneur!"

The Governor looked at her; did not speak.

"I—I at first did not know who he was—not until this man came—and the priest! And when he, the Black Seigneur, saw I had learned the truth, he asked me to promise—not for himself—but because of this man!—to say nothing of having met him there, or the others! And I did promise, and—he sent me back—and that is all—"

"All!" Did the Governor speak the word? He sat as if he had hardly comprehended; a deeper flush dyed her cheek.

"You—you can not blame me—after what he did. He saved me—saved my life. You are glad of that, mon père, are you not? And it must have been hard doing it, for his clothes were torn, and his hands were bleeding—he can't be all bad, mon père! He knew who I was, yet trusted me—trusted!"

The Governor looked at her; touched a bell; the full-toned note vibrated far and near.

"What are you going to do?" Something in his face held her.

Again the tones startled the stillness. "Remember, it is I who am responsible for—"

"Your Excellency?" Across the court appeared Beppo, moving quickly toward them. "Your Excellency?"

"One moment!" The servant stepped back; the Governor looked first at the girl; then toward the entrance of the cloister.

"You want me to go?" Her voice was low: strained; in it, too, was a hard, rebellious accent. "But I can't—can't—until—"

"What?"

"You promise to set him free! This man who brought me back! Don't you see you must, mon père? Must!" she repeated.

His thin lips drew back disagreeably; he seemed about to speak; then reached among the papers and, turned them over absently. "Very well!" he said at length without glancing up.

"You promise," her voice expressed relief and a little surprise, "to set him free?"

"Have I not said so?" His eyelids veiled a peculiar look. "Yes, he shall be liberated—very shortly."

"Thank you, mon père." A moment she bent over him; the proud, sweet lips brushed his forehead. "I will go, then, at once." And she started toward the door. Near the threshold she paused; looked back to smile gratefully at the Governor, then quickly went out.

CHAPTER XII

AT THE COCKLES

A rugged mass of granite, rent by giant fissures, and surrounded by rocks and whirlpools, the Norman English isle, so-called "Key to the Channel," one hundred miles, or more, northwest of the Mount, had from time immemorial offered haven to ships out of the pale of French ports. Not only a haven, but a home, or that next-best accommodation, an excellent inn. Perched in the hollow of the mighty cliff and reached by a flight of somewhat perilous stone stairs, the Cockles, for so the ancient tavern was called, set squarely toward the sea, and opened wide its shell, as it were, to all waifs or stormy petrels blown in from the foamy deep.

Good men, bad men; Republicans, royalists; French-English, English-French, the landlord—old Pierre Laroche, retired sea-captain and owner of a number of craft employed in a dangerous, but profitable, occupation—received them willingly, and in his solicitude for their creature comforts and the subsequent reckoning, cared not a jot for their politics, morals, or social views. It was enough if the visitor had no lenten capacity; looked the fleshpots in the face and drank of his bottle freely.

The past few days the character of old Pierre's guests had left some room for complaint on that score. But a small number of the crew of the swift-looking vessel, well-known to the islanders, and now tossing in the sea-nook below, had, shortly after their arrival toward dusk of a stormy day, repaired to the inn, and then they had not called for their brandy or wine in the smart manner of seamen prepared for unstinted sacrifice to Bacchus. On the contrary, they drank quietly, talked soberly, and soon prepared to leave.

"Something has surely gone wrong," thought their host. "Why did not your captain come ashore?" he asked. "Not see his old friend, Pierre Laroche, at once! It is most unlike him."

And on the morrow, the islanders, or English-French, more or less privateersmen themselves, were equally curious. Where had the ship come from? Where was it going? And how many tons of wine, bales of silk and packages of tobacco, or "ptum," as the weed was called, had it captured? Old Pierre would soon find out, for early that day, despite the inclemency of the weather, he came down to the beach, and, followed by a servitor, got into a small boat moored close to the shore.

"He is going aboard!"

"Who has a better right? His own vessel!"

"No; André Desaurac—the Black Seigneur's! They say he long ago paid for it from prizes wrested from the Governor of the Mount."

"At any rate, old Pierre entered into a bargain to build the boat for him—"

"And added to his wealth by the transaction."

Later that morning the old man came ashore, but, according to habit, preserved a shrewd silence; in the afternoon a small number of the crew landed to take on stores and ammunition—of which there was ever a plentiful supply at this base; that night, however, all, including their master, betook themselves to the Cockles.

"Glad to see you ashore, mon capitaine!" Pierre Laroche, standing at the door, just beyond reach of the fierce driving rain, welcomed the Black Seigneur warmly; but the young man, one of whose arms seemed bound and useless, cut short his greetings; tossed bruskly aside his dark heavy cloak, and called for a room where he might sit in private with a companion. This person the landlord eyed askance; nevertheless, with a show of bluff heartiness, he led the way to a small chamber, somewhat apart, but overlooking the long low apartment, the general eating and drinking place of the establishment, now filled by the crew and a number of the islanders.

"Your capitaine has been hurt? How?" A strapping, handsome girl, clad in red and of assured mien, passing across the room, paused to address a man of prodigious girth, who drank with much gusto from a huge vessel at his elbow.

"Did not your father, Pierre Laroche, tell you?"

"He? No; all he thinks of is the money."

"Then must le capitaine speak for himself, Mistress Nanette."

"You are not very polite, Monsieur Gabarie," she returned, tossing her head; "but I suppose there is a reason; you have been beaten. In an encounter with the Governor's ships? Did you sink any of them? It would be good news for us islanders."

"You islanders!" derisively.

"Yes, islanders!" she answered defiantly. "But tell me; a number of you wear patches, which make you look very ugly. They were acquired—how?"

"In a little clerical argument!" growled the poet.

She glanced toward the secluded apartment; its occupants—the subject of their conversation, and a priest, a feeble-looking man of about seventy, whose delicate, sad face shone white and out-of-keeping in that adventuresome company. "At any rate, the Black Seigneur hasn't lost his good looks!"

"Take care you don't lose your heart!"

"Bah!" Her strong bold eyes swept back. "Much good it would do me!"

"And for that reason—"

"Messieurs!" the landlord's voice broke in upon them; "behold!" it seemed to say, as pushing through the company, he preceded a lanky lad who bore by their legs many plucked fowls and birds—woodcock, wild duck, cliff pigeons—and made his way to the great open fireplace at one end of the room. There, bending over the glowing embers, the landlord deliberately stirred and spread them; then, reaching for a bar of steel, he selected a poulet from the hand of the lanky attendant and prepared to adjust it; but before doing so, prodded it with his finger, surveyed it critically, and held it up for admiring attention.

"Who says old Pierre Laroche doesn't know how to care for his friends? What think you of it, my masters?"

"Plump as the King's confessor," muttered the poet.

"Or your King himself!" said one of the islanders.

"On with the King! Skewer the King!" exclaimed a fierce voice.

"And then we'll eat him!" laughed the girl, showing her white teeth.

"Thoughtless children!" From his place at the table in the small room adjoining, the priest, attracted by the grim merriment of the islanders, looked down to regard them; the red fire; the red gown.

"Here, at least, will you find a safe asylum, Father," said his companion, the Black Seigneur, in an absent tone; "a little rough, perhaps, to suit your calling—"

"The rougher, the more suitable—as I've often had occasion to learn since leaving Verranch."

"Since being driven from it, you mean!" shortly.

"Ah, those revolutionary documents—placed in my garden!"

"To make you appear—you, Father!—a sanguinary character!" But the other's laugh rang false.

"Alas, such wickedness! But I was too content; the rose-covered cottage too comfortable; its garden, an Eden! It was more meet I should be driven forth; go out into the highways, where I found—such misery! I reproached myself I had not sought it sooner—voluntarily. From north to south peasants dying, women and children starving, no one to administer the last rites—on every side, work, work for the outcast priest! For ten years it has occupied him—a blessed privilege—"

"And then," the young man, who had seemed absorbed in other thoughts, hardly listening, looked mechanically up, "you came back?"

"A weakness of age! To see the old place once more! The little church; God's acre at its side; to stand on the hill at Verranch and look out a last time over the beautiful vale toward the Mount!" Briefly he paused. "Yet I am glad I yielded to the temptation; otherwise should I not have met your old servant, Sanchez; who told me all—how you had long been looking for me, and arranged our meeting for that day—on the island of Casque!"

"But not," the young man's demeanor at once became intent; his eyes gleamed with sudden fierce lights, "for what followed!"

The priest sighed. "Shall I ever forget it? The terrible night, the troop-ship, the killed and wounded. And the poor fellows taken prisoners! I can not but think of them and their fate. What will it be?"

The other did not answer; only impatiently moved his injured arm and, regarding him, the down-turned, dark countenance, the knit brows, quickly the priest changed the subject of conversation.

In the large room some one began to play, and before the fire, where now the birds were turning and the serving-lad, with a long spoon was basting, the dark-browed girl started to dance. At the side of the hearth old Pierre smoked stolidly, gazed at the coals, and dreamed—perhaps of the past, and dangers he had himself encountered, or of the present, and his ships scattered—where?—on profitable, if precarious errands. Somberly, in no freer mood than on the occasion of their first visit to the inn, the crew looked on; but a tall, savage-appearing islander soon matched her step; a second took his place; from one partner to another she passed—wild, reckless men whose touch she did not shun; yet it might have been noticed her eyes turned often, through wreaths of smoke, mist-like in the glare and glimmer of dips and torches, toward the Black Seigneur.

Why—her gaze seemed to say—did he not join them, instead of sitting there with a priest? She whirled to the threshold; her flushed face looked in. "Are you saying a mass for the souls of your men who were captured?"

"I see," he returned quietly, "you have been gossiping."

"A woman's privilege!" she flashed back. "But how did it happen? And not only your arm," more sharply regarding him, "but your head! I fancy if I were to push back a few locks of that thick hair I should discover—it must have been a pretty blow you got, my Seigneur Solitude!" He made no reply and she went on. "You, who I thought were never beaten! By a mere handful of troops, too! Did you have to run away very fast? If I were a man—"

"Your tongue would be less sharp," he answered coolly, the black eyes indifferent.

"Much you care for my tongue!" she retorted.

"No?"

"No!" she returned mockingly, when above the din of voices, the crackling of the fire, and the wild moaning of the wind in the chimney, a low, but distinct and prolonged call was heard,—from somewhere without, below.

"What is that?" Quickly Nanette turned; superstitious, after the fashion of most of her people, a little of the color left her cheek. Again was it wafted to them, nearer, plainer! "The voices of dead men from the sea!"

"More like some one on the steps who would like to get in—some fisherman who has just got to shore!" said old Pierre Laroche, waking up and emptying his pipe. "Throw open the door. The stones are slippery—the night dark—"

One of the crew obeyed, and, as the wind entered sharply, and the lights flickered and grew dim, there half staggered, half rushed from the gloom, the figure of a man, wild, wet, whose clothes were torn and whose face was freshly cut and marked with many livid signs of violence.

"Sanchez!" From his place the Black Seigneur rose.

The others looked around wonderingly; some with rough pity. "What's the matter, man?" said one. "You look as if you had had a bad fall."

"Fall!" Standing in the center of the room, where he had come to a sudden stop, the man gazed, bewildered, resentful, about him; then above the circle of questioning faces, his uncertain look lifted; caught and remained fixed on that of the Black Seigneur. "Fall?" he repeated, articulating with difficulty. "No; I had—no fall—but I will speak—with my master—alone!"

CHAPTER XIII

THE SEETHING OF THE SEA

"'I have concluded to deal leniently with you,' said the Governor; 'set you free!' I could not believe."

Alone in the little chamber, the door of which now was closed, shutting them from sight of the company in the general eating and drinking room adjoining, Sanchez and the Black Seigneur sat together. Before them the viands that had been placed on the table were untouched; the filled glasses, untasted. As he spoke, the man bent forward, his words disjointed; his eyes gleaming.

"'But,' the Governor added, 'the criminal must be taught not to forget'; then turned to his soldiers. 'Beat me this fellow from the Mount!' he commanded."

"What!" The blood sprang to the dark face of the listener; he half started from his chair. "And they did! A merry chase, down the streets, across the sands! I, an old soldier!" His voice choked. "Beaten like a dog!"

For some moments the young man looked at him; then again sank back; stared straight ahead. Without, the laughter and harsh voices of the islanders had become louder; within the little chamber, the only sound now was the hard, persistent ticking of the clock on the shelf.

"But how," at length Desaurac made a movement, "did he—"

"Learn!" violently. "The way I told you he would!"

"You mean—"

"That I was betrayed and you were—by the Lady Elise—"

"Impossible!" the Black Seigneur exclaimed with sudden violence.

"Because she has a pretty face!" sneered the other.

"Silence! Or—"

"That is it!" The servant's voice rose stridently. "Beaten at one end, threatened at the other!"

The arm the young man had reached out fell to his side. "Hush! You're mad; you don't know what you're saying!"

"And you did not know what you were doing! Oh, I dare say it—I tell you now I little liked the task of taking her back; expecting some sort of treachery, and, when it came, was not surprised! Any more than, when they had brought me before the Governor, I saw her at the cloister—watching, hiding—"

"Hiding!"

"Behind the coping to listen when he, her father, was questioning me! And, when I looked up and caught her, she walked out—to show me I might as well confess!"

"She did that?"

"Then tried to cozen me into believing it was not through her," went on the man bitterly, as if speaking to himself. "But I know the lying blood—none better—and when she saw it was no use," he paused and looked up, the marks of the stripes on his face seeming suddenly to burn and grow livid, "she acknowledged it to my face! 'I won't deny.' Those were her words! And when she left the place, she turned around to look back at me—and laugh—"

"You are not mistaken?"

"Perhaps," said the man, a venomous light in his obstinate eyes, "it was all a fancy; or—I am lying!"

Outside, the wind, blowing sharper, whistled about the eaves, beat at the window and shook the blinds angrily; far below, a steady monotone to those other sounds, could be heard the rush and breaking of the surf.

"Why did I cross myself that day on the island, when I saw her—behind you?" Sanchez's taciturnity—the reticence of years—suddenly burst its bonds. "Because she made me think of the former lady of the Mount—the Governor's wife—who betrayed the Seigneur, your father! I promised him to keep the secret—he would have it, for the sake of the lady; but now—to you! Your father was stabbed at the foot of the Mount by the Governor!—"

"Stabbed! By him!"

"It was given out," sourly, "by rogues—again to shield her!"

"But—"

"That same day he had a letter—from her. As evening fell he walked near the Mount—was followed by the Governor, who sprang, struck in the back and left him for dead! I found him and took him home. But before he recovered, it was reported my lady had died—"

"How?"

"I know not; a punishment, perhaps! She was always delicate—or liked to be considered such—a white-faced, pretty, smiling thing whose beauty and treachery this other one, the daughter, inherits. It was the ghost of herself looking over your shoulder that day on the island, with the same bright, perfidious eyes—"

"Enough!" Angrily the Black Seigneur brought down his hand. "I will hear no more!"

"Because she has caught your fancy! Because you—"

"No more, I say! Think you I would not avenge your wrongs at once, were it possible? That I would not strike for you, on the instant? But now? My hands are tied. Another matter—of life, or death—presses first!"

Sanchez looked at him quickly; said no more; between them, the silence grew. The servant was the first to move; turning to the table, he began to eat; at first mechanically; afterward faster, with the ravenous zest of one who has not tasted food for many hours. The other, for his part, showed no immediate desire to disturb that occupation; for some time waited; and it was not until the servant stopped; reached out his arm for a glass, to drink, that the young man again spoke.

"The palace? The plan of the Mount? Did you notice? Tell me something of it—how it is laid out—"

Sanchez swallowed; set down the glass hard. "Yes, yes! I saw much—a great deal!" he answered with eager zest. "Oh, I kept my eyes open, although I seemed not to, and was mindful of learning all I could!"

"Here!" From his pocket the young man took a note-book; pencil. "Set it down; everything! I know something, already, from the old monks—the rough diagrams in their books. You entered where? Take the pencil and—"

The minutes passed and still Sanchez traced; seemed almost to forget his injuries in his interest in the labor. Plan after plan was made; torn up; one finally remained in the hand of the Black Seigneur.

"You think—" Anxiously the servant watched his master's face; but the latter, straight, erect, with keen eyes fixed, did not answer.

"You think—" again began the man when the ancient time-piece, beating harshly the hour, interrupted.

"Eleven o'clock! High tide!" The Black Seigneur pushed back his chair and rose.

"Good!" Sanchez's alacrity indicated a quick comprehension of what the movement portended.

"You—had better remain here!" shortly.

"Me?" said the servant with a hoarse laugh. "Me?"

"Have you not had enough of my family—my service?" the young Seigneur demanded bitterly.

"Bah!" muttered the other. "The dog that's beaten springs at the chance to bite! You go to rescue your comrades. I—will go with you!"

"In which case, death—not vengeance—will most likely be your reward!"

"I care not!" stubbornly.

A moment the Black Seigneur regarded him; then made a gesture.

"Well, have your way!" He listened. "The wind is in the west."

"A little south of west," answered the man.

"A rough night for your boat to have crossed!"

"Oh, I was bound to come! And if you hadn't been here, I'd have gone on, on,—till I found you—"

The hand of the young man touched the other's shoulder. "Come!" he said, and threw open the door.

"You are going in the storm?" The girl, Nanette, intercepted them.

The Black Seigneur nodded shortly.

"It must be an important mission to take you to sea on such a night. Why don't you stay where it's warm and comfortable? Or," with a laugh, "at least until Monsieur Gabarie," indicating the corpulent figure intrenched behind a barricade of dishes and bottles on a small table near the fire, "has finished the little puppet play he is writing."

"It is finished!" As he spoke, the poet rose. "I had but written 'curtain' when you spoke. Your wine, fair Nanette, hath a rarely inspiring quality!"

"Oh, I care not for your compliments!" she returned. "Your capitaine," again studying the Black Seigneur with dark sedulous eyes, "has not found it so much to his liking! He has neither asked for more, nor drunk what he ordered; and now would venture out—"

Unmindful of her words the young man called to old Pierre.

"Well," she went on, throwing back her head, "if you lose your ship, come to me, and—I'll see you have another!"

Above in his chamber at the inn, not long thereafter, the priest, looking out of the window, saw a line of men file down the narrow stairs; embark in the small boats from the sheltered nook where they lay, and later, in the light of the moon, breaking from between scudding clouds and angry vapors, a ship that got under way—glided like a phantom craft from the haven and set seaward through the foam.

CHAPTER XIV

THE PILGRIMAGE

From far and near the peasants and the people of the towns and villages, joined in the customary annual descent upon—or ascent to—the Mount. None was too poor, few too miserable, to undertake the journey. A pilgrimage, was the occasion called; but although certain religious ceremonies were duly observed and entered into by some with fanatical warmth, many there were, who, obliged to pay tithes, nourished the onerous recollection of the enforced "ecclesiastical tenth" to the exclusion of any great desire to avail themselves of the compensating privilege of beholding and bowing before the sacred relics. To these recalcitrant spirits, license and a rough sort of merrymaking became the order of the hour.

Early in the morning the multitude began to arrive—in every manner of dilapidated vehicle, astride starved-looking donkeys and bony horses, or on foot. Many who had camped out the night before, by wayside or in forest, brought with them certain scanty provisions and a kitchen pot in which to boil thin soup, or some poor makeshift mess; others came empty-handed, "pilgrims" out at the elbow and shoeless, trusting to fortune for their sustenance, and looking capable even of having poached in one of the wide forests they had traversed, despite a penalty, severe and disproportionate to the offense, for laying hand on any lord's wild birds or rabbits.

Savage men; sodden men—good, bad and indifferent! Like ants thronging about the hill, they straightway streamed to the Mount; took possession of it, or as much as lay open to them; for around the top, chosen abode of the Governor, extended a wall; grim, dark and ominous; bristling with holes which seemed to look blackly down; to watch, to listen and to frown. Without that pretentious line of encircling masonry, the usual din, accompaniment to the day and the presence of so many people, prevailed; within, reigned silence, a solemn hush, unbroken by even a sentinel's tread.

"I shall be glad when it's all over!" Standing at the window of her chamber the Lady Elise had paused in dressing to look out upon the throng—a thousand clots upon the sand, dark moving masses in the narrow byways, and motionless ones near the temporary altars.

"Oh, my Lady!" Her companion, and former nurse, a woman about fifty years of age, ventured this mild expostulation.

"There, Marie! You can go!"

"Yes, your Ladyship—"

"One moment!" The slender figure turned. "This fastening—"

In an instant the woman was by her side.

"Have you heard anything more about the prisoners, Marie?" abruptly. "Those who were tried, I mean?"

"Nothing—only Beppo said they are to be hanged day after to-morrow—when the pilgrimage is over."

"Day after to-morrow!" The brown eyes looked hard and bright; the small white teeth pressed her lip. "And the man my fa—the Governor had—whipped from the Mount—you have heard nothing more of him—where he has gone?"

"No, my Lady; he seems to have disappeared completely; fled this country, perhaps, for those islands where so many like him," half bitterly, "have gone before!"

The girl looked up in a preoccupied manner. "Poor Marie! Your only sister died there, didn't she?"

"Yes, my Lady; I never saw her after she left France with her husband and baby girl. He was an unpatriotic fellow—Pierre Laroche!"

"No doubt," said the Governor's daughter absently, as the other prepared to leave the room.

Alone, the girl remained for several moments motionless before the great Venetian mirror; then mechanically, hardly looking at the reflection the glass threw back at her, she finished her toilet. This task accomplished, still she stood with brows closely drawn; afar the flute-like voices of the choir-boys arose from different parts of the Mount, but she did not seem to hear them; made a sudden quick gesture and walked toward the door in the manner of one who has arrived at some resolution.

Passing down a corridor, she reached an arched opening whose massive door swung easily to her touch, and let herself out by a private way, which had once been the ancient abbot's way, to an isolated corner of a small secluded platform. From this point a stairway led up to a passage spanning a great gulf. Below and aside, where the red-tiled houses clung to the steep slope of the rock, fluttered many flags; yet the girl did not pause either to contemplate or admire. Only when her glance passed seaward and rested on the far-away ocean's rim of light, did she stop for an instant—mid-way on the bridge—then, compressing her lips, moved on the faster; down the incline on the other side; up winding stairs between giant columns, reaching, at length, that bright and grateful opening, the cloister. With an unvarying air of resolution she stepped forward; looked in; the place was empty—silent save for the tinkling of the tiny fountain in the center.

"Are you looking for some one, my Lady?"

The voice was that of Beppo, who was regarding her from an angle in the cloister walk.

"I am looking for his Excellency. I suppose he is—"

"In the apartments of state, my Lady. But—"

The girl frowned.

"But, but!" she said. "But what?"

"His Excellency has left word—he was expecting a minister from Paris—that no one else was to be admitted; the matter was so important that he wished no interruptions."

She had already turned, however; moved on past him without answer. At the inner entrance to the "little castle" or châtelet, which presently she reached, the girl stopped. Here, without, in the shadow of two huge cylindrical towers, that crowned the feudal gate-house, a number of soldiers, seated on the steps, clinked their swords and talked; within, beneath the high-vaulted dome of the guard-room lolled the commandant and several officers on a bench before a large window. Immediately on her appearance they rose, but, merely bowing stiffly, she started toward a portal on the left. Whereupon the commandant started forward, deferentially would have spoken—stopped her, when at the same moment, the door she was approaching opened, and the Governor himself appeared. At the sight of her he started; a shade of annoyance crossed his thin features, then almost immediately vanished; his cold eyes met hers expectantly.

"I have been told you were very busy, yet I must see you; it is very important—"

A fraction of a moment he seemed to hesitate; then with an absent air: "Certainly, I was very busy; nevertheless—" he stepped aside; permitted her to pass, and softly closed the door. With the same preoccupied air he walked to his table before one of the large fireplaces whose pyramidal canopies merged into the ribs of the vaulting of a noble chamber, and, seating himself in a cushioned chair, looked down at a few embers.

"I came," standing, with her fingers straight and stiff on the cold marble edge of the table, the girl began to speak hurriedly, constrainedly, "I wanted to see you—about the prisoners—"

He did not answer. Gently stroking his wrist, as if the dampness from some subterranean place had got into it, he evinced no sign he had heard; and this apathy and his apparent disregard of her awoke more strongly the feeling she had experienced so often since that day in the cloister, when he had promised to set free the servant of the Black Seigneur; had kept his word, indeed, but—

"Can't you see," she forced herself to continue, "after what the man Sanchez thought—suspected about me, what he said that day at the Mount, after what he, the Black Seigneur, did for me"—the Governor started—"that you, if you care for me at all," he looked at her strangely, "at least, should—"

"As I told you the other day," his accents were cold, "why concern yourself about outlaws and peasants clamoring for 'rights'!"

"But it is my concern," she said passionately. "Unless—"

"Neither yours nor mine," he answered in the same tone. "Only the law's!"

"The law's!" she returned. "You are the law—"

"Its servant!" he corrected.

"But—you could spare their lives! You could deal with them more mercifully!"

"The law is explicit. In the King alone rests the power to—"

"The King! But before word could reach him—"

"Exactly!" As he spoke, the Governor rose. "And now—"

"You will not hear me?"

"If there is anything else—"

Her figure straightened. "Why do you hate him so?" she asked passionately. "You have hastened their trial, and would carry out the sentence before there is time for justice. And the man whom that day you ordered whipped from the Mount—after letting me think him safe! After all that his master did for me! Why was he lashed? Because of him he served or of the old

Seigneur before that? I heard you ask about him—of his having gone to America? Why did you care about that?"

"You seem to have listened to a great deal!"

 "You seem to have listened to a great deal."

"You seem to have listened to a great deal."

"And why did he go to America?" she went on, unheeding. "Did you hate him, too? What for?"

"If you have nothing else to talk about—" He glanced at the door.

"And the lands!" she said. "They were his; now they are yours—"

"Unjustly, perhaps you think."

"No, no!" she cried. "I didn't mean—I didn't imply that. Of course not! Only," putting out her hands, "I try to understand, and—you have never taken me into your confidence, mon père! You have been indulgent; denied me nothing, but—I don't want to feel the way I have felt the last week, as if—" quickly she stopped. "No doubt there are reasons—although I have puzzled; and if I knew! Can't you," abruptly, "treat me as one worthy of your confidence?"

"You!" he said with quiet irony. "Who—listen!"

The girl flushed. "I had to, because—"

"And who misrepresent facts, as in the case of—Saladin!"

"But—"

"How long," standing over her, "were you on the island?"

"I—don't know!"

"You don't?" His voice implied disbelief.

"Part of the time I was unconscious—"

"In the watch-tower with him!"

She made a gesture. "Would you rather—"

"What did he say?"

The girl's eyes, that had been so steadfast, on a sudden wavered. "Nothing—much."

"And you? Nothing, too? Then how was the deception devised—the pact entered into—"

Her figure stiffened. "There was no pact."

"Treason, then? The law holds it treason to—"

"You are cruel; unjust!" she cried. "To me, as you were to him. That old man you had whipped! I wonder," impetuously, "if you are so to all of them, the people, the peasants. And if that is the reason they have only black looks for me—and hatred? As if they would like to curse us!"

He turned away. "I am very busy."

"Mon père!"

He walked to the door.

"Then you won't—won't spare them?"

He opened wide the door. Still she did not move, until the sight of the commandant without, the curious glance he cast in their direction, decided her. Drawing herself up, she walked toward the threshold, and, bowing perfunctorily, with head held high, crossed it.

CHAPTER XV

THE VOICE FROM THE GROUP

"No one from the household is allowed through without an order!"

"You will, however, let me pass."

"Because you have a pretty face?" The sentinel at the great gate separating the upper part of the Mount from the town, answered roughly. "Not you, my girl, or—"

But she who importuned raised the sides of the ample linen head-dress and revealed fully her countenance.

"My Lady!" Half convinced, half incredulous, the soldier looked; stared; at features, familiar, yet seeming different, with the rebellious golden hair smoothed down severely above; the figure garbed in a Norman peasant dress, made for a costume dance when the nobles and court ladies had visited the Mount.

"You do not doubt who I am?" Imperiously regarding him.

"No, my Lady; only—"

"Then open the gate!" she commanded.

The man pushed back the ponderous bolts; pressed outward the mass of oak and iron, and, puzzled, surprised, watched the girl slip through. Of course it was none of his affair, my lady's caprice, and if she chose to go masquerading among the people on such a day, when all the idle vagabonds made pretext to visit the Mount, her right to do so remained unquestioned; but, as he closed the heavy door, he shook his head. Think of the risk! Who knew what might happen in the event of her identity being revealed to certain of those in that heterogeneous concourse without? Even at the moment through an aperture for observation in the framework to which he repaired upon adjusting the fastenings, he could see approaching a procession of noisy fanatics.

The apprehension of the soldier was, however, not shared by the girl, who, glad she had found a means to get away from the chilling atmosphere of her own world, experienced now only a sense of freedom and relief. In her tense mood, the din—the shouting and unwonted sounds—were not calculated to alarm; on the contrary, after the oppressive stillness in the great halls and chambers of the summit, they seemed welcome. Her pulses throbbed and her face still burned with the remembrance of the interview with her father, as she eyed unseeingly the approaching band, led by censer- and banner-bearers.

"Vierge notre espérance—" Caught up as they swept along, she found herself without warning suddenly a part of that human stream. A natural desire to get clear from the multitude led her at first to struggle, but as well contend with the inevitable. Faces fierce, half-crazed, encompassed her; eyes that looked starved, spiritually and physically, gleamed on every side. Held as in a vise, she soon ceased to resist; suddenly deposited on a ledge, like a shell tossed up from the sea, she next became aware she was looking up toward a temporary altar, garish with bright colors.

"Etends sur nous—" Louder rose the voices; more uncontrollable became the demeanor of the people, and quickly, before the unveiling of the sacred relics had completely maddened them, she managed to extricate herself from the kneeling or prostrate throng; breathless, she fled the vicinity.

Down, down! Into the heart of the village; through tortuous footpaths, where the pandering, not pietistic, element held sway; where, instead of shrines and altars, had been erected booths and stands before which vendors of nondescript viands or poor trumpery vented their loquacity on the pilgrims:

"All hot! All hot!"

"A la barque! A l'écaille!"

"La vie! Two drinks for a liard!"

"Voilà le plaisir des dames!"

The Mount, in olden times a glorious and sacred place for royal pilgrimages, where kings came to pray and seek absolution, seemed now more mart than holy spot. But those whom the petty traders sought to entice—sullen-looking peasants, or poorly clad fishermen and their families—for the most part listened indifferently, or with stupid derision.

"Bah!" scoffed one of them, a woman dressed in worn-out costume of inherited holiday finery. "Where think you we can get sous for gew-gaws?"

"Or full stomachs with empty pockets?" said another. "The foul fiend take your Portugals!"

The nomadic merchants replied and a rough altercation seemed impending, when, pushing through the crowd, the girl hurried on.

Down, down, she continued; to the base of the rock where the sand's shining surface had attracted and yet held many of the people. Thither they still continued to come—in bands; processions; little streams that, trickling in, mingled with and augmented the rabble. An encampment for the hour—until the "petite" tide should break it up, and drive it piecemeal to the shore or up the sides of the Mount—it spread out and almost around the foundations of the great rock. Only the shadows it avoided—the chilling outlines of pinnacles and towers; the cold impress of the saint, holding close to the sunlit strand and basking in its warmth.

Some, following the example of their sea-faring fellows, dug half-heartedly in the sands in the hope of eking out the meager evening meal with a course, salt-flavored; others, abandoning themselves to lighter employment, made merry in heavy or riotous fashion, but the effect of these holiday efforts was only depressing and incongruous.

"Won't you join?" Some one's arm abruptly seized my lady.

"No, no!"

Unceremoniously he still would have drawn her into the ring, but with a sudden swift movement, she escaped from his grasp.

"My child!" The voice was that of a wolfish false friar who, seeing her pass quickly near by, broke off in threat, solicitation and appeal for sous, to intercept her. "Aren't you in a hurry, my child?"

"It may be," she answered steadily, with no effort to conceal her aversion at sight of the gleaming eyes and teeth. "Too much so, to speak with you, who are no friar!"

"What mean you?" His expression, ingratiating before, had darkened, and from his mean eyes shot a malignant look; she met it with fearless disdain.

"That you make pretext of this holy day to rob the people—as if they are not poor enough!"

"Ban you with bell, book and candle! Your tongue is too sharp, my girl!" he snarled, but did not linger long, finding the flashing glance, the contemptuous mien, or the truth of her words, little to his liking. That he profited not by the last, however, was soon evident, as with amulets and talismans for a bargain, again he moved among the crowd, conjuring by a full calendar of saints, real and imaginary, and professing to excommunicate, in an execrable confusion of monkish gibberish, where the people could not, or would not, comply with his demands.

"So they are—poor enough!" Leaning on a stick, an aged fishwife who had drawn near and overheard part of the dialogue between the thrifty rogue and the girl, now shook her withered head. "Yet still to be cozened! Never too poor to be cozened!" she repeated in shrill falsetto tones.

"And why," sharply my lady turned to the crone, "why are they so poor? The lands are rich—the soil fertile."

"Why?" more shrilly. "You must come from some far-off place not to know. Why? Don't you, also, have to pay métayage to some great lord? And banalité here, and banalité there, until—"

"But surely, if you applied to your great lord, your Governor; if you told him—"

"If we told him!" Brokenly the woman laughed. "Yes; yes; of course; if—"

"I don't understand," said the Governor's daughter coldly.

Muttering and chuckling, the woman did not seem to hear; had started to hobble on, when abruptly the girl stopped her.

"Where do you live?"

"There!" A claw-like finger pointed. "On the old Seigneur's lands—a little distance from the woods—"

"The old Seigneur? You knew him?"

"Knew him! Who better?" The whitened head wagged. "And the Black Seigneur? Wasn't he left, as a child, with me, when the old Seigneur went to America? And," pursing her thin lips, "didn't I care for him, and bring him up as one of my own?"

"But I thought—I heard that he, the Black Seigneur, when a boy, lived in the woods."

"That," answered the old creature, "was after. After the years he lived with us and shared our all! Not that we begrudged—no, no! Nor he! For once when I sent word, pleading our need, that we were starving, he forgave—I mean, remembered me—all I had done and," in a wheedling voice, "sent money—money—"

"He did?" Swiftly the girl reached for her own purse, only to discover she had forgotten to bring one. "But of course," in a tone of disappointment at her oversight, "he couldn't very well forget or desert one who had so generously befriended him."

"There are those now among his friends he must needs desert," the crone cackled, wagging her head.

A shadow crossed the girl's brow. "Must needs?" she repeated.

"Aye, forsooth! His comrades—taken prisoners near the island of Casque? His Excellency will hang them till they're dead—dead, like some I've seen dangling from the branches in the wood. He, the Black Seigneur, may wish to save them; but what can he do?"

"What, indeed?" The girl regarded the Mount almost bitterly. "It is impregnable."

"Way there!" At that moment, a deep, strong voice from a little group of people, moving toward them, interrupted.

CHAPTER XVI

THE MOUNTEBANK AND THE PEOPLE

In the center walked a man, dressed as a mountebank, who bent forward, laden with various properties—a bag that contained a miscellany of spurious medicines and drugs, to be sold from a stand, and various dolls for a small puppet theater he carried on his back. It was not for the Governor's daughter, or the old woman, however, his call had been intended. "Way there!" he repeated to those in front of him.

But they, yet seeking to detain, called out: "Give the piece here!"

Like a person not lightly turned from his purpose, he, strolling-player as well as charlatan, pointed to the Mount, and, unceremoniously thrusting one person to this side and another to that, stubbornly pushed on. As long as they were in sight the girl watched, but when with shouts and laughter they had vanished, swallowed by the shifting host, once more she turned to the crone. That person, however, had walked on toward the shore, and indecisively the Governor's daughter gazed after. The woman's name she had not inquired, but could find out later; that would not be difficult, she felt sure.

Soon, with no definite thought of where she was going, she began to retrace her steps, no longer experiencing that earlier over-sensitive perception for details, but seeing the picture as a whole—a vague impression of faces; in the background, the Mount—its golden saint ever threatening to strike!— until she drew closer; when abruptly the uplifted blade, a dominant note, above color and movement, vanished, and she looked about to find herself in the shadow of one of the rock's bulwarks. Near by, a scattering approach of pilgrims from the sands narrowed into a compact stream directed toward a lower gate, and, remembering her experience above, she would have avoided the general current; but no choice remained. At the portals she was jostled sharply; no respecters of persons, these men made her once more feel what it was to be one of the great commonalty; an atom in the rank and file! At length reaching the tower's little square, many of them stopped, and she was suffered to escape—to the stone steps swinging sharply upward. She had not gone far, however, when looking down, she was held by a spectacle not without novelty to her.

In the shadow of the Tower of the King stood the mountebank she had seen but a short time before on the sands. Now facing the people before his little show-house, which he had set up in a convenient corner, he was calling attention to the entertainment he proposed giving, by a loud beating on a drum.

Rub-a-dub-dub! "Don't crowd too close!" Rub-a-dub-dub! "Keep order and you will see—"

"Some trumpery miracle mystery!" called out a jeering voice.

"Or the martyrdom of some saint!" cried another.

"I don't know anything about any saint," answered the man, "unless,"—rub-a-dub-dub!—"you mean my lord's lady!"

And truly the piece, as they were to discover, was quite barren of that antique religious flavor to which they objected and which still pervaded many of the puppet plays of the day. The Petit Masque of the Wicked Peasant and the Good Noble, it was called; an odd designation that at once interested the Lady Elise, bending over the stone balustrade the better to see. It interested, also, those official guardians of the peace, a number of soldiers and a few officers from the garrison standing near, who, unmindful of the girl, divided their attention between the pasteboard center of interest and the people gathered around it.

Circumspectly the little play opened; a scene in which my lord, in a waistcoat somewhat frayed for one of his station, commands the lazy peasant to beat the marsh with a stick that the croaking of the frogs may not disturb at night the rest of his noble spouse, seemed designed principally to show that obedience, submission and unquestioning fealty were the great lord's due. On the one hand, was the patrician born to rule; on the other, the peasant, to serve; and no task, however onerous, but should be gladly welcomed in behalf of the master, or his equally illustrious lady. The dialogue, showing the disinclination of the bad peasant for this simple employment and the good lord's noble solicitude for the nerves of his high-born spouse, was both nimble and witty; especially those bits punctuated by a cane, and the sentiment: "Thus all bad peasants deserve to fare!" and culminating in an excellent climax to the lesson—a tattoo on the peasant's head that sent him simultaneously, and felicitously, down with the curtain.

"What think you of it?" At my lady's elbow one of the officers turned to a companion.

"Amusing, but—" And his glance turned dubiously toward the people. Certainly they did not now show proper appreciation either for the literary merits of the little piece or the precepts it promulgated in fairly sounding verse.

"The mountebank!" From the crowd a number of discontented voices rose. "Come out, Monsieur Mountebank!"

"Yes, Monsieur Mountebank, come out; come out!"

With fast-beating heart the Lady Elise gazed; as in a dream had she listened—not to the lines of the puppet play; but to a voice—strangely familiar, yet different—ironical; scoffing; laughing! She drew her breath quickly; once more studied the head, in its white, close-fitting clown's covering; the heavy, painted face, with red, gaping mouth. Then, the next moment, as he bowed himself back—apparently unmindful of a missile some one threw and which struck his little theater—the half-closed, dull eyes met hers; passed, without sign or expression!—and she gave a nervous little laugh. What a fancy!

"Act second!" the tinkling of a bell prefaced the announcement, and once more was the curtain drawn, this time revealing a marsh and the bad peasant at work, reluctantly beating the water to the Song of the Stick.

"Beat! beat!

At his lordship's command;

For if there's a croak,

For you'll be the stroke,

From no gentle hand."

A merry little tune, it threaded the act; it was soon interrupted, however, during a scene where a comical-looking devil on a broomstick, useful both for transportation and persuasion, came for something which he called the peasant's soul. Again the bad peasant protested; would cheat even the devil of his due, but his satanic Majesty would not be set aside.

"You may rob your master," he said, in effect; "defraud him of banalité, bardage and those other few taxes necessary to his dignity and position; but you can't defraud Me!" Whereupon he proceeded to wrest what he wanted from the bad peasant by force—and the aid of the broomstick!—accompanying the rat-a-tat with a well-rhymed homily on what would certainly happen to every peasant who sought to deprive his lord of feudal rights. At this point a growing restiveness on the part of the audience found resentful expression.

"That for your devil's stick!"

"To the devil with the devil!"

"Down with the devil!"

The cry, once started, was not easy to stop; men in liquor and ripe for mischief repeated it; in vain the mountebank pleaded: "My poor dolls! My poor theater!" Unceremoniously they tumbled it and him over; a few, who had seen nothing out of the ordinary in the little play took his part; words were exchanged for blows, with many fighting for the sake of fighting, when into the center of this, the real stage, appeared soldiers.

"What does it mean?" Impressive in gold adornment and conscious authority, the commandant himself came down the steps. "Who dares make riot on a day consecrated to the holy relics? But you shall pay!" as the soldiers separated the belligerents. "Take those men into custody and—who is this fellow?" turning to the mountebank, a mournful figure above the wreckage of his theater and poor puppets scattered, haphazard, like victims of some untoward disaster.

"It was his play that started the trouble," said one of the officers.

"Diable!" the commandant frowned. "What have you to say for yourself?"

"I," began the mountebank, "I—" he repeated, when courage and words alike seemed to fail him.

The commandant made a gesture. "Up with him! To the top of the Mount!"

"No, no!" At once the fellow's voice came back to him. "Don't take me there, into the terrible Mount! Don't lock me up!"

"Don't lock him up!" repeated some one in the crowd, moved apparently by the sight of his distress. "It wasn't his fault!"

"No; it wasn't his fault!" said others.

"Eh?" Wheeling sharply, the commandant gazed; at the lowering faces that dared question his authority; then at his own soldiers. On the beach he might not have felt so secure, but here, where twenty, well-armed, could defend a pass and a mob batter their heads in vain against walls, he could well afford a confident front. "Up with you!" he cried sternly and gave the mountebank a contemptuous thrust.

For the first time the man's apathy seemed to desert him; his arm shot back like lightning, but almost at once fell to his side, while an expression, apologetically abject, as if to atone for that momentary fierce impulse, overspread his dull visage. "Oh, I'll go," he said in accents servile. And proceeded hurriedly to gather up the remains of his theater and dolls. "I'm willing to go."

CHAPTER XVII

THE MOUNTEBANK AND THE HUNCHBACK

Up the Mount with shambling step, head down-bent and the same stupid expression on his face, the mountebank went docilely, though not silently. To one of the soldiers at his side he spoke often, voicing that dull apprehension he had manifested when first ordered into custody.

"Do you think they'll put me in a dungeon?"

"Dungeon, indeed!" the man answered not ill-naturedly. "For such as you! No, no! They'll keep the oubliettes, calottes, and all the dark holes for people of consequence—traitors, or your fine gentry consigned by lettres de cachet."

"Then what do you think they will do with me?"

"Wait, and find out!" returned the soldier roughly, and the mountebank spoke no more for some time; held his head lower, until, regarding him, his guardian must needs laugh. "Here's a craven-hearted fellow! Well, if you really want to know, they'll probably lock you up for the night with the rest of rag-tag," indicating the other prisoners, a short distance ahead, "in the cellar, or almonry, or auberge des voleurs; and in the morning, if you're lucky and the Governor has time to attend to such as you, it may be you'll escape with a few stripes and a warning."

"The auberge des voleurs!—the thieves' inn!" said the man. "What is that?"

"Bah! You want to know too much! If now your legs only moved as fast as your tongue—" And the speaker completed the sentence with a significant jog on the other's shoulder. Whereupon the mountebank quickened his footsteps, once more ceased his questioning. It was the soldier who had not yet spoken, but who had been pondering a good deal on the way up, who next broke the silence.

"How did it end, Monsieur Mountebank?—the scene with the devil, I mean."

The man who had begun to breathe hard, as one not accustomed to climbing, or wearied by a long pilgrimage to the Mount, at the question ventured to stop and rest, with a hand on the granite balustrade of the little platform they had just reached. "In the death of the peasant, and a comic chorus of frogs," he answered.

"A comic chorus!" said the soldier. "That must be very amusing."

"It is," the mountebank said, at the same time studying, from where he stood, different parts of the Mount with cautious, sidelong looks; "but my poor frogs!—all torn! trampled!"

"Well, well!" said the other not unkindly. "You can mend them when you get out."

"'When!' If I only knew when that would be! What if I should have to stay here like some of the others?—pour être oublié!—to be forgotten?"

"If you don't get on faster," said the soldier who had first spoken, "you won't be buried alive for some time to come, at least!"

"Pardon!" muttered the mountebank. "The hill—it is very steep."

"You look strong enough to climb a dozen hills, and if you're holding back for a chance to escape—"

"No, no!" protested the man. "I had no thought—do I not know that if I tried, your sword—"

"Quite right. I'd—"

"There, there!" said the other soldier, a big, good-natured appearing fellow. "He's harmless enough, and," as once more they moved on, "that tune of yours, Monsieur Mountebank," abruptly; "it runs in my head. Let me see—how does it go? The second verse, I mean—"

"Beat! beat!

Mid marsh-muck and mire,

For if any note

Escapes a frog's throat,

Beware my lord's ire!"

"Yes; that's the one. Not bad!" humming—

"For if any note

Escapes a frog's throat

Beware my lord's ire!"

"Are the verses your own?"

"Oh, no! I'm only a poor player," said the mountebank humbly. "But an honest one," he added after a pause, "and this thieves' inn, Monsieur?" returning to the subject of his possible fate, "this auberge des voleurs—that sounds like a bad place for an honest lodging."

"It was once under the old monks, who were very merry fellows; but since the Governor had it restored, it has become a sober and quiet place. It is true there are iron bars instead of blinds, and you can't come and go, as they used to, but—"

"Is that it—up there?" And the mountebank pointed toward a ledge of rock, with strong flanking buttresses, out jutting beneath a mysterious-looking wall and poised over a sparsely-wooded bit of the lower Mount. "The gray stone building you can just see above the ramparts, and that opening in the cliff to the right, with something running down—that looks like planking—"

"Oh, that is for the wheel—"

"The wheel?"

"The great wheel of the Mount! It was built in the time of the monks, and was used for—"

"Hold your tongue!" said the other soldier, and the trio entered the great gate, which had opened at their approach, and now closed quickly behind them.

For the first time in that isolated domain of the dreaded Governor, the mountebank appeared momentarily to forget his fears and gazed with interest around him. On every side new and varying details unfolded to the eye; structures that from below were etched against the sky in filmy lines, here resolved themselves into vast, solid, but harmonious masses.

Those ribbons of color that had seemed to fall from the wooing sky, to adorn these heights, proved, indeed, fallacious; more somber effects, the black touches of age, confronted the eye everywhere, save on one favored front— that of a newer period, an architectural addition whose intricate carvings and beautiful roses of stone invited and caught the warmer rays; whose little balcony held real buds and flowers, bright spots of pink dangling from, or nestling at, the window's edge.

"Yonder looks like some grand lady's bower," as he followed his captors past this more attractive edifice, the mountebank ventured to observe. "Now, perhaps, lives there—"

"Hark you, my friend," one of the soldiers bruskly interrupted; "a piece of advice! His Excellency likes not babblers, neither does he countenance gossip; and if you'd fare well, keep your tongue to yourself!"

"I'll—I'll try to remember," said the mountebank docilely, but as he spoke, looked back toward the balcony; at the gleaming reflection full on its windows; then a turn in the way cut off the pleasing prospect, and only the grim foundations of the lofty, heavier structure on one hand and the massive masonry of the ramparts on the other greeted the eye.

For some distance they continued along the narrow way, the mountebank bending lower under his load and observing the injunction put upon him, until the path, broadening, led them abruptly on to a platform where a stone house of ancient construction barred their further progress. But two stories in height, this building, an alien edifice amid loftier piles, stood sturdily perched on a precipitous cliff. The rough stonework of its front, darkened by time, made it seem almost a part of the granite itself, although the roof, partly demolished and restored, imparted to it an anomalous distinctness, the bright new tile prominent as patches on some dilapidated garment. In its doorway, beneath a monkish inscription, well-nigh obliterated, stood a dwarf, or hunchback, who, jingling a bunch of great keys, ill-humoredly regarded the approaching trio.

"What now?" The little man's welcome, as mountebank and soldiers came within earshot, was not reassuring. "Isn't it enough to make prisoners of all the scamps in Christendom without taking vagabond players into custody?"

"Orders, good Jacques!" said one of the soldiers in a conciliatory tone. "The commandant's!"

"The commandant!" grumbled the grotesque fellow. "It is all very well," mimicking: "'Turn them over to Jacques. He'll find room.' If this keeps on, we'll soon have to make cages of confessionals, or turn the wine-butts in the old cellar into oubliettes."

"If any of the ancient flavor lingers in the casks, your guests would have little reason to complain!" returned the other soldier. "But this fellow, he'll make no trouble—"

"Oh, I suppose we'll have to take care of him!" muttered the dwarf. "In the thieves' inn there's always room for one more!" Obeying the gesture, at once menacing and imperious, that accompanied these words, the mountebank, who had been eying his prospective host not without visible signs of misgiving, reluctantly entered.

But as he did so, he looked back; toward the soldier who had displayed half-friendly interest in the play.

"If you care to know more about the piece—" he began, when the maledictions and abuse of the misshapen keeper put a stop to further conversation and sent the mountebank post-haste into the darkness of the cavern-like hall intersecting the ground floor.

On either side closed doors, vaguely discerned, hinted at the secrets of the chambers they guarded; the atmosphere, dark and close, proclaimed the sunlight long a stranger there. At the end of the hall the dwarf, who had walked with the assurance of one well acquainted with that musty interior and all it contained, paused; shot sharply a bolt and threw open a door. The action was the signal for a chorus of hoarse voices from within, and the little man stayed not on the order of his going, but, thrusting the mountebank across the threshold, leaped nimbly back, slammed hard the door, and locked it.

Cries of disappointment and rage followed, and, facing the company that crowded the dingy little room almost to suffocation, the latest comer found himself confronted by unkempt people who shook their fists threateningly and execrated in no uncertain manner. A few, formerly spectators of his little play, inclined again to vent their humor on him, but he regarded them as if unaware of their feeling; pushed none too gently to a tiny window, and, depositing his burden on the stone floor, seated himself on a stool with his back to the wall.

As a squally gust soon blows itself out, so their temper, mercurial, did not long endure; from a ragged coat one produced dice, another cards, and, although there were few sous to exchange hands, the hazard of tossing and shuffling exercised its usual charm and held them. The minutes wore away; motionless in his corner, the mountebank now watched; then with his head on his elbow, seemed sunk in thought. Once he rose; stood on his stool and looked out between the heavy bars of the narrow window.

"Not much chance to get out that way," observed a fellow prisoner. "What did you see?"

"Only a chasm and the sands."

"The sands!" said the man. "Cursed the day I set foot on them!"

To this malediction the other did not answer; stepped down and, again seated in his corner, waited, while the light that had grudgingly entered the narrow aperture grew fainter. With the growing darkness the atmosphere seemed to become closer, more foul; but although he breathed with difficulty, the mountebank suffered no sign of impatience or concern to escape him; only more alertly looked, and listened—to a night bird cleaving the air without; to muttered sounds, thieves' patois, or snatches of ribald mirth within; and, ere long, to new complainings.

"Our supper! What of our supper?"

"The foul fiend take the auberge des voleurs and its landlord?"

"Vrai dieu! Here he comes!" as footsteps were heard without.

And the door, opening, revealed, indeed, in the rushlight, now dimly illuminating the hall, the hunchback; not laden, however, with the longed-for creature comforts, but empty-handed; at his back the commandant and a number of soldiers.

"You fellow with the dolls!" Blinking in the glare of the torches, the dwarf peered in. "Where are you? Come along!" as the mountebank rose, "you are wanted."

"Wanted?" repeated the player, stepping forward. "Where?"

"At the palace," said the commandant.

"The palace!" stopping short. "Who can want me there?"

"Who?" The dwarf made a grimace. "Who?" he repeated mockingly.

"Her ladyship," said the commandant, with a reproving glance at the jailer.

"Her ladyship!"

"Haven't you ears, my man?" The commandant frowned and made an impatient gesture. "Come, bestir yourself! The Governor's daughter has commanded your presence."

CHAPTER XVIII

THE MOUNTEBANK AND MY LADY

"The Governor's daughter!" Had the light been stronger they must have seen the start the mountebank gave. "Impossible!"

"Eh? What?" Surprised in turn, the officer gazed at him. "You dare—out with him!" To the soldiers.

But in a moment had the mountebank recovered his old demeanor, and, without waiting for the troopers to obey the commandant's order, walked voluntarily toward the door and into the passage.

"Our supper! Our supper!" A number of the prisoners, crowding forward, began once more to call lustily, when again was the disk-studded woodwork swung unceremoniously to, cutting short the sound of their lamentations.

"Dogs!" Malevolently the dwarf gazed back. "To want to gorge themselves on a holy day!"

"Pious Jacques!" murmured the commandant. "But I always said you made a model landlord!"

"When not interfered with!" grumbled the other.

"At any rate he doesn't seem to appreciate his good fortune," with a glance at the mountebank.

"No," jeering. "A gallant cavalier to step blithely at a great lady's command! 'Your Ladyship overwhelms me!'" bowing grotesquely. "'Your Ladyship's condescension'—"

"Why, then, need you take me?" interposed the mountebank quickly. "Can you not tell her ladyship I am not fit to appear in her presence—an uncouth clown—"

"Bah! I've already done that," answered the commandant.

"But how came her ladyship to know of me—here—?"

"How indeed?"

"And what does she want of me?"

"That," roughly, "you will find out!" and stepped down the hall, followed by the soldiers, mountebank and dwarf, the last of whom took leave of them at the door.

Clear was the night; the stars, like liquid drops about to fall, caressed with silvery rays the granite piles. In contrast to the noisome atmosphere of the prison, faint perfumes, borne from some flowery slope of the distant shore, swept languorously in and out the open aisles and passages of the Mount. In such an hour that upper region seemed to belong entirely to the sky; to partake of its wondrous stillness; to share its mysteries and its secrets. Like intruders, penetrating an enchanted spot, now they trod soft shadows; then, clangorous, beat beneath foot delicate laceworks of light.

"Here we are!" The officer stopped. At the same time upon a near-by balcony a nightingale began to sing, tentatively, as if trying the scope and quality of its voice. "You are to go in!" he announced abruptly.

"Such a fine palace! I—I would rather not!" muttered the fellow, as they crossed an outer threshold and proceeded to mount some polished stairs.

"Stubborn dolt! Now in you march," pausing before a door. "But, hark you! I and my men remain without. So, mind your behavior, or—"

A look from the commandant completed the sentence.

Alone, in an apartment of the palace, some moments later, the mountebank's demeanor underwent a quick change; he glanced hastily toward the door the commandant had closed in leaving, and then, with sudden brightening gaze, around him, as if making note of every detail of his surroundings. Set with columns of warm-hued marble, relieved with ornate carvings and designs, the spacious chamber presented an appearance at once graceful and charming. Nor were its furnishings at variance with its architectural elegance; on every hand soft colors met the eye, in rugs of ancient pattern; in tapestries, subdued; in the upholstering of Breton oak. A culminating note was in the center of the room, where a great bunch of roses opened wide their petals.

But briefly, however, the clown permitted himself to survey, or study, these details of refinement and luxury; the swift eager interest that had shone from the dark eyes gave way to an expression, lack-luster and stupid; his countenance once more resumed its blank, stolid aspect. As if unconscious of the anomalous figure he presented, mechanically had he seated himself; was gazing down, when through a doorway, opposite the one by which the commandant had left, a slender form appeared. Under the heavy, whitened lids a slight movement of the clown's eyes alone betrayed he was aware of that new presence. A moment the girl stood there, her glance resting on the grotesque, bent figure before her; then with a quizzical lift of the delicate brows she entered.

"You believe, no doubt, in making yourself at home?"

Crossing to the table, once more she stopped; her figure, sheathed in a gown of brocade of rose, glowed bright and distinct in contrast to the faint, vari-colored tints of ancient embroideries on the wall. Above, the light threw a shimmer on the deep-burnished gold of her hair; the sweeping lashes veiled the half-disdainful, half-amused look in her brown eyes. "Or, perhaps, you are one of those who think the peasants will some day sit, while the lords and ladies stand?"

"I don't know," he managed to answer, but got up, only to appear more awkward.

"You do not seem to know very much, indeed!" she returned, her tone changing to one of cold severity. "Not enough, perhaps, to perceive the mischief you may cause! That play of yours, which I witnessed to-day—"

"You! To-day? Your Ladyship was—"

"Yes," imperiously, "I was there! And heard and saw the effect it had on the people; how it stirred all their baser passions! But you, of course, could not know—or care, thinking only of the sous!—that, instead of teaching a lesson, the piece would only move them to anger, or resentment."

"I—your Ladyship—great lords have commended the play—"

"Great lords!" she began, but stopped; regarded her listener and shrugged her shoulders.

A few moments silence lasted, the fellow apparently not knowing what to say, or if he was expected to say anything, while, for her part, the girl no longer looked at him, but at the flowers, taking one, which she turned in her fingers.

"Your Ladyship would command me—"

"To give the play no more!"

"But—" Expostulation shone from his look.

"In which event you shall be suffered to go free to-morrow."

"But my livelihood! What shall I do, if I am forbidden to earn—"

She gave him a colder look. "I have spoken to the commandant; told him what I had seen, and that I did not think you intended to make trouble. Your case will, therefore, not be reported to his Excellency. Only," with a warning flash, "if you are again caught giving the play, you must expect to receive your deserts."

"Of course! If your Ladyship commands!" dejectedly.

"I do! But, as an offset to the coppers you might otherwise receive, I will give you a sum of money sufficient to compensate you."

"Your Ladyship is so generous!" He made an uncouth gesture of gratitude and covetousness. "May I ask your Ladyship how much—"

 "May I ask your ladyship how much--?"

"May I ask your ladyship how much—?"

"How much?" scornfully. "But I suppose—"

The words died away; her glance fell; lingered on the hand he had extended. Muscular, shapely, it seemed not adapted to the servile gesture; was most unlike the hand of clod or clown. Moreover, it was marked with a number of wounds, half-healed, which caught and held her look.

"Of course, I am so poor, your Ladyship—" he began, in yet more abject tone, but stopped, attracted in turn by the direction of her gaze; then, meeting it, quickly withdrew the hand and thrust it into his pocket. Not in time, however, to prevent a startled light, a swift gleam of recollection from springing into her eyes! The very movement itself—ironically enough!—was not without precedent.

"You!" She recoiled from him. "The Black—"

As a man who realizes he has betrayed himself, he bit his lips; but attempted no further subterfuge. The shambling figure straightened; the dull eyes grew steady; the bold self-possession she remembered well on another occasion again marked his bearing.

"Your Ladyship has discerning eyes," he remarked quietly, but as he spoke glanced and moved a little toward the window.

My lady stood as if dazed. He, the Black Seigneur, there, in the palace! Mechanically she raised her hand to her breast; she was very pale. On the balcony the nightingale, grown confident, burst into a flood of variations; a thousand trills and full-throated notes filled the room.

"I understand now," at length she found voice, "why that fancy came to me below, when I was listening to the play on the platform. But why have you come—to the very Mount itself?" Her voice trembled a little. "You! On the beach the people tried to stop you—"

"You saw that, too?"

"And you knew the play would make trouble! You wanted it to," quickly. "For what purpose? To get into the upper part of the Mount? To have them arrest—bring you here?" She looked at him with sudden terror. "My father! Was it to—"

A low, distinct rapping at the door she had entered, interrupted them. She started and looked fearfully around. At the same time the mountebank stepped back to the side of a great bronze in front of the balcony, where, standing in the shadow, he was screened.

"Elise!" a voice called out.

The flower the girl had been holding, fell to the floor.

"My—" she began, when the door opened and the Governor stood on the threshold.

CHAPTER XIX

THE MOUNTEBANK AND THE GOVERNOR

In his hand the Governor held a paper; his usually austere face wore a slightly propitiatory expression, while the eyes he turned upon her, as slowly he entered the room, suggested a respite of differences. Pausing, he toyed with the missive, turning it around and around in his fingers, as if something in his thoughts were revolving with it. Had he been more watchful of her, less bent on some matter uppermost in his mind, he could not have failed to mark the pallor of her face, or the agitation written there. As it was, his glance swept without studying.

"I hoped to find you here," he began complacently; "hoped that you had not yet retired."

She made some faint response, but her voice, despite herself, wavered. Whereupon his look sharpened; then almost immediately relapsed; constraint on her part could easily be accounted for; not many hours had elapsed since their last interview.

"Yes," he continued, "I have here to consider," indicating a paper he held, "a rather important matter." He waited a moment before adding: "A matter that concerns—you!"

"That concerns me?" Her hands tightened.

"Yes."

"Since it is important," she said hastily, "would it not—shall we not leave it until to-morrow? I—I am rather tired to-night, and—"

"What?" he returned in the same unruffled tone. "Would you postpone considering the command of the King!"

"Command!" she repeated nervously. "Of the King?"

"Or request," he said, "which is the same."

"But—" she began, and stopped; held by a sound, as of some one moving, near the window.

"Shall I read it, or—"

She had started to look behind her; but abruptly caught herself, and seemed about to frame some irrelevant response, when his voice went on: "The King desires to change the date set for your marriage with his kinsman, the Marquis de Beauvillers."

"Change?" she echoed.

"Yes; to hasten it." If the Governor had expected from her hostility, or perverseness, he was agreeably disappointed; the girl evinced neither pleasure nor disapproval; only stood in the same attitude of expectancy, with head half turned.

"His Majesty's reasons for this step—"

"Can't we—can't we, at least, postpone considering them?"

Again he regarded her more closely. "What better time than the present?"

"But I don't want—"

"Elise!" A slight frown appeared on his brow. "His Majesty," once more looking at the paper, "hints at an important political appointment he desires to confer on the Marquis de Beauvillers which would take him abroad; but whether as ambassador, or as governor in the colonies, his Majesty does not disclose. Obviously, however, the bestowing of the honor—a high one, no doubt!—depends on his early marriage, and a wife to grace the position. The letter," weighing it, "is a tentative one; the courteous precursor of a fuller communication when he has learned our—your—pleasure."

She did not at once express it; indeed, at the moment, seemed scarcely to have comprehended; her glance, which had swept furtively behind when he was studying the document, returned more uneasily to his, but not before he had caught the backward look.

"Well?" he said with a touch of asperity. "Well?" he repeated, when his gaze, following the direction hers had taken, paused.

Although well lighted in the center by a great Venetian candelabrum, the far ends of the spacious hall lay somewhat in obscurity; notably the space adorned with tropical plants and a life-size bronze before the entrance to the balcony. It was on this dim recess the Governor permitted his eye to rest; at first casually; then with a sudden appearance of interest.

"Eh?" he muttered, and before my lady could prevent him, if she had been mindful so to do, walked quickly forward; but as he advanced, a white figure stepped boldly out from behind that partial screen. With a sharp exclamation, which found a startled echo from the girl, the Governor stopped; stepped back as far as the table.

"What mummery is this?" His lips shaped the words uncertainly; his hand, reaching out with that first startled instinct of danger, touched the bell.

"Your Ladyship rang?" On the opposite side of the room was the door thrown suddenly open. The look of expectancy on the face of the commandant, who had so promptly appeared, gave way to one of surprise; consternation. "His Excellency!" he muttered, and mechanically saluted.

Over the Governor's visage a faint trace of relief flitted; dryly he looked from the mountebank, now erect and motionless, to the girl; but the face was averted and his Excellency could not see the sudden whiteness of her cheek; again he regarded the officer.

"You answer our summons with alacrity," he observed to this last subject of his scrutiny.

The commandant reddened. "I—your Excellency—the truth is, I was waiting without, at the door."

"What you have just stated," returned the Governor, "is patent; what I should like to know, however," with subtle change of tone, "is why you were stationed there."

"To take this mountebank player away, when it pleased her Ladyship to—"

"Yes; to take him away!" interrupted the lady in hurried tones, the agitation of which she strove to conceal. "And I was about to call him, when—"

The Governor continued to address the commandant. "You brought him here?" incisively.

"Yes; your Excellency; a stupid fellow we arrested below for making trouble with his dolls, and—but with her ladyship's permission—" awkwardly turning to the Governor's daughter, "I will explain."

To this appeal the girl, however, made no answer; as if fascinated, watched them, the commandant, her father, the still, white figure at one side—not far away!

"I think," the Governor spoke softly, "you will do that, anyway!"

"Exactly, your Excellency! It happened in this wise," and not without evidence of constraint and hesitation, the officer slowly related the story of the disturbance on the platform; the taking into custody of the rogues and knaves, and my lady's interest in the vagabond clown whose play had occasioned the riot.

"Because it was seditious, designed to set authority at naught?" interrupted the listener, grimly eying for an instant the motionless form of the mountebank.

"On the contrary, your Excellency!" quickly. "Her ladyship assured me it was the loyal and faithful sentiments of the play that caused the unruly rascallions to make trouble, and that the clown deserved no punishment, because he had intended no mischief."

"Her ladyship?" The Governor's brows went suddenly up. "How," he asked at length in a voice yet softer, "should her ladyship have known about the 'loyal and faithful sentiments' of a piece, given in the town, before a crowd of brawlers?"

"Because I was a spectator!" said his daughter, a red spot now on her cheek; changing lights in her eyes.

"A spectator?" repeated, in mild surprise, the Governor.

"I will explain—after!" she added in tones, low, constrained.

"Hum!" His Excellency's glance swept to the commandant.

"Her ladyship was so good," murmured the latter in some embarrassment and yet feeling obliged to speak, with that bright insistent gaze of the high official of the Mount fastened upon him, "as to inform me that, desiring to mingle with the people, and, knowing it might not be expedient to do so—in her own proper character—her ladyship saw fit to assume a humbler costume—that of a Norman peasant maid—"

From the Governor's lips fell an ejaculation; he seemed about to speak sternly, but the words failed on his lips; instead, "Continue!" he said curtly.

"That, I believe, is all, your Excellency, except that her ladyship expressed the desire the stupid fellow be set at liberty on the morrow, as not worth the keeping—and—"

The mountebank started, as expecting now the Lady Elise to speak; to denounce him, perhaps; but it was his Excellency who interrupted.

"You were going to do so? To set him at liberty?"

"I, your Excellency? The auberge des voleurs is so full of the scum of the sands, there is hardly room for them to squirm; but if your Excellency wishes all these paltry ragamuffins and beggars brought before you—"

"Well, well!" The Governor looked down; his hand crushed impatiently the paper he held. "Here is much ado about nothing! Have you," to his daughter, "aught to add?"

She lifted her head. Standing in a careless pose, apparently regardless of what was taking place, the mountebank, at the Governor's question, shot a quick glance from him to her. Although but an instant his look met my lady's, in that brief interval she read all that was lost on the other two; the sudden, desperate purpose, the indubitable intention, his warning glance conveyed. At the same time she noticed, or fancied she did, the hand thrust into his breast, as if grasping some weapon concealed there, draw out a little, while simultaneously, lending emphasis to the fact, he moved a shade nearer the Governor, her father!

"Nothing," said the girl hastily; "nothing!"

"Then," his Excellency waved a thin, aristocratic hand, "take him away!"

"And your—her ladyship's instructions?" murmured the commandant.

"Are to be obeyed, of course!" answered the Governor, complacently regarding his letter.

"You hear, fool?" said in a low voice the commandant, as he approached the clown. "Thank his Excellency! Don't you know enough? Clod! Dolt!"

But the man made at first no effort to obey; immovable as a statue, seemed not to see the speaker, and once more, the officer half whispered his injunction.

"Eh?" The Governor turned.

"I thank your Excellency! Your Excellency is most kind!" said the mountebank in a loud, emphatic tone.

"And her ladyship?" prompted the officer.

The clown looked at the girl; her breath came fast through her parted lips.

"Speak, fool! To her ladyship you also owe much."

"Much!" repeated the clown, a spark in the dull gaze still fastened upon her.

"Is that all you can say?"

"Take him away!" My lady spoke almost wildly.

"Yes; take him away!" With a querulous gesture his Excellency put an end to the matter. "Am I to be interrupted in important affairs by every miserable farceur, or buffoon, you pick up on the beach? To the devil with the fellow!"

When the door had closed on the mountebank and the commandant, he turned to his daughter. "A madcap trick!" Frowningly his Excellency regarded her. "To have gone into the town and mingled with the rabble! But," shaking his head and then suffering that expression of disapproval to relax into severity, "say no more about it! Here," indicating the letter, "is something of greater moment, to be attended to and answered!"

CHAPTER XX

THE MOUNTEBANK AND THE SOLDIER

As the mountebank walked out of the apartment of the Governor's daughter, he drew himself up with an air of expectancy, like a man preparing for some sudden climax. Once beyond the threshold, his eyes glanced furtively back at the closed door, and, descending the stairs to the floor below, he carried his head a little forward, as if intent to catch unwonted sound or outcry. But no raised voice or unusual noise reached his ear, and his footsteps, as the party issued forth into the street, responded briskly to the soldiers' pace. Still with the same air of strained attention, now mingled with a trace of perplexity, he followed his guard until called upon to stop.

"You are to sleep here!" As he spoke, the commandant opened the door of what seemed a low out-building, not very far from the general barracks, and motioned the mountebank to enter. The latter, after glancing quickly at the speaker and the soldiers behind, bent to step across the dark threshold, and, still stooping, on account of the low roof, looked around him. By the faint glimmer of light from a lantern one of the soldiers held, the few details of that squalid place were indistinctly revealed: A single stall whose long-eared occupant turned its head inquiringly at the abrupt appearance of a companion lodger; bits of harness and a number of traps hanging from pegs on the wall, and, near the door, on the ground, a bundle of grass, rough fodder from the marshes close by the shore. This last salt-smelling heap, the officer, peering in with a fastidious sniff, indicated.

"That's your bed! A softer one than you would have had but for the Lady Elise!"

The prisoner returned no answer, and in the voice of a man whose humor was not of the best, the commandant uttered a brief command. A moment or two the light continued to pass fitfully about the stable; then it and the moving shadows vanished; a key grated in the door, and the sound of the officer's receding footsteps was followed by the diminishing clatter of men's heels on the flagging stone. Not until both had fairly died away in the distance and the silence was broken only by certain indications of restiveness from the stall, did the prisoner move.

First, to the door, which he tried and shook; then, avoiding the pile of fodder, to the wall, where, feeling about the rough masonry with the energy of one who knew he had no time to spare, his hands, ere long, encountered the frame of a small window. Any gratification, however, he might have experienced thereat found its offset in the subsequent discovery that the window had heavy iron blinds, closed and fastened, and was further guarded by a single strong bar set in the middle, dividing the one inconsiderable aperture into two spaces of impassable dimensions. But as if spurred by obstacles to greater exertions, fiercely the man grasped the metallic barrier, braced himself, and put forth his strength. In its setting of old masonry, the rod moved slightly; then more and more, and the prisoner, breathing a moment hard, girded himself anew. A wrench, a tug, and the bar, partly disintegrated, snapped in the middle, and holding the pieces, the prisoner fell somewhat violently back. Armed now with an implement that well might serve as a lever, he, nevertheless, paused before endeavoring to force the formidable fastenings of the blinds; paused to tear off the tight-fitting clown's cap; to doff the costume of the mountebank covering the rough, dark garments beneath, and vigorously to rub his face with some mixture he took from his pocket. He had made but a few passes to remove the distinguishing marks of paint and pigment, when a sound without, in the distance, caused him to desist.

Footsteps, that grew louder, were coming his way, and, gripping his bar tighter the prisoner grimly waited; but soon his grasp relaxed. The sound was that of a single person, who now paused before the entrance; fumbled at the lock, and, with an impatient exclamation, set something down. At the same time the prisoner dropped his weapon and stooped for the discarded garments; in the dark, they escaped him and he was still searching, when the bolt, springing sharply back, caused him to straighten.

"Are you there, Monsieur Mountebank?" The door swung open; an uncertain light cast sickly rays once more within, and beneath the lantern, raised above his head, innocent of the danger he had just escaped, the round visage of the good-natured soldier who had escorted the mountebank to the auberge des voleurs looked amicably and inquiringly into the darksome hovel.

"Yes; what do you want?" the answer came more curt than courteous.

"What do I want?" the fellow repeated with a broad smile. "Now that's good! Perhaps it would be more to the point to ask what do you want? And here," indicating a loaf and jug in his hand, "I've got them, though why the commandant should have cared, and ordered them brought—"

"He did?" said the prisoner, with a flash of quick surprise. "Well, I'm not hungry, but you can leave them."

"Not hungry?" And the soldier, who seemed a little the worse for liquor, but more friendly in consequence, walked in. "I don't wonder, though," he went on, closing the door, hanging his lantern above and placing the jug on the ground; "in such a foul hole! What you need, comrade, is company, and," touching significantly his breast, "something warmer than flows from the spring of St. Aubert."

"I tell you," began the mountebank, when the soldier, staring, got a fair look at the other for the first time and started back.

"Eh? What's this?"

"Oh, I took them off! You don't suppose I'd sleep in my white clothes in such a dirty—"

"Right you are, comrade!" returned the other, seating himself before the door on a three-legged stool he found in a corner. "But for the moment you gave me a start. I thought you some other person."

"What—person?"

"No one in particular. You might," unbuttoning his coat to draw forth a bottle, "have been any one! But I dare say you have had them off in worse places than this—which, after all, is not bad, compared to some of the rooms for guests at the Mount!"

"You mean?" The mountebank looked first at the closed blinds; then at the door, and a sudden determination came to his eyes.

"Those especially prepared for the followers of the Black Seigneur, taken prisoners near Casquc, for cxample!"

"They are dungeons?"

"With Jacques for keeper! The little sexton, we call him, because the prisoners go generally from the cells to the pit, and the quicklime is the hunchback's graveyard!"

"This Jacques—" A growing impatience shone ominously from the prisoner's glance; his attention, that of a man straining to catch some expected sound without, focused itself on the speaker. "This Jacques—what sort of quarters has he?"

"Oh, he lives anywhere; everywhere! Sometimes at the thieves' inn; again in one of the storehouses near the wheel. They say, though, he is not a great hand to sleep, but passes most of his time like a cat, prowling in and out the black passages and tunnels of the Mount. But," abruptly breaking off, "the play—that's what I want to know about! The end! How did it end?"

"I'm in no mood for talking."

"Take the bottle, an' it'll loosen your tongue!"

"No."

"What! you refuse?"

"Yes."

"Then," philosophically, "must I drink alone."

"Not here!"

"Eh?"

"Will you get out, or—" and the mountebank stepped toward the other with apparently undisguised intention.

"So that's your game?" Quickly the soldier sprang to his feet. "I must teach you a little politeness, my friend—how we deal with uncivil people in the army!" And throwing off his coat, as ready for a bout at fisticuffs as for an encounter of words, the soldier confronted the clown. "When I'm done, you'll sing that song of the stick out of the other side of the mouth, and think your wicked peasant received a coddling from his master in comparison!"

But the mountebank did not answer—with words—and the soldier was still threatening, and painting dire prophetic pictures of what he intended doing, when a strong arm closed about him; fingers like iron gripped his throat, and, for some moments thereafter, although of unusual size and vigor, the man was more concerned in keeping his feet than in searching his vocabulary for picturesque imagery. Then, in spite of his struggles and best endeavors to free himself, he felt his head forced backwards; the grasp on his neck tightened. Still he could not shake off that deadly hold, and, aware that consciousness was gradually leaving him, his efforts relaxed. After that, for an interval, he remembered nothing; but with returning realization and a vague sense of stiffness in his throat, in a rough sort of way was prepared to accept defeat; acknowledge the other's supremacy, and seal that acknowledgment over the bottle.

Only the mountebank afforded him no opportunity thus to toast the "best man"; with a long strap of leather snatched from one of the pegs, he had already bound the hands and feet of his bulky antagonist, and was just rising to survey his handiwork, when the other opened his eyes.

"Here! What do you mean?" exclaimed the soldier, when even the power vocally to express further surprise or indignation was denied him, in consequence of something soft being thrust between his teeth; and mute, helpless, he could but express in looks the disgusted inquiry his lips refused to frame.

"No! it's no joke," answered the mountebank, rapidly passing an end of the strap, binding the soldier, about a post of the stall and securing it, sailor-wise. "A poor return for hospitality, yet needs must, when the devil drives!" quickly seizing a handful of marsh grass from the ground and rubbing it over his face. "Anyhow, you'll be none the worse on the morrow," stepping toward the lantern, "while I—who can say? He laughs best—" About to blow out the flame, he stopped, attracted by something his foot had thrust aside; a garment; the soldier's! A moment he surveyed it; stooped; picked it up. "Unless I am mistaken," casting aside his own coat, slipping on that of the soldier, and then donning the latter's cap, which had fallen in the struggle, "we are about of a size. And this sword," unfastening the belt from the prostrate jailer, "should go with the coat." A moment his words, tense, reckless, continued to vibrate in the soldier's ears, then: "I'll leave you the lantern!" And darkness fell over the place.

Boldly, a little uncertainly, as the soldier had walked, the mountebank, now, to all appearance, a man of the ranks in the service of his Excellency, the Governor, strode down the wide, stone-paved way separating the outhouses and a number of desultory ancient structures from the officers' quarters, hard against the ramparts. In the sky's dome the stars still shone, although a small mottled patch of cloud obscured the moon; on either side no lights appeared in windows, and friendly shadows favored him, until he approached at the end of the way the broad, open entrance between the soldiers' barracks and the officers' row. There, set in the stone above the key of the time-worn arch, flared a smoky lamp, dimly revealing the surrounding details; but the young man did not stop; had drawn quite close to the medieval structure, when unexpectedly another tread, on the soldiers' side of the entrance, mingled with his own; rang for a moment in unison; then jingled out of time. He who approached came to a sudden standstill; cast a quick glance over his shoulder, only to be brought to an abrupt realization that it was now too late to retreat. A black silhouette, suddenly precipitated across the pavement, preceded a dark figure that stepped quickly out and barred the way, while at the same time, a voice, loud and incisive, challenged.

CHAPTER XXI

THE STAIRWAY OF SILVER

The stillness of the moment that followed was tense; then thickly the young man answered something irrelevant about a clown, a bottle and a loaf; with cap drawn down and half-averted face, he lurched a little forward in the darkness, and the sentinel's weapon fell. "Oh, that's you, is it, Henri?" he said in a different tone, stepping back. "How did you leave the fellow?"

"Eating the bread and calling for more!" As he spoke, the other stopped, swaying uncertainly; above the arch, the wick, ill-trimmed, brightened and darkened to the drafts of air through break and slit of the old lamp; and briefly he awaited a favorable moment, when the flame blew out until almost extinguished; then with hand near sword-hilt, somewhat over-briskly, but in keeping with the part, he stepped toward the arch; through it, and quickly past the sentinel.

"You seem to have been feasting and drinking a little yourself, to-night, comrade?" called out the latter after him. "I noticed it when you went in, and— But aren't you taking the wrong way?" As the other, after starting toward the barracks, straightened, and then abruptly wheeled into the road, running up the Mount.

"Bah!" A moment the young man paused. "Can't a soldier," articulating with difficulty, "go to see his sweetheart without—"

"Eh bien!" The sentinel shrugged his shoulders. "It isn't my business. I think, though, I know where they'll put you to-morrow, when they find out through the guard at the barracks."

To this ominous threat the other deigned no response, only, after the fashion of a man headstrong in insobriety, as well as in affairs of gallantry, continued his upward way; at first, speedily; afterward, when beyond hearing of the man below, with more stealth and as little noise as possible, until the road, taking a sudden angle, brought him abruptly to an open space at the foot of a great flight of stone stairs.

Broad, wide, broken by occasional platforms, these steps, reaching upward in gradual ascent, had designedly, in days gone by, been made easy for broken-down monarchs or corpulent abbots. Also they had been planned to satisfy the discerning eye, jealous of every addition or alteration at the Mount. My lord, the ancient potentate, leisurely ascending in ecclesiastical gown, while conscious of an earthly power reaching even into England, could still fancy he was going up a Jacob's ladder into realms supernal.

Saint Louis, with gaze benignly bent toward the aërial escalier de dentelle of the chapel to the left, might well exclaim no royal road could compare with this inspiring and holy way; nor is it difficult to understand a sudden enchantment here, or beyond, that drew to the rock on three pilgrimages that other Louis, more sinner than saint, the eleventh of his name to mount the throne of France.

But those stones, worn in the past by the footsteps of the illustrious and the lowly, were deserted now, and, for the moment, only the moon, which had escaped from the cloud, exercised there the right of way; looking squarely down to efface time's marks and pave with silver from top to bottom the flight of stairs. It played, too, on façades, towers and battlements on either side, and, at the spectacle—the disk directly before him—the Black Seigneur, about to leave the dark and sheltering byway, involuntarily paused. Angels might walk unseen up and down in that effulgence, as, indeed, the old monks stoutly averred was their habit; but a mortal intrusion on the argent way could be fraught only with visibility.

To reach the point he had in mind, however, no choice remained; the steps had to be mounted, and, lowering his head and looking down, deliberately he started. As he proceeded his solitary figure seemed to become more distinct; his presence more obtrusive and his echoing footsteps to resound louder. No indication he had been seen or heard, however, reached him; to all appearances espionage of his movements was wanting, and only the saint with the sword at the top of the steeple—guardian spirit of the rock—looked down, as if holding high a gleaming warning of that unwonted intrusion.

Yet, though he knew it not, mortal eye had long been on him, peering from a window of the abbot's bridge spanning the way and joining certain long unused chambers, next to the Governor's palace, with my lady's abode. Against the somber background of that covered passage of granite, the face looking out would still have remained unseen, even had the young man, drawing near, lifted his glance. This, however, he did not do; his eyes, with the pale reflections dancing in them, had suddenly fastened themselves lower; toward another person, not far beyond the bridge; some one who had turned in from a passage on the other side of the overhead architectural link, and had just begun to come down. An old man, with flowing beard, from afar the new-comer looked not unlike one of the ancient Druids that, in days gone by, had lighted and watched the sacred fires of sacrifice on the rock. He, too, guarded his light; but one set in the tall, pewter lamp of the medieval watchman.

"Twelve o'clock and all's—" he began when his glance, sweeping down, caught sight of the ascending figure, and, pausing, he leaned on his staff with one hand and shaded his eyes with the other.

A half-savage exclamation of disappointment was suppressed on the young man's lips; had he only been able to attain that parallelogram of darkness, beneath the abbot's passage, he would have been better satisfied, his own eyes, looking ahead, seemed to say; then gleamed with a bolder light.

"A sword and blade

A drab and a jade;

All's one to the King's men of the army!"

he began to hum softly, as with a more reckless swing, quickly he went up in the manner of a man assigned some easy errand. At the same time the patriarch slowly and rather laboriously resumed his descent, and just below the bridge, without the bar of shadow, the two came together.

"Think you it is too late for his Excellency, the Governor, to receive a message?" at once spoke up the younger, breaking off in that dashing, but low-murmured, song of the barracks.

"That you may learn from the guard at the palace," was the deliberate answer, as, raising his lamp, the watchman held it full in his questioner's face.

"Thanks! I was going to inquire." As he answered, at the old abbot's window in the bridge above, the face, looking out, bent forward more intently; then quickly drew back. "Good night!"

But the venerable guardian of the inner precinct was not disposed thus lightly to part company. "I don't seem to know you, young man," he observed, the watery, but keen and critical eyes passing deliberately over the other's features.

"No?" Unflinching in the bright glare of the lamp, the seeming soldier smiled. "Do you, then, know all at the Mount—even the soldiers?"

"I should remember even them," was the quiet reply.

"Those, too, but lately brought from St. Dalard?"

"True, true! There may be some of those—" uncertainly.

"No doubt! So if you will lower your lamp, which smells rather vilely—"

"From the miscreants it has smelled out," answered the old man grimly, but obeyed; stood as if engrossed in the recollections his own response evoked; then turned; walked on, and, a few moments later, his call, suddenly remembered, rang, belated, in the drowsy air: "Twelve o'clock and all's well! A new day, and St. Aubert guard us all!"

"A sword and a blade;

A drab and a jade—"

The words, scarcely begun, above his breath, died away on the seeming soldier's lips, as the watcher on the bridge, looking down to follow first the departing figure of the old custodian, crossed quickly to the opposite window, and, from this point of vantage, gazed up after the young man rapidly vanishing in the track of the moonlight. A moment the onlooker stood motionless; then, ere the figure, so vividly defined in shine and shimmer, had reached the top of the stairway, made an abrupt movement and swiftly left the window and the passage.

At the head of the steps, which without further incident or interruption, he reached, the Black Seigneur, stepping to the shadow of a small bush against the wall, glanced about him; with knit brows and the resolute manner of one who has come to some definite conclusion, he left the spot for observation, almost the apex of the Mount, and plunged diverging to the right. From glint and shimmer to darkness unfathomable! For some time he could only grope and feel his way, after the fashion of the blind; fortunately, however, was the path narrow; although tortuous, fairly well paved, and no serious mishap befell him, even when he walked forward regardlessly, in feverish haste, beset with the conviction that time meant all in all, and delay the closing of the toils and the failure of a desperate adventure. Several times he struck against the stones; once fell hard, but picked himself up; went on the faster, only, after what seemed an interminable period, to stop.

"Am I, can I be mistaken?"

But the single star he could see plainest from the bottom of the deep alley, and to which he looked up, answered not the fierce, half-muttered question; coldly, enigmatically it twinkled, and, half running, he continued his way, to emerge over-suddenly into a cooler well of air, and—what was more to be welcomed!—an outlook whereof the details were in a measure dimly shadowed forth.

On one side the low wall obscured not the panorama below—a ghost-like earth fading into the mist, and nearer, the roof of the auberge des voleurs, a darkened patch on the slope of the rock; but in this direction the man hardly cast a glance. Certain buildings ahead, austere, Norman in outline, absorbed his attention to the exclusion of all else, and toward them, with steps now alert and noiseless, he stole; past a structure that seemed a small salle des gardes whose window afforded a view of four men nodding at a table within; across a space to another passage, and thence to a low door at the far corner of a little triangular spot, alongside the walk and near a great wall. At once the young man put out his hand to the door; tried it; pushed it back and entered. Before him a wide opening looked out at the sky, framing a multitude of stars, and from the bottom of this aperture ran a strand, or rope, connecting with an indistinct object—a great wheel, which stood at one side!

CHAPTER XXII

THE WHIRLING OF THE WHEEL

As old as church or cloister, the massive wheel of the Mount had, in the past, played prominent part in the affairs of succeeding communities on the rock. It, or the hempen strand it controlled, had primarily served as a link between the sequestered dwellers, and the flesh-pots and material comforts of the lower world. Through its use had my lord, the abbot, been ever enabled to keep full the mighty wine-butts of his cellars; to provide good cheer for the tables of the brethren, and to brighten his cold stone interiors with the fresh greens of Flemish tapestry, or the sensuous hues of rugs and fabrics from seraglio or mosque. Times less ancient had likewise claimed its services, and even in recent years, by direction of his Excellency, the Governor, had it occasionally been used for the hoisting of goods, wares, or giant casks, overcumbersome for men or mules.

Toward this simple monkish contrivance, the summit's rough lift, or elevator, wherein serfs or henchmen had walked like squirrels in a cage to bring solace to generations of isolated dwellers, the Black Seigneur had at first stepped impetuously; then stopped, hardly breathing, to look over his shoulder at the door that had been left unfastened. An involuntary question flashing through his brain—the cause of this seeming carelessness—found almost immediate answer in his mind, and the certainty that he stood not there alone—a consciousness of some one else, near, became abruptly confirmed.

"What are you doing, soldier?" A voice, rough, snarling, drew swiftly his glance toward a presence, intuitively divined; an undersized, grotesque figure that had entered the place but a few moments before and now appeared from behind boxes and casks where he had been about to retire to his mattress in a corner.

"What do you want?" repeated this person, the anger and viciousness on his distorted features, revealed in the moonlight from the large opening, like that of some animal unwarrantedly disturbed.

"You, landlord of the thieves' inn!" And inaction giving way to movement on the intruder's part, a knife that had flashed back in the hand of the hunchback, with his query, was swiftly twisted from him and kicked aside, while a scream of mingled pain and rage became abruptly suppressed. Struggling and writhing like a wildcat, Jacques proved no mean antagonist; with a strength incredible for one of his size, supplemented by the well-known agility of his kind, he scratched, kicked, and had managed to get the other's hand in his mouth, when, making an effort to throw off that clinging burden, the Black Seigneur dashed the dwarf's head violently against the wooden support of the place. At once all belligerency left the hunchback, and, releasing his hold, he sank to the ground.

An instant the intruder regarded the inert form; then, going to the door, latched and locked it with a key he found inside. Having thus in a measure secured himself from immediate interruption without—for any one trying the door would conclude the wheel-room vacant, or that the dwarf slept there or in the store-house beyond—the Black Seigneur walked to the aperture, and reaching up, began to pay out the rope from a pulley above. As he did so, with feet braced, he leaned over to follow in its descent a small car along the almost perpendicular planking from the mouth of the wheel-room to the rocks, several hundred feet below.

A sudden slackening of the rope—assurance that the car, at the end of the line, had reached the loading-spot below without the fortifications—and the young man straightened; in an attitude of attention, stood listening. But the stillness, impregnated only with a faint underbreath, the far-away murmur of water, or the just audible droning of insects near the fig-trees on the rocks, continued unbroken. An impatient frown gathered on his brow; more eagerly he bent forward to gaze down, when through the air a distant sound—the low, melancholy hoot of an owl—was wafted upward.

Upon him at the aperture, this night-call, common to the Mount and its environs, acted in magical manner, and swiftly had he stepped toward the wheel, when an object, intervening, stirred; started to stagger to its feet. At once was the young man's first impelling movement arrested; but, thus forcibly drawn from his purpose, he did not long pause to contemplate; his hand, drawing the soldier's sword, held it quickly at the hunchback's throat.

"A sound, and you know what to expect!"

With the bare point at his flesh, Jacques, dully hearing, vaguely comprehending, could, indeed, guess and the fingers he had involuntarily raised to push the bright blade aside, fell, while at the same time any desire to attempt to call out, or arouse the guard, was replaced by an entirely different emotion in his aching brain. Never before had he actually felt that sharp touch—the prelude to the final thrust. At the sting of it, a tremor ran through him, while cowardice, his besetting quality, long covered by growl and egotism in his strength and hideousness to terrify, alone shone from his unprepossessing yellow features.

"You were brave enough with the soldiers at your beck!" went on a determined voice whose ironical accents in no wise served to alleviate his panic. "When you had only a mountebank to deal with! But get up!" contemptuously. "And," as the hunchback obeyed, his crooked legs shaking in the support of his misshapen frame, "into the wheel with you!"

"The wheel!" stammered the dwarf. "Why—what—"

"To take a little of your own medicine! Pardi! What a voluble fellow! In with you, or—"

With no more words the hunchback, staggering, hardly knowing what he did, entered the ancient abbot's machine for hoisting. But as he started to walk in the great wheel at the side of his captor, a picture of the past—the times he, himself, had forced prisoners to the wheel, stimulating with jeer and whip—arose mockingly before him, and the incongruous present seemed, in contrast, like a black waking dream.

That it was no dream, however, and that the awakening would never occur, he well knew, and malevolently though fearfully he eyed the rope, coming in over the pulley at the aperture; to be wound around and around by a smaller wheel, attached to the larger, and—drawing up what?

An inkling of the sort of merchandise to be expected, under the circumstances, could but flash through his mind, together with a more vivid consciousness of the only course open for him—to cry out, regardless of consequences! Perhaps he might even have done so, but at that instant—as if the other had read the thought—came the cold touch of a bare blade on his neck; and with a sudden chill, the brief heroic impulse passed.

More stealthily now he began to study his companion in the wheel, while a question, suddenly occurring, reiterated itself in his brain. This man—who was he? And what did he know of the mountebank, or his, Jacques', dealings with the clown? That his captor was no soldier of the rock, or belonged there, the hunchback felt by this time assured, and a growing suspicion of the other's identity brought home with new force to the dwarf the thankless part chance, perhaps, had assigned to him in that night's work. And at the full realization of the consequences, should his surmise prove correct—what must ultimately happen to himself in that event, when unwilling coöperation at the wheel should become known—almost had he again reached the desperate point of calling out; but at that moment a turn in the wheel brought to the level of the aperture, the car. In it, or clinging thereto, were a number of figures who, as soon as the rope stopped, sprang noiselessly to the platform.

"Seigneur, we hardly dared hope—"

"We obeyed orders, but—"

Gazing through the spokes of the wheel, and listening to their whispered exclamations, any lingering doubt as to who his captor was could no longer be entertained by the hunchback. These new-comers took no pains to conceal it; even when the dwarf's presence became known to them and unceremoniously was he dragged forth—they displayed a contemptuous disregard of him as a factor to interfere, not calculated to dull the edge of his apprehension! Too late now might he regret that pusillanimity that had caused him to draw back from an immortal rôle; already was the car again descending!

It came up loaded; went down once more, reappeared. On the little platform now were more than a dozen men assembled, but to Jacques this force looked multiplied. Amid the confusion of his thoughts, vaguely could he hear orders given; caught something about the need for quiet, haste, overpowering the guard; then saw the door open, and the men, like shadows, go out; leaving him alone. No; with two black figures; ominous; armed. He could see the glitter of their weapons, and ventured to move his thick tongue, when, fiercely silenced, he crouched down; waited, with hands clenched, an interminable period; until faintly from afar sounded the note of a night-bird.

Roughly jerked to his feet, between them he walked to the door; heard it close; stepped out into the night. Many times had he made his way between wheel-room and guard-house, but now the route seemed strange, and, looking around near the structures at the entrance to his dungeons Jacques shook his head as if to rid his brain of some fantasy. But the scene did not change; the guard-house remained—familiar; unlike, with unknown faces peering from it, and an imperious voice issuing commands to him, once unquestioned commander here!

And comprehending what was being said, he struck his breast violently; with curses would have answered that the keys were his own; the dungeons, too, and what they held, and that he would never lead them there; never open those doors! But this grim, savage, determined band beat down his arms, and his courage; and, with the shadow of the grave again before him, the dwarf walked on; past the stable into the guard-house, where familiar forms once had been seated, and into the passage leading to the dungeons beyond.

CHAPTER XXIII

AT THE VERGE OF THE APERTURE

The footfall of the Black Seigneur, near the guard-house of the dungeons, was measured, yet noiseless, as he stepped on the soft earth, alongside the stone walk, now toward the passage in the direction of the wheel-room, then back into the little square. That his thoughts, however, moved not in accord with that deliberate stride, the brows impatiently knit, and the quick glances he continued to cast over his shoulder, bore testimony.

Stopping at length near the Tour Bernard, he looked fixedly down at the town, wrapped in a stillness that should have reassured him. Nevertheless he appeared not satisfied; and had stepped out into the court again, when some sound he heard, or fancied, sent him quickly to an embrasure in the wall. From this opening—formerly for cannon in defense of the fenils, and the poulain, or planking for the hoisting of goods—he leaned far out, his glance instinctively turning toward the barracks, some distance to the right and far below. As he stood thus, that which had first attracted his attention—the sound of a voice giving orders—was repeated; at the same time where had been only darkness now shone many windows, while to the left, near the entrance he had passed after leaving the stable, lights began to dance like fireflies.

At these signs of activity and the sounds breaking the general quietude, an exclamation fell from his lips; then, pausing only a moment to listen and observe, he sprang toward the guard-house. Crossing the threshold, defined by a faint glimmer from a distant corner, he madc his way past several motionless forms, into a low passage beyond. Here he called out impatiently; but from those depths, leading down into the dungeons where his comrades had gone, no answer was returned. His voice, hollow, mocking, seemed stifled in a tomb; more loudly he shouted; walked farther in, when an indistinct response was followed by a pin-point of light, and, ere long, by the bearer of a little lamp, Sanchez.

"The others?" At the head of a dark stairway into which he would inadvertently have plunged, had he gone farther, the Black Seigneur confronted the man, as he approached.

"They will soon be here," said the old servant, springing up the steps and walking after his master, who had already turned back toward the guard-room. "Jacques—curse him!"—putting out his light in obedience to a gesture from the other—"fumbled with the keys; pretended he couldn't find the right ones! So it took longer to open the doors."

"The prisoners?"

"I left our men working at the last dungeon to come on ahead—to let you know you might soon expect them."

"Soon," ironically, "may be too late."

"You mean—?"

"The hue and cry is out! I have long been expecting it; I do not understand why it didn't come before; unless a mountebank, locked up, was considered safe enough for the night—"

"Then some one knew—?"

"Some one?" A bitter laugh was quickly suppressed on the young man's lips. "Hark! Listen!"

"Sounds below! the soldiers!" exclaimed Sanchez, and started toward the window to look out, only to fall quickly back.

"What is it?" With his hand on the other's shoulder, the Black Seigneur whispered the question.

"A face! At the window!"

"So soon? The hounds are quicker than I thought! Or," drawing his sword, "it may be only one or two in advance. In that case—"

But no enemy, single or plural, met their view, either in front, or at the side of the guard-house; only the darkness, void, empty, and the bare rampart wall winding around the head of the Mount like a monster guardian dragon, asleep at his post.

"Here is no one!"

"No one! Yet am I sure I saw—"

"A shadow!" answered the other. "And we have nothing worse to fight!"

"Some one was there, Seigneur," stubbornly, "and fled!"

"Eh bien! He's gone!"

"He? It looked like a—"

"Back with you, quick! Is this a time for talk? Call those who can come—if they would save their necks!"

"Here they are now," exclaimed the servant, and, as he spoke, the first of their men, blowing out the light he carried, ran quickly across the guard-chamber and into the open air. Others hastily followed, until the gathering, swelled by those brought with them from the dungeons, stood expectantly before the little stone structure.

"All the prisoners are here?"

"All!"

"To the wheel-house, then!"

But as they hastened across the square and into the narrow way, the Black Seigneur again spoke to the man just ahead:

"The hunchback?"

"We left him below, locked up in the Devil's Cage!"

"The Devil's Cage! Quelle bonne plaisanterie! Although," looking back, "it may cost us dear!"

And indeed, behind the sound of pursuit came nearer; the clatter of soldiers' feet grew louder, until, reaching the little square and the guard-house, all tumult suddenly ceased. A momentary silence, strange, ominous, was broken by a din of voices, as the flaring here and there of torches threw grotesque reflections high against the grim background of black masonry.

To those now within the wheel-room, the cause of that abrupt clamor was not difficult to divine; his Excellency's soldiers had found the sentinels overpowered in the guard-house! Would the former stop to investigate; search first those subterranean passages? Already had the prisoners, the weaker of the Black Seigneur's men, filled the car, or hung clinging to the rope above; already was the wheel turning—almost before the key had turned in the lock at the entrance.

"Seigneur!"

"Sanchez?"

"When we left the wheel-room, we closed the door."

"When we got back, it—"

A footfall without interrupted, followed by the sound of a hand at the door, and other steps drawing near.

"Jacques!" An expectant voice spoke; waited; called louder. Then those outside listened; some one exclaimed, and hurried footsteps retreated toward the guard-house.

As they died away, in the wheel-room the car came up for the second time empty, and inquiringly the men there looked from one to the other; but, even in that moment of danger, not one of them moved, or made sign of impatience. Some must go; others remain, and stoically they awaited the word of their leader.

"Down with all of you! I'll let you out the line," taking a turn with the rope around a stanchion near the wall, "and then come down myself."

The command was unexpected; for the first time those that had never questioned their leader's authority, hesitated, and more sharply was the order repeated; whereupon they obeyed; all save one.

"I'll let it out myself," said Sanchez.

"Get in!"

"No!" was the obdurate reply, when the Black Seigneur made a sign; hands reached up, seized Sanchez, and a moment later the car started down. The line strained; as it played out, now running free about the stanchion, then stopping with jerks, the man in the wheel-house almost looked to see it part. The hempen strand, however, proved sound; held its human freight; but another danger pressed near.

Scarcely had the car begun its downward journey than an attack, indications of whose approach had not been wanting, manifested itself without. Beneath a sudden, savage assault, the door shook; yet engrossed at the line, every muscle strained, the man at the stanchion heeded not. Swiftly, mechanically he worked, apparently as unconscious of the clamorous soldiers without as of a silent presence within—some one that had been concealed in the little store-room adjoining, opening into the wheel-house, and now peered out; but at once drew back, as, with a crash, the door fell in.

At first, in the comparative darkness, with only the sky at the aperture staring them in the face, the in-rushing black figures paused, uncertain; lights soon were pushed forward, however, and then could they see the great wheel going round, unwinding the rope; the man at the stanchion.

"The prisoners! He's letting them down."

"Cut the line!"

Some one with a knife rushed forward, severed the strand; but at that moment the car touched the bottom. Then did the solitary man at the rope for the first time awaken to his own situation; with a backward sweep of the arm he struck so fiercely the foremost of those to rush at him that the fellow fell, hitting hard the stone floor. Those nearest stumbled, and drawing his sword, with a thrust of point or blow of hilt, the Black Seigneur, for a moment withstood the first confused on-coming; then extricated himself and leaped to the narrow space behind the wheel. Here was he protected behind by the wall; at one end, by the masonry jutting out, while, at the other, only one or two could attack at the same time. But in front, through the spokes of the broad wheel, they might well hope to reach him.

At once the soldiers sprang forward, when, seizing the wheel, the man behind, with a savage jerk, set it in motion. The swords thrust at him were turned aside, one or two of his assailants were caught in the ponderous mechanism, and, before those attacking him had recovered from their surprise, the blade of the Black Seigneur shot in and out; to the right, to the left. Those ahead fell back upon their comrades; two, however, were unable to withdraw, and sank to the ground before the wheel. A third, with his hand to his throat and making strange sounds, staggered back to the wall.

Momentarily disconcerted, the others hesitated. "In the fiend's name, fear ye one man?" shouted an authoritative voice.

"A devil!"

"'Tis the Black Seigneur! I had a good sight of him."

"Beat! beat!

'Mid marsh-muck and mire—"

came in mocking tones from behind the wheel.

"The mountebank!"

"Sacre tonnerre! But mountebank, or outlaw, you shall pay! This way!" And at the unprotected side of the wheel the commandant sought to bring the issue to a conclusion. One blade the Black Seigneur struck down, while his own weapon retorted with more effect, though as it did so, another soldier made a lunge, and his sword entered the shoulder of the man behind the wheel. A shout of triumph that fell from the lips of the Governor's trooper was, however, abruptly checked; lurching forward with the stroke, ere he could recover, something heavy—a brass hilt—beat like a hammer on his head and he dropped to his knees. The others pressed closer; but with the desperation of a man resolved to sell his life dearly, the Black Seigneur fought on; regardless of cut and thrust, was holding the narrow entrance, when from the rear, somewhere, came the report of a firearm.

"Back! Stand back!"

Those nearest the wheel, not unwilling, perhaps, to desist, drew away; other detonations followed and smoke filled the place, obscuring the gaze. In the yellow fog they waited; until first it was swept aside close to the opposite wall by a draft of air from the aperture of the adjoining store-room, and the commandant, in an effort to see, moved impatiently forward. Ere, however, he could reach the wheel, near the threshold of the store-room, he felt his arm suddenly seized.

"Look, listen!"

The warning cry—a girl's voice—rang through the wheel-room; but the commandant did not at once heed it; at that abrupt touch he had involuntarily wrested his arm away; he stared, not in the direction she who had called out pointed, but at her! The white, drawn face, the eyes dilated—

"You, my Lady! Here?" he stammered. But she only made a wild movement; again grasped, drew him forward.

"Quick, or—" And suddenly was he brought to a realization of what she wished him to see: a figure drawing itself along, slowly, painfully, toward the verge—

"Don't you see? Rather than be taken, he's going to throw himself over!"

The excited, admonishing sound of her voice aroused the commandant. He gave a sharp order and the soldiers sprang forward; laid roughly hold of the prostrate form; drew it back. The Black Seigneur yet struggled, but not for long! A moment, and his eyes turned to the Governor's daughter.

"Ma foi! I must needs yield—to your Ladyship! Yet, what matter, since I have done what I came to do!"

His gaze, darkly glowing, seemed to envelope the shrinking figure whose cloak only partly concealed the gay, rich gown beneath; lifted to the brilliant affrighted brown eyes. "Your Ladyship has bright eyes, forsooth!" An ironical laugh burst from his lips. "But sharper than their swords!" He strove to speak further, when a hand holding a weapon fell heavily. At that a cry escaped the girl's lips.

"No, no; you shall not!"

The Black Seigneur lay still.

"Ciel! It's fortunate we got him," ruefully the commandant gazed around. "It would have made a pretty tale, if—" he turned to the Governor's daughter, "I have your Ladyship to thank—" he began, and stopped.

My lady's figure had at that moment relaxed and fallen to the ground!

CHAPTER XXIV

THE HALL OF THE CHEVALIERS

The report of the capture of the Black Seigneur spread from Mount to town; from rock to shore. Pilgrims repeated, peasants circulated it; many credited; a few disbelieved. Like shadows had his comrades and the escaped prisoners vanished, leaving no trace, save one—an over-turned car and severed rope at the foot of the poulain, without the fortifications. And flocking to that point, of greater interest now than shrine or sanctuary, the pilgrims gazed around; down the rocks; up the almost perpendicular planking to what looked like a mere pigeon-hole in the side of the cliff. Then ominous grumblings escaped them; some shook their fists at the black wall; others scoffed at distant sounds of priestly hallelujahs. Had the soldiers that day appeared in the town or on the beach, serious trouble would have ensued. For the time, however, they remained discreetly housed, while supplies for pilgrims' needs were, by the commandant's orders, so curtailed, many of the indigent multitude, urged by pinched stomachs, began, ere night, to wend their way from strand to shore. But as they left the vicinity of the Mount, they turned last looks of hatred toward the rock.

His Excellency, the Governor, wasted no time considering the humor of the masses; their resentment, or displeasure, signified nothing; his own complacency left little room for speculation on that score. He was undeniably satisfied; even the escape of the prisoners and the loss of the soldiers at the guard-house, or in the wheel-room, was overshadowed by the single capture. This contentment, however, he kept to himself; instigated a rigorous inquiry, and prepared to punish certain offenders. But the principal of these he could not reach; when released from the iron cage, the hunchback, knowing he would be called upon to answer for his part in the night's work, had made the best use of his short legs to place a long distance between himself and the Mount.

The sentinel that allowed the Black Seigneur to pass through the entrance near the barracks; the watchman encountered on the stairway, and the soldier that had been overpowered in the stable, his Excellency could, however, lay hands on, and promptly ordered into custody to await his official attention. For this last culprit, the commandant—mindful, perhaps, of bolstering his own position—interceded; pointing out that the man had to get the gag from his mouth and give the alarm; also, that the mountebank's appearance and acting had been calculated to deceive even one of the Governor's discernment. Which remark his Excellency had received with sphinx-like, and not altogether reassuring, gravity; had reserved his verdict, and continued, after his own fashion, to collect the details of the affair.

This searching process should have led him almost at once to his daughter—a puzzling figure in the maze of events; but the Governor exhibited no haste in approaching that important witness. Only when he had marshaled his other testimony and put it in order did the scope of his sifting extend to the girl. And then had his manner been strictly judicial: maintaining an imperturbable mask, he professed not to notice the pallor of her face, the unnatural brightness of her glance.

"When you sent for the mountebank to come to your apartments, did you know who he was?" the Governor had asked.

"No."

"When did you find out?"

"When you entered the room."

"Why did you not give the alarm then?"

"Because," she hesitated; her face changed, "he would have killed you, I think—if I had!"

"Was that solicitude for me the only reason?"

"Why, what other could there be?"

"What other truly? And after he left with the commandant—why did you not, then, inform me?"

"You remember you had something important, from the King, to consider!" hastily.

"More important than this?"

"He was going to be locked up," was the best reply she could make.

"And in the morning set free!"

She did not answer.

"And yet, you gave the word that enabled us to capture him at the wheel-house! How, by the way, came you there—in the wheel-house?"

"I saw him from the abbot's bridge; heard him tell the watchman he had a message to deliver at your palace, and followed."

"Again feeling solicitude for me?"

"I did not know—he would dare much; and what does it matter now?" almost wildly. "You have captured him, shut him up somewhere in some terrible, deep dungeon, where—"

"He is safe? True; that is the main consideration."

Thereafter had the subject of the Black Seigneur been dropped between them; the pilgrimage over, the Mount resumed its normal aspect, but only for a little while! One day about a week later, a bright cortége whose appearance was in marked contrast to that of the beggarly multitude, late visitors to the rock, came riding down the road through the forest to the sea; at the verge of the sands, stopped for a first distant impression of the rock.

"Noble monument, I salute you!" Smiling, debonair, the Marquis de Beauvillers removed his hat.

"And the noble mistress thereof?" suggested one of his train.

"She, of course!" he said, still surveying a scene different from that final memory he had carried away with him. Then had the rock reared itself in all the glamour of a sunny day; now was the sky overcast, while through a sullen mist the Mount loomed like a shadow itself.

"A cold place for our gay Elise!" One or two who viewed the sight for the first time looked disappointed; even the Marquis appeared for the instant more sober; but immediately regained his lively demeanor.

"Wait until you have seen it at its best," he retorted carelessly, and set the pace across the sands.

Midway, where once on the sands the men of Brittany had engaged in fierce conflict the ancient abbot's forces, were the new-comers met by an imposing guard; escorted with due honor through the gates, and up the narrow street of the town.

As he climbed the winding highway, my lord, the Marquis, bestowed approving nod and smile this way and that; it may be that he already felt a nearer affiliation with these people; for his glance, gracious, condescending in passing, was that of a man armed with the knowledge that he, kinsman of the King, might some day be called upon to govern here. But to these advances, the townspeople responded ill, and the young noble's brow went delicately up, as if a little amused! Mon dieu! did not unfriendly eyes peer from every lurking place around the royal palaces and pleasure grounds near Paris; and had they not encountered them all the way to the sea? People were the same everywhere; must be treated like bad children, and, with relays of troops from the capital to the sea, from the strand to the Mount's high top, one could afford to smile at their petty humors. Above all, when one had more momentous matter for consideration! And my lord lifted his head higher, toward a rampart, where some one had once bid him au revoir, and where he might yet in fancy see a fluttering ribbon wave a bright adieu!

But to-day my lady, the Princess of the Rock, was not there; waited above, with her father, to receive him—then—in the great Hall of the Chevaliers. Until that morning she had not known of the coming of the Marquis, an impatient suitor, following the courier and the perfumed missive acquainting her with the noble's near approach. Certainly had she shown surprise; but whether she was pleased or not, his Excellency could not tell.

He was still uncertain; standing, near the raised gallery, in the ancient salle des chevaliers, from time to time regarded her furtively! Often had she looked from one of the round windows, commanding a view of the shore and the sands; many times turned away. At first sight of the company on the beach, the Governor had seen the girl's face alter and noted the involuntary start she had given. Whereupon, moving toward one of the giant fireplaces, had he sought for the sake of diplomacy and the end in view, to turn their conversation into a channel that should have interested her; spoke of plans to be made; preparations for festivities and merrymaking commensurate with the circumstances. But to these suggestions of gaieties, the prelude to a stately ceremony, had she hardly listened; paused absently before the blazing logs; once or twice seemed about to say something and stopped.

She was silent now, a slender figure beneath that great canopy of stone designed for the shelter of a score of knights; nervously twining and intertwining her fingers, she looked out at the shadows moving between the columns, playing around the bases, or melting in the vaulting.

"They should be almost here now," observed his Excellency, again seeking to break that spell of constraint, when suddenly she stepped to him.

"Mon père," her voice sounded strained, unnatural, "it was you who wanted this marriage?"

"Yes," he had answered in some surprise; "yes."

"And I have not opposed you—the King—"

"Opposed? No! Of course not!"

"Then," more hurriedly, "must you do something in return for me! I do not want my—the wedding festivities—marred by anything unpleasant! Promise that nothing will happen to him, the Black Seigneur, until after—"

"Impossible!" The sudden virulence her unexpected request awoke could not be concealed.

"Very well!" Before the anger in his gaze, her own eyes flashed like steel. "In that case, you can send the Marquis back! For I will not see him—to-day, to-morrow or any time again!"

Long he looked at her; the white face; the tightly compressed lips; the eyes that would not flinch! They reminded him of another's—were of the same hue—so like, and yet so different! Unlike, in bespeaking a will he could not break! What he said, matters not; his face wore an ashy shade. She did not answer in words; but he felt, with strange bitterness, a revulsion; she seemed almost suddenly to have become hostile to him.

Gay voices sounded without; nearer; she walked to a door opposite the entrance their visitors were approaching. An instant, and she would have passed out, when the Governor spoke.

But the Marquis, stepping quickly in a few moments later, noted nothing amiss between them. "Your Excellency!" With filial respect he greeted the Governor. "My Lady!" Gaily, approvingly, his eye passed over her; then in that hall dedicated to chivalry, a graceful figure, he sank to his knee; raised a small cold hand, and pressed it to his lips.

CHAPTER XXV

THE UNDER WORLD

A coterie of brilliant folk soon followed in the wake of my lord, the Marquis' retinue; holy-day banners were succeeded by holiday ribbons; the miserere of the multitude by pæans of merriment. Hymen, Io Hymen! In assuming the leading rôle to which circumstances now assigned her, the Governor's daughter brought to the task less energy than she had displayed on that other occasion when visitors had sojourned at the rock. Her manner was changed—first, lukewarm; then, almost indifferent; until, at length, one day she fairly waived the responsibility of planning amusements; laid before them the question: What, now, would they like to do?

"Devise a play," said one.

"With shepherds and shepherdesses!"

The Marquis, however, qualified the suggestion. "A masque! that is very good; but, for this morning—I have been talking with the commandant—and have another proposal—"

"Which is?"

"To visit the dungeons."

"The dungeons?" My lady's face changed.

"And incidentally inspect their latest guest! Some of you heard of him when we were here before—Le Seigneur Noir—the Black Seigneur!"

"Le Seigneur Noir!" They clapped their hands. "Yes, let us see him! Nothing could be better. What do you say, Elise?"

She started to speak, but for the instant her lips could frame no answer; with a faint, strained smile, confronted them, when some one anticipated her reply—

"Did she not leave it to us? It is we who decide."

And a merry party, they swept along, bearing her with them; up the broad stairway, cold, gray in the morn; beneath the abbot's bridge—black, spying span!—to the church, and thence to the isolated space before the guard-house to the dungeons. Here, at the sound of their voices, a man, carrying a bunch of keys—but outwardly the antithesis to the hunchback—peered from the entrance.

"Unless I am mistaken, the new jailer!" With a wave of his hand, the Marquis indicated this person. "The commandant was telling me his Excellency had engaged one—from Bicêtre, or Fort l'Evêque, I believe?"

"Bicêtre, my Lord!" said the man gravely. "And before that, the Bastille."

"Ah!" laughed the nobleman. "That pretty place some of the foolish people are grumbling about! As if we could do without prisons any more than without palaces! But we have come, my good fellow, to inspect this lower world of yours!"

The man's glance passed over the paper the Marquis handed him; then silently he moved aside, and unlocked the iron doors.

"Are you not coming?" At the threshold the Marquis looked back. When first they had approached the guard-house, involuntarily had the Governor's daughter drawn aside to the ramparts; now, with face half-averted, stood gazing off.

"Coming?" Surprised, the Marquis noted her expression; the fixed brightness of her eyes and her parted lips. "Oh, yes!" And turning abruptly, she hastened past him.

Would they have to be locked in?—the half-apprehensive query of one of the ladies caused the jailer at first to hesitate and then to answer in the negative. He would leave the doors from the outer room open, and himself await there the visitors' return. With which reassuring promise, he distributed lights; called a guardsman, familiar with the intricate underground passages, and consigned them to his care.

One of the gay procession, the Lady Elise stepped slowly forward; the guide proved a talkative fellow, and seemed anxious to answer their many inquiries concerning the place. The salle de la question? Yes, it existed; but the ancient torture devices for the "interrogatory ordinary" and the "interrogatory extraordinary" were no longer pressed into service; the King had ordered them relegated to the shelves of the museum. The cabanons, or black holes? Louis XI built them; the carceres duri and vade in pace, however, dated from Saint Mauritius, fourth abbot of the Mount.

"And the Black Seigneur? How have you accommodated him?"

"In the petit exil; just to the left! We are going there now."

"I—am going back!" A hand touched the arm of the Marquis, last of the file of visitors, and, lifting his candle, he held it so that the yellow glimmer played on the face of the Governor's daughter. Her eyes looked deeper; full of dread, as if the very spirit of the subterranean abode had seized her. He started.

"Surely you, Elise, are not afraid?"

"I prefer the sunlight," she said hurriedly in a low tone. "It—it is not cheerful down here! No; do not call to the guide—or let the others know. I'll return alone, and—wait for you at the guard-house."

He, nevertheless, insisted upon accompanying her; but, indicating the not distant door through which they had come, she professed to make light of objections, and when he still clung to the point, replied with a flash of spirit, sudden and passionate. It compelled his acquiescence; left him surprised for a second time that day; a little hurt, too, perhaps, for heretofore had their intimacy been maintained on a strictly ethical and charming plane. But he had no time for analysis; the others were drawing away to the left, into a side passage; and, with a last backward glance toward the retreating figure, the Marquis reluctantly followed the majority.

Despite, however, her avowed repugnance for that under-world, my lady showed now no haste to quit it; for scarcely had the others vanished than she stopped; began slowly to retrace her way in the direction they had taken. When the narrow route to the petit exil connected with the main aisle, a sudden draft of air extinguished her light; yet still she went on, led by the voices, and a glimmer afar, until reaching a room, low, massive, as if hewn from the solid rock, again she paused. Drawing behind a heavy square pillar, she gazed at the lords and ladies assembled in the forbidding place; listened to a voice that ran on, as if discoursing about some anomalous thing. Again was she cognizant of their questions; a jest from my lord, the Marquis; she saw that several stole forward; peered, and started back, half afraid.

But, at length, they asked about the oubliettes, and, chatting gaily, left. Their garments almost touched the Governor's daughter; lights played about the gigantic pillars, and like will-o'-the-wisps whisked away. Now, staring straight ahead toward the chamber they had vacated, my lady's attention became fixed by a single dot of yellow—a candle placed in a niche by the jailer's assistant. It seemed to fascinate; to draw her forward; across the portals—into the room itself!

How long she stood there in the faint suggestion of light, she did not realize; nor when she approached the iron-barred aperture, and what she first said! Something eager, solicitous, with odd silences between her words, until the impression of a motionless form, and two steady, cynical eyes fastened on her, brought her to an abrupt pause. It was some time before she continued, more coherently, an explanation about her apprehension on account of her father, which had entirely left her when she had peered through the window of the guard-house.

"You thought me, then, but a common assassin?" a satirical voice interposed.

"My father hates you, and you—"

"My Lady has, perhaps, a standard of her own for judging!"

Unmindful of ironical incredulity, she related how she had been forced to take refuge in the wheel-house; how, when Sanchez had seen her, alarmed she had fled blindly down the passage; waited, then hearing them all coming, at a loss what else to do, had opened the wheel-house door; run into the store-room! What she had seen from there, disconnectedly, also she referred to; his rescue of the others; his remaining behind to bear the brunt—as brave an act as she knew of! Her tone became tremulous.

"Who betrayed me?" His voice, bold and scoffing, interrupted.

She answered. It was like speaking to some one in a tomb. "The soldier you bound gave the alarm."

From behind the bars came a mocking laugh.

"You don't believe me?" She caught her breath.

"Believe? Of course."

"You don't!" she said, and clung tighter to the iron grating. "And I can't make you!"

"Why should your Ladyship want to? What does it matter?"

"But it does matter!" wildly. "When your servant accused me that day in the cloister I did not answer nor deny; but now—"

"Your Ladyship would deny?"

"That I betrayed you at Casque? Here? Yes, yes!"

"Or at the wheel-house when you called to warn the soldiers?"

"You were about to—to throw yourself over!" she faltered.

"And your Ladyship was apprehensive lest the Black Seigneur should escape?"

"Escape?" she cried. "It was death!"

"And the alternative? My Lady preferred to see the outlaw taken—die like a felon on the gallows!"

"No; no! It was not that."

"What then?" His eyes gleamed bright; her own turned; shrank from them. A moment she strove to answer; could not. Within the black recess a faint light from the flickering candle played up and down. So complete the stillness, so dead the very air, the throbbings of her pulses filled the girl with a suffocating sense of her own vitality.

"I spoke to my father to try to get your cell changed," she at last found herself irrelevantly saying; "but could do nothing."

"I thank your Ladyship! But your Ladyship's friends will be far away. Your Ladyship may miss something amusing!"

"I did not bring them—did not want them to come!"

"No?"

Her figure straightened.

"Perhaps, even, they are not aware you are here?"

"They are not, unless—"

"Elise!" From afar a loud call interrupted; reverberating down the main passage, was caught up here and there. "Elise! Elise!" The whole under-world echoed to the name.

"I promised to meet them at the guard-house," she explained hurriedly. And hardly knowing what she did, put out her hand, through the bars, toward him. In the darkness a hand seized hers; she felt herself drawn; held against the bars. They bruised her shoulder; hurt her face. The chill of the iron sent a shudder through her; though the pain she did not feel; she was cognizant only of a closer view of a figure; the chains from him to the wall; the bare, damp floor—then, of a voice low, tense, that now was speaking:

"Your Ladyship, indeed, found means to punish a presumptuous fellow, who dared displease her. But ma foi! she should have confined her punishment to the offender. Those stripes inflicted on him, my old servant! Think you I knew not it was my Lady's answer to the outlaw, who had the temerity to speak words that offended—"

"You dream that! You imagine that!"

The warmth of his hand seemed to burn hers; her fingers, so closely imprisoned, to throb with the fierce beating of his pulses.

"I do not want you to think—I can't let you think," she began.

"Elise!" The searchers were drawing nearer.

She would have stepped back, but the fingers tightened on her hand.

"They will be here in a moment—"

Still he did not relinquish his hold; the dark face was next hers; the piercing, relentless eyes studied the agitated brown ones. The latter cleared; met his fully an instant. "Believe!" that imploring wild glance seemed to say. Did his waver for a moment; the harshness and mockery soften on his face?

"Elise!" From but a short distance came the voice of the Marquis.

A moment the Black Seigneur's hand gripped my lady's harder with a strength he was unaware of. A slight cry fell from her lips, and at once, almost roughly, he threw her hand from him.

"Bah!" again he laughed mockingly. "Go to your lover."

Released thus abruptly she wavered, straightened, but continued to stand before the dungeon as if incapable of further motion.

"Elise! Are you there?"

"There!" Caverns and caves called out.

"There!" gibed voices amid a labyrinth of pillars, and mechanically she caught up the candle; fled.

"Here she is!" Coming toward her quickly out of the darkness, the Marquis uttered a glad exclamation. "We have been looking for you everywhere. Did I not say you should not have attempted to return alone? Mon dieu! you must have been lost!"

CHAPTER XXVI

A NEW ARRIVAL

Thrice had the old nurse, Marie, assisting her mistress that night for the banquet, sighed; a number of times striven to hold my lady's eye and attention, but in vain. Only when the adorning process was nearly completed and the nurse knelt with a white slipper, did she, by a distinctly detaining pressure, succeed in arresting, momentarily, the other's bright strained glance.

"Is anything the matter?" My lady's absent tone did not invite confidences.

"My Lady—" the woman hesitated; yet seemed anxious to speak. "I—my Lady," she began again; with sign of encouragement from the Governor's daughter, would have gone on; but the latter, after waiting a moment, abruptly withdrew the silken-shod foot.

"The banquet! It is past the hour!"

An instant she stood, not seeing the other or the expression of disappointment on the woman's countenance; then quickly walked to the door. Nor, as the Governor's daughter moved down the long corridor, with crimson lips set hard, was she cognizant of another face that looked out from one of the many passages of the palace after her—the face of a younger woman whose dark, spying eyes glowed and whose hands closed at sight of the vanishing figure!

The sound of gay voices, however, as she neared the banqueting hall, perforce recalled my lady to a sense of her surroundings; at the same time a figure in full court dress stepped from the widely opened doors. An adequate degree of expectancy on his handsome countenance, my lord, the Marquis, who had been waiting, lover-fashion, for the first glimpse of his mistress that evening, now gallantly tendered his greetings.

Seldom, perhaps, had the ancient banqueting hall presented a more festive appearance. Fruits and flowers made bright the tables; banners medieval, trophies of many victories, trailed from the ceiling; a hundred lights were reflected from ornaments of crystal and dishes of gold. On every hand an almost barbaric profusion impressed the guests with the opulence of the Mount; that few could sit in more state than this pale lord of the North, or few queens preside over a scene of greater splendor than their fair hostess, his daughter!

With feverish semblance of spirit, she took her place; beneath the keen eyes of his Excellency responded to sallies of wit, and only when between courses the music played, did her manner relax. Then, leaning on her elbow, with cheeks aflame and downcast eyes, she professed to listen to dainty strains— the sighing of the old troubadours, as imitated by a group of performers in costume on a balcony at one end of the hall.

"Charming!" The voice was the Marquis'; she looked at him, though her eyes conveyed but a shadowy impression. "You have quite recovered from your trip to the dungeons?"

"Quite!" With a sudden lift of the head.

"The dungeons?" His Excellency's gaze was on them. "I understand," looking at Elise, "you had a slight adventure?"

The glow on her cheek faded. "Yes." She seemed to speak with difficulty. "It—was too stupid!"

"To get lost? Say, rather, it was venturesome to have attempted to return alone."

"Just what I said to the Lady Elise!" broke in the Marquis. "And to have left us at a most interesting moment!"

"Interesting?" The Governor's steel-gray eyes regarded the speaker inquiringly.

"We were about to visit the Black Seigneur!"

"Ah!" A look flashed from his Excellency to his daughter; her glance failed to meet it.

Yet paler, she turned over-hurriedly to the Marquis. "What is that air they are playing now?" His response she heard not, was only conscious that, across the board, the eyes of her father still scrutinized; studied!

At length, however, the evening wore away; a signal from his Excellency, and of one accord they rose and crossed to the star-illumined cloister adjoining. There at the entrance, my lady, who toward the last had listened with an air of distraction, hardly concealed, to her noble suitor's graceful speeches, held back, and, as the others went in, quickly effected her escape and hastened to her own apartments.

"At last!" She threw back her arms; breathed deeper. "Ah, mon père, you are hard—unyielding as the iron doors and bars of your dungeons!" She pressed her hand to her forehead. "And I can do nothing—nothing!" she repeated; stood for a moment motionless and then mechanically moved toward the bell-rope at the other end of the chamber. But the hand she started to raise was arrested; through the slightly opened door to the adjoining apartment, she heard voices; words that caused her involuntarily to listen.

"I have made up my mind to tell her ladyship, Nanette!" The old nurse was speaking, in tones that betrayed excitement and anxiety. "It is, to say the least, embarrassing for me—your coming here! You, the daughter of Pierre Laroche, who emigrated to the English Isles! Who has always shown disloyalty for the monarchy at home!"

My lady, surprised, drew nearer; caught the answer, which came in tones, deep and strong.

"At least, aunt, you are frank!"

"I must be! Under ordinary circumstances, I should be glad; of course, the child of my dead sister ought to be welcome."

"So I thought," dryly, "when I stopped off a few days ago to see you, on my way to Paris."

"If you had let me know, it is I who would have gone somewhere, near by, to have seen you!" was the troubled reply. "His Excellency—what would he say if he knew? Pierre Laroche, who has been called friend of privateersmen, perhaps even of the Black Seigneur, himself! I should have gone to his Excellency at once and asked if he objected, only you begged me not, and—"

"Were you so anxious to be rid of me?" quickly.

"I shouldn't speak as I do now, perhaps, only—"

"Only?"

"Your conduct, since you have been here—"

"What do you mean?" The other's tone had a sudden defiant ring.

"It is not seemly for a girl of your age and condition to be out alone so late, nights!"

"I just went down into the town to get something," was the careless response, "and the sands looked so attractive—"

"That's no excuse! And now," the old nurse's voice showed a trace of embarrassment, "we've had our visit, and you had better carry out your plan of going to Paris."

"You want me to leave here—at once?" The girl drew her breath sharply.

"Perhaps it would be as well."

"You treat me as if—I were a spy!" angrily.

"I don't wish to do that," returned the woman in a constrained tone. "But now, after so many years of service with her ladyship! And her mother, the former lady of the Mount! If I should incur the Governor's displeasure—" the words died away. "If I can be of any help to you, if you need assistance—money—"

"Money!" Nanette's derisive laugh rang out; was suddenly hushed by the tinkling of a bell!

"Her ladyship!"

For a few moments the Governor's daughter, now standing in the center of her apartment, heard no sound from the other room; then a timid footstep approaching the door was followed by an indecisive rap.

"Your Ladyship rang?" inquired Marie, turning a half-guilty glance on her mistress.

"Yes! Did I hear voices, as I came in?"

"Did your Ladyship? I mean, I was going to speak to your Ladyship. It's my niece!" suddenly. "On her way to Paris!"

"Your niece!" The Governor's daughter looked at the other. "And you—are pleased?"

"Your Ladyship—" The woman flushed.

"Of course, though, you must be! She is out there? Show her in!" quickly.

"But—"

"At once!"

"Very well, my Lady!" Marie's manner, however, was depressed, as, stepping to the threshold, reluctantly she beckoned.

Erect, with mien almost antagonistic, Nanette entered and stood before the Lady Elise. The latter did not at once speak; for a few moments the observant brown eyes passed in quick scrutiny over her visitor; noting the aggressive brows; the broad, strong face; the self-assertive pose of the well-developed figure. A woman to do—to dare!—What?

 "A woman to do--to dare!"

"A woman to do—to dare!"

"You wished to see me?" Nanette first spoke.

Marie lifted an expostulatory hand. What bad manners, thus to dare! But my lady did not seem to notice. "You are from one of the islands?" she began.

"Yes."

"Say 'my Lady'!" broke in the old nurse. "I trust your Ladyship will pardon—"

"Never mind, Marie!" with a quick gesture. "Your aunt tells me you are on your way to Paris?"

"Yes—my Lady!" with the slightest hesitation before the last two words. "To seek a situation as lady's maid!"

"When are you leaving?"

"To-morrow morning, your Ladyship!" interposed Marie quickly.

"So soon?" My lady continued to address the girl. "You have had experience?"

"No, my Lady!"

"Then how can you secure what you wish?"

"How? At least, I can try!"

"To be sure! You can try." My lady's eyes fell; she seemed to be thinking. "Still, it may be difficult; Paris is far away. And if you should fail," her fingers tapped nervously on the chair, "we are very busy at the Mount just now," she added suddenly, directing her glance full upon the other, "and there may be something here—"

"Here! Your Ladyship will keep me here!"

Marie made a movement as if to speak, but her niece intercepted her.

"I will do my best, my Lady!"

"Very well! Then shall you have a trial!"

"Your Ladyship!" interposed Marie.

The Governor's daughter got up quickly. "I am very tired, Marie, and wish now to be alone! You need not remain—I shall not want you again to-night."

The old nurse murmured a dejected response; turned away.

"I thank your Ladyship!" The girl's last look was one of indubitable satisfaction ere she followed her aunt from the room.

My lady stared after them. "'Daughter of Pierre Laroche! Friend of the Black Seigneur!'" Marie's words continued to ring in her ears. She threw herself into a chair; sat long very still, her eyes bent straight before her, on either cheek now a bright spot of color.

CHAPTER XXVII

A STROLL ON THE STRAND

"You are in a hurry, Monsieur Beppo?" arms akimbo, Nanette, standing in an embrasure of the rampart, called out to the Governor's man as he passed by.

"Ah, Mistress Nanette," Beppo stopped readily enough, "I didn't see you at first."

"Because you have more important matters to think of," she laughed, showing her strong white teeth.

The fat old man looked pleased; a few days before, Nanette had flashed a radiant smile at him from her casement, and, ever since, he had been inclined to regard her with favor.

"Not more important, but duties that must be attended to! The wedding hour draws near." The island girl half turned her head; a shadow seemed to pass over the bold, sunburned features. "And her ladyship gives to-morrow a riding party for her guests—a last celebration before she is led to the altar. I am on my way now to arrange about the escort."

"A riding party!" Nanette spoke quickly. "You mean on horseback?"

"How else?" said Beppo. "It is a pastime her ladyship has always been very fond of, even as a child. In those days," not without an accent of self-importance, "it was my privilege—"

"Do they ride far?" interrupted Nanette with ill-suppressed eagerness.

"To the old Monastery St. Ranulphe; an imposing ruin of tenth century architecture, my dear," he added pompously.

"And where is it?"

"Off the Paris highway, some ten miles from the Mount."

"Ten miles? And the country is beautiful? Not open; sandy, like the shore?"

"It partakes of a rugged grandeur."

"With forests around?" quickly.

"Yes," indulgently. "You like forests, Mistress Nanette?"

"When they are thick and wild—"

"Then would you like these!"

The girl asked no further questions; yet still Beppo lingered, his glance seeming loath to withdraw from this exuberant specimen of vigorous young womanhood. "Which way were you going, good Mistress Nanette?" he asked finally. "On second thoughts, I have a little time to spare and will walk along."

Nanette, looking down from the rampart toward the sands and the shore, did not answer, and, more insinuatingly, Beppo repeated his proposal. Nanette started.

"La, Monsieur Beppo! I—I'm afraid it wouldn't do. There's my aunt," tossing her head, "that careful of me! Won't even let me go walking on the beach alone! Do you ever go walking on the beach, Monsieur Beppo?" she inquired suddenly, regarding him with an eloquent look.

"I—it has not been my custom," he murmured. "But," the fishy eyes growing brighter, "with you—if I might accompany you—"

"Oh, I didn't mean that! No; no! Of course not! And I couldn't think of it. My aunt—"

But when a few moments later, she turned, to walk quickly away, the round and shining face of Beppo, watching her disappear, wore not the look of a man who had allowed himself to be rebuffed.

Out of his sight, Nanette's expression changed to one of somber thoughtfulness; it lingered as she entered the palace, with free swing, mounted the steps to her mistress' apartments; was still there, when she took a bit of embroidery from a table, and seating herself at the window of an antechamber, bent over her task. Soon, however, she stopped, to sweep abruptly cloth and colored silks from her lap to the floor, and, leaning forward, her firm, brown hands clasped over her knees, she seemed to be asking herself questions, or weighing some problem.

"Yes; it is our only chance." In her eyes a steady glow replaced the varying lights, and, getting up with a sudden air of determination, Nanette crossed the room to where, near the door, stood a small desk. Glancing quickly around, she seated herself and, reaching for paper and pen, wrote carefully and somewhat laboriously a few words. She had finished and was contemplating the result of her eager efforts when a hand at the door caused her hurriedly to dash down the pen and spring to her feet. As her aunt entered, Nanette took a few steps forward, and, bending to pick up her work from the floor, turned partly away and thrust the paper into the bosom of her gown.

"I came to tell you supper is ready," said Marie quietly.

At the table with her aunt the girl's manner was subdued and deferential; she observed the nicest proprieties, and bestowed on the other's slightest word a meed of attention calculated to soften the old woman's attitude and suspicions. And possibly succeeded; or, it may be, Marie's own conscience had begun to reproach her; for a number of days had passed and nothing had as yet occurred to justify the early apprehensions she had entertained. Under the circumstances the meal was a little prolonged; the first shafts of twilight had entered the courtyard and had begun to steal into the narrow chamber with darkening effect, ere of an accord the two women pushed back their chairs.

"It gets dark early," said the girl, "or time has passed quicker than I thought. Perhaps it was what you were telling me of the former lady of the Mount. She must have been very beautiful!"

"She was," answered the woman; "and as good as beautiful!"

"Heigh-ho!" Nanette sighed; through the window watched the shadows that like dark, trailing figures seemed creeping up the ancient wall to caress and linger on green leaves of vines, bright flowers and other living things. "But I suppose she had everything she wanted." The girl stirred restlessly. "What sort of a man is Monsieur Beppo, aunt?"

"Beppo?" Recalled as from a long train of recollections, the woman did not seem to notice the abruptness of the inquiry. "Oh, he is an old and faithful servant. For almost as many years as I have been here," with an accent of pride, "has he served at the Mount!"

"And his moral character, aunt?" demurely.

"Monsieur Beppo has a reputation for piety, no doubt deserved!" returned the woman, with an accent of surprise. "At any rate, he seldom misses a mass. But why do you ask?"

"Because I met him to-day and he invited me to walk with him this evening."

"He did?" Marie's mouth grew firmer. "And you?"

"I didn't exactly know how to refuse; he—looked so old and respectable! I thought, too, you wouldn't mind and—I'm glad you think so well of him, aunt."

In the gathering gloom the listener's face seemed suddenly to grow graver; her eyes, which had returned to the girl's, expressed once more doubt and misgiving. With her glance lifted upward, however, Nanette did not seem to notice this quick change. A star—faint forerunner of a multitude of waiting orbs—peeping timorously down from above the gray, gaunt mass of stone, alone absorbed the girl's gaze and attention.

"Where were you thinking of going?" after a silence of some length the older woman asked.

"I don't recall that Monsieur Beppo mentioned," was the low-murmured response. "But, of course, aunt, if you object—"

"I do not know that I do," said the other slowly. "Only," as if the thought had suddenly come to her, "what were you writing at her ladyship's desk when I went to call you?"

"Writing?" Nanette regarded her blankly. "I don't understand you, aunt."

"Weren't you writing something that you hid in your dress when I came?"

"No!" The girl looked full at the other; denied point-blank the accusation. "Now that you speak of it, I believe I did step to the desk," she answered glibly, "to look at some ornament; but as for writing, or daring to, I should not have presumed."

A low discreet rap at the door interrupted, and, with a whispered "There he is now!" Nanette cut short further argument by rising.

"She is not telling the truth!" For some time the woman stood looking down in gloomy thought after the two had gone. "What does it mean?" Moving to a peg, she took down a shawl. "What can it mean?" she asked herself again, and, wrapping the garment about her head and shoulders, left the room.

Half an hour later, at Beppo's side, on the beach, Nanette measured her steps to his; listened to the old man's platitudes, and even turned a not unwilling ear to sundry hints and innuendos of a tenderer nature. The girl was in her most complaisant mood, and, in his rôle of discreet gallant to young and blooming womanhood, the fat factotum strove to make the most of the opportunity. He sighed; bethought him of a sentimental tale, and carped of the beauty of the moon, then gilding the edge of the Mount's high towers! She answered; looked; but soon her eloquent glance swerved to the sands, dotted by desultory seekers of cockles, or belated stragglers from the shore, and fastened itself on a jutting point of the Mount.

Near it, before a large rock of peculiar shape, a man was engaged in that common nocturnal labor of the locality, digging! As the couple drew near, quickly he raised his gaze; almost at once let it fall; engrossed in his work, continued to toss the sand and stoop over it searchingly. But when they had gone by, once more he straightened, and, at the same time, the girl looked back. Stalwart, black-bearded, a sailor by his dress, the fellow made a sign, and, apparently any doubt as to who he was vanished from Nanette's mind; for from the fingers of the free hand she held behind her, something fluttered to the beach.

Leaning to his implement, the man regarded the paper, but not until the girl's low laugh was heard, as she and Master Beppo vanished in the darkness, did he step forward and secure it.

"So! That was it!" Breathless, indignant, Marie, standing in the black shade of one of the Mount's projections, watched the fellow read and regard carefully the message in his hand; then tearing it, crumple the bits and thrust them toward his pocket as he walked off. "Brazen huzzy! But her ladyship shall know; and if she doesn't pack you off, bag and baggage—Eh? What is that?" And springing forward, the woman pounced upon something that lay on the sand.

CHAPTER XXVIII

THE HESITATION OF THE MARQUIS

The day of my lady's riding party dawned; in the east a tender flame burned, and, vanishing, left the heavens an unbroken blue. Shoreward the mists rolled up, until only in the neighborhood of the forest did the white, soft vapor linger. On the Mount itself sunshine held sway; it radiated from the fortifications, "cuirass of the rock," and gleamed on the church, "tiara of its majesty." It warmed a cold palace of marble; looked in at its windows, and threw bold shafts to lighten dark nooks and corners.

But my lady, mistress of the Mount, seemed not to feel its beneficent touch; standing in the full glow and looking from her casement she shivered a little. Already was she dressed, and her habit of dark green, fitting close, served to accentuate the whiteness of her cheek which general absence of color, in turn, made the more manifest certain dark lines beneath the restless, bright eyes.

"Your Ladyship!" After knocking in vain, Marie had entered the room and set down the small tray she carried. "There is something your Ladyship ought to know!" with an air of excitement. The Governor's daughter half turned. "What now, Marie?" she said sharply.

"It's about Nanette!" My lady made a quick movement of annoyance, impatience. "I did not tell your Ladyship, but I was averse to having her remain here. Your Ladyship does not understand, of course, and—"

"I do understand," said my lady unexpectedly. "And—you need not explain. I overheard you talking with her that night of the banquet!"

"Your Ladyship!" startled.

"And I heard you speak of her father, Pierre Laroche, friend of the Black Seigneur."

"And engaged her—after that!"

"Why not? I could watch—and I have! But you were wrong, Marie." My lady's manner was feverish. "Your suspicions were ridiculous. There has been nothing—nothing! And day after to-morrow is the wedding celebration, and the next day, he, the Black Seigneur—" She broke off abruptly.

Had Marie been less wrought up, less excited, less concerned with the information she had to impart, she could not have failed to notice the odd break in her young mistress' voice; something unusual, almost akin to despair, in her manner. As it was, that which weighed on the old nurse's mind precluded close observation of the other.

"But something has happened, my Lady!" the woman half stammered.

"Comment!" The girl turned to her sharply. "What? Explain, Marie!"

Disconnectedly, the woman launched into a narration of the events of the night before; my lady listened closely, with an interest and excitement she strove to conceal, half turning so that the other saw no longer her face.

"And here," ended Marie, extending a crumpled fragment of paper, "is a piece of the note she dropped on the beach. The man tore it up, but in thrusting the bits of paper into his pocket this fell out, and, after he walked away, I picked it up myself from the sand. I can't read, as your Ladyship knows, and there isn't much on it—only a word or two! But it may tell something."

My lady's face was now composed; the hand she extended, steady; for several moments she regarded the fragment.

"What does it say?" asked the woman anxiously. "Is it—is it important?"

Her mistress did not at once answer; twisting the bit of paper in her fingers, stood as if in thought, and the old nurse repeated her question.

"This note might have been intended for some admirer!" said, at length, the Governor's daughter slowly.

"He looked more like an old privateersman!" murmured the woman. "And there may be some plot—some plan!"

"Privateersman!" The girl's manner underwent a change; she shrugged her shoulders. "What could they hope to do at the Mount! You are imaginative, Marie!" lightly. "Nanette is good-looking, and what little is here would seem to signify a rendezvous. There may be no great harm in that."

"I am sorry, my Lady, to seem to think ill of my own kin," muttered the woman dejectedly, "but—"

"Think no more of it! You have done your duty. Now leave the matter to me, and—thank you, Marie!"

When, however, the old nurse had gone, all pretense of lightness faded from the face of the Governor's daughter, and, opening the bit of paper, once more she scrutinized it swiftly, intently.

"To-morrow—Monastery St. Ranu—" she read. "Yes; it must mean St. Ranulphe—where we are going. And where Beppo knew we were going! Beppo, she went down on the beach with!" Again she studied the fragment, striving to make out a word that had been blotted and was almost illegible. She frowned as she endeavored to decipher it. "Lady E." She gave an exclamation. "That refers, of course, to— But why?" She kept asking herself the question. "Why?" she repeated, when suddenly the brown eyes widened—changed; a new light shone in their depths. "It must be they intend to—what else?"

The sound of horns—signal for the party to gather—broke upon the air, and, nervously crushing in her palm the piece of the message, she stepped to the table, to the untasted breakfast. Like one in a dream, who yet feels the need for haste, she poured out the coffee; with unsteady hand raised the cup and drank; started to serve herself again; as if forgetful of the impulse, paused.

"And I?" she said with deeper breath. "To ride to the ambush they have so cleverly planned? Allow myself to be taken prisoner by these desperate men? No; no; I could not! And yet—" A trampling of horses' hoofs in the court below interrupted. "They are ready to start!" Uncertainly she lifted her head; looked around her; then mechanically stepped forward and left the room.

A scene of animation greeted her in the court, alive with lords and ladies, for the most part already in the saddle and waiting.

"Hail to Diana, who will lead us in the forests!"

"Fair nymph, let us away!" and the Marquis extended his hand.

With a seemingly merry nod she acknowledged their greetings; put out a foot, and lightly sprang to her place on the back of the nervous thoroughbred. But ere giving the signal to start, the girl's glance swung around to a window opposite, where stood an austere figure, imperturbably looking down to watch them ride off.

"Au revoir, mon père!" Her voice rose with an odd, unusual thrill. "Au revoir!" she repeated, when a mistiness in her eyes suddenly blurred sight of him, and she tightened the reins. Yet hesitating to go, her gaze cleared, and swerving, was abruptly arrested by another and more interested spectator, who, partly concealed by flowers and plants, peered with anxious expectancy from her own balcony. As Nanette's eyes met those of the Governor's daughter, they wavered half guiltily; suddenly became steady, held by something—a flash of impelling intelligence in the other's gaze. A moment or two, my lady continued to regard the girl; then touching her horse, wheeled sharply, and set a pace downward not easy to follow.

At the base of the Mount they were met by a numerous guard bright in holiday trappings, and, under the care of the commandant, with flourish of horse, the party swept gaily from sands to shore.

"A gallant company, Monsieur le Commandant!" observed the Marquis to the officer in charge, as they reached the green line at the yellow basin's edge. "Now if we were to meet an enemy—"

"He would find us prepared, my Lord!" the officer declared.

"True!" And the nobleman complacently touched the jeweled hilt of his own blade, accompanying the action with a tender glance at the Lady Elise.

She, however, a little ahead, appeared not to hear; spoke suddenly to her horse, and, as they swung from the sward, started at a brisk gallop down the road. Laughing, the others came after, lords and ladies first; behind, with tumult and clatter, the commandant and his men. As they advanced, on either side the way thick trunks of moss-grown monarchs uplifted their gnarled and hoary branches, to meet overhead; through leafy interstices bright flashes of sunlight shot downward, danced on fine garments and accoutrements, and then whisked elfishly away. In dim recesses finches and sparrows sang; beyond, murmured streams and rivulets, while at the feet of the riders, gay restless flowers nodded, as if in accompaniment to the glad music of the morn.

"Small wonder his Excellency should have desired to add this fair principality to his own!" muttered the Marquis, looking around. "Of the seven forests of Brittany, none will compare with this, the Desaurac woods. What think you, Elise?" spurring his horse near his betrothed's. "Are you not taken by its beauties?"

She looked at him with a start; since leaving the sands she had not spoken, and now, tugging at the reins, only said abruptly: "My saddle! I believe it is loose."

"Loose!" repeated the nobleman. "Careless lackeys! Let us see!" And grasping the bridle of her horse, pulled in his own, and drew both animals to a standstill at the side of the road.

As he dismounted to examine straps and fastenings, the others dashed up; my lady lightly motioned them on. "We'll soon overtake you! Don't wait!" Unquestioning, they obeyed; though the commandant, to whom a few moments later she delivered a similar injunction, brought his men to a halt and proffered his services. Whereupon the Marquis repeated the girl's words more sharply; reddening, the officer wheeled and started to ride on.

"I can't find anything wrong here!" Puzzled, the Marquis straightened.

But her eyes were directed ahead and she pointed with her whip to a break in the woody barrier to the right—a path that, springing from the roadside, seemed to plunge into the very heart of the labyrinth.

"Look! the short cut!—that would bring us half an hour before them to the ruins! Let us take it!"

A light seemed suddenly to break on her companion, and he sprang airily to his saddle. "As my Lady wills!" gallantly.

"Then call to the commandant, and tell him we'll meet them there!"

The Marquis obeyed, and, without awaiting answer, or demur from the officer in charge of the guard, the girl flicked her horse and sent him over a low bush into the narrow way.

Fairly in the path, she rode fast, and pressing hard behind, my lord soon found reason for doubt as to the advisibility of that route, and a suspicion of regret at his own hasty assent to the departure from the main thoroughfare. As their surroundings grew wilder and the slender green figure flitted more and more recklessly before him, he even ventured to voice his misgivings— advise greater care. A shake of the fair head was all he received for answer and, regardless of the increasing roughness of the way, she continued to sweep on, now uphill, then down, avoiding by a quick turn one obstacle here, leaping another there! From a black ambush, a branch like the arm of a Titan reached out to seize, but adroitly she swayed from its grasp and only the twigs and leaves touched lightly the bent figure.

My lord, however, they struck sharply, and at the sudden smart and a quick realization of falling behind, frowningly he drove his horse harder. The tête-à-tête he had naturally expected from her request to pursue the lonelier way promised now not to materialize; the idea that she was fleeing, he pursuing, possessed him. The forest, a tangle of shrubs and strange creepers, was the scene of the idyl; she, a sprite of the greenwood, danced illusively through the maze. At length when my lord had begun to grow weary of vainly endeavoring to overtake her, fate favored his efforts; brought to a standstill, at the edge of a torrent, the object of his pursuit.

"Are you mad, Elise?" A shadow on his brow, the Marquis rode down.

She made no reply; regarded only the water.

"I hope it is not in your mind to attempt to cross," he went on, a shade of petulance in his accents.

She urged her horse forward; it stopped.

"Elise! I beg of you! It is dangerous; better go back, and around!"

But the girl set her red lips, raised her whip, and brought it down hard. The animal sprang into the foam; breasting the current, it slipped once or twice, recovered, and, after an effort, managed to reach the bank opposite. My lord—less blithely than he had first embarked on the adventure—followed; the cold waters surged around, and he almost expected to be swept away. At length, however, chilled by the icy touch of the torrent and somewhat more out of humor, he found himself on the other side. Near the top of the bank, where the Governor's daughter had now the grace to await him, he rejoined her, disapproval on his face, reproach in his eyes. Yet still did the girl remain unconscious of her lover's wounded sensibilities; her own eyes, like stars beneath the flurry of hair, were turned, not to the young man, but away, toward a gaunt-looking ruin that had suddenly uplifted itself, as if by magic, through a rift in the forest. But a few hundred yards distant, the black crumbling walls bristled with rough, jagged edges—big, broken teeth that snarled at the rim of the ever-young wood. The very brightness of the day seemed only to emphasize the ominous aspect of the place; to reveal more plainly the solitary character of its wildness.

"The monastery, I suppose?" following the direction of her gaze, the Marquis, after a pause, grudgingly vouchsafed.

"Yes," said the girl in a low tone; "yes!"

"Shall we go on?"

Her eyes, passing over a tangle of shrubs, bushes and thick, natural screens, slowly settled on a spot, not far away, where a wild bird, about to alight, fled off with a scream.

"Shall we go on?"

With a start the girl turned; the clear-cut features were very grave; in her gaze shone sudden compunction. She raised her hand. "My veil!" she said quickly. "I—dropped it. Do you mind? You—you will find it on this side of the stream—a little way down."

"Mind?" He regarded her doubtfully a moment; then moved by the irresistible appeal in her eyes, rather abruptly he wheeled, and as he did so, she gathered up the reins. Ere proceeding farther upon this errand of gallantry, my lord looked around.

"You seem to set great store on this veil," he, observed suspiciously. "And I believe you were about to ride off!" he added, noting her expression, when, before she had time for pretext or answer, a heavy body stirred in the bushes, near at hand, and a gruff voice called out.

"Stand where you are!"

The nobleman's face changed; his gaze, as if fascinated, now rested on a score of rough figures who, following the order, so unexpected and startling, sprang simultaneously from neighboring thicket or covert, and advanced to surround them. Held by their grim aspect—the desperate determined visages; the black, threatening looks—in the surprise of the moment, too late my lord's hand sought the sword at his side. Roughly plucked from his horse, he found himself flung to the sward; unceremoniously pinioned, and heard the voice of my lady raised in his behalf.

CHAPTER XXIX

THE MARQUIS INTERVENES

The evening of the same day, his Excellency, in the seclusion of a small private chamber adjoining the salle du gouvernement, stood looking down at his desk on which were strewn papers and messages containing the latest news from Paris and received at the Mount but a few hours before. That the character of this information, political and social, was little to his liking, seemed manifest from his manner; he stared at the missives resentfully; then frowned and threw down the pen he had been using to mark, or make note of, their contents.

"Versailles—a mob! Sugar-plums to placate them! Sugar-plums!" he repeated; and, impatiently turning away, walked to the window. There for some time he stood peering out, when, the current of his thoughts slowly changing, he took from his pocket a watch, and examined the jeweled face. "Time they were back!" About to return to his table and task, a loud knocking arrested the impulse, and testily the Governor called out; glanced toward the threshold and surveyed the intruder.

"A message from the commandant, your Excellency!" said the man, a trooper of the Mount, with a respectful, though nervous salute.

"Why," returned the Governor in a dry tone, "didn't he bring it himself?"

"Because," the trooper shifted; looked away; "because Monsieur le Commandant is engaged in scouring the country for miscreants, your Excellency."

"Miscreants!" sharply. "What miscreants?"

"Monsieur le Commandant hopes to overtake those who have carried off the Lady Elise," said the messenger hurriedly, in the tone of one anxious to be done with his task.

"Carried off!" The thin figure wavered as if struck by a cold breath. "Carried off!" he repeated, laying his hand on the back of the chair.

"By a band of the Black Seigneur's men! His lordship, the Marquis, they left behind bound and secured, but the Lady Elise they took with them."

For some time his Excellency said nothing; like a ghost of himself, leaned hard against his support and looked at the trooper.

"But how could it have happened?" at length in a voice, low, intense, he inquired. "Monsieur le Commandant! The guard—you—all are alive?"

Stumblingly, as best he could, the soldier explained, and when he had done, his Excellency made no sign that he had heard.

"Monsieur le Commandant further ordered me to say he had no doubt he would return with the Lady Elise," added the messenger hastily.

"Monsieur le Commandant!" The Governor's eyes suddenly blazed; swiftly he put question after question, and, having probed to the core the consistency of the tale, with a gesture, brusk and contemptuous, dismissed the bearer.

But whatever feeling the lord of the Mount might entertain toward his chief officer, no course at the moment seemed open save to await the return of that person and the Marquis. So, curbing his impatience as best he might, his Excellency kept vigil; and not alone! Tidings of what had happened spread at the top of the rock; sifted through closed gates and thick walls into the town. The late arrival at the Mount of the lords and ladies, companions of the Governor's daughter for the day, but added to the questionings of the multitude. All night life and expectancy reigned; lights gleamed from high places; responded in low ones.

"Is it true, my dear, what we hear about the Lady Elise?" the landlady of the inn on the Mount near the strand called out to a stalwart, dark young woman, hurrying down the narrow way shortly after the Paris contingent had gone up.

"I've heard no more than you have," came the curt answer of this person— none other than Nanette—who carried a small bundle and seemed anxious to move on.

"Oh, I didn't know but you came from the palace!" observed the mistress of the inn, and returned to her customers, drinking and nodding with heads close together.

On the morrow, however, all doubts were removed and speculations put at rest; for hardly had the sun set its seal in the sky than from the forests the appearance of a body of troops rewarded the watchers. From hovel to hut the word went, and men, women and children, unkempt and curious, ran down to the beach to await the approach of the guard. Proudly had it departed, with waving of plumes; slowly it returned, a bedraggled procession of staggering horses and heavy-eyed men. Had it come back a little earlier, the dark might have kept the truth from the people; now the pitiless red glare revealed to the full the plight of the troopers. It told, too, the disappointment of Monsieur le Commandant, who looked neither to the right nor to the left; and the despair of my lord, the Marquis, pale counterfeit of his debonair self.

"Her ladyship!" "They haven't brought her back!" Low murmurs arose; grew louder; some one laughed. But sullenly, without answer, the soldiers dragged by, into the town, and laboriously up to the top of the Mount.

At the gate his Excellency waited; cast one glance at the company—their leader—and silently turned. Later, however, was he closeted with both the commandant and the Marquis—a brief period with the former who departed, carrying a look eloquent of the unpleasantness of the interview.

"And now," said the Governor in tones somewhat strained, as the officer's dejected footfall died in the distance, "we've got rid of that dolt, let us consider, my Lord, the purport of this outrage."

"Purport?" repeated the Marquis petulantly, stretching his stiff legs. "Did they not tell me that if anything happened to the Black Seigneur, they would hold her, Elise, answerable for it? You see they had learned," bitterly, "of your intention to hang him after the wedding!"

"From which you infer?"

"They will keep her as hostage! Indeed, they said as much, when—"

"They bound you, my Lord?"

The color came to the young man's face. "It was a trap," he said, his voice pitched higher; "and they came prepared, not for one man, but the guard!"

"Still was it very ill-advised—a great mistake—to have taken the shorter way through the forest alone."

"The proposal did not originate with me! Elise suggested it. She seemed in a wild, headstrong mood; nothing would stop her. Now," moodily he rose, "mon dieu! What has she brought upon herself? Where is she now?"

His Excellency did not stir; his face, like a pale mask, was turned aside. "I do not think," he said slowly, as arguing to convince himself, "she is in any immediatc danger."

But my lord caught irritably at the word. "No danger! She is surrounded by it. And we? what are we to do? Sit idly here? Give me a ship, your Excellency, and I will follow the boat of this Black Seigneur, and, when I find it, force them to—"

"What?" The Governor's eyes swerved dully. "Have you forgotten their threat? Their last words to you that if we attempted to follow, to rescue—that, rather than give her up—"

"They would not dare!" cried my lord with sparkling glance.

But his Excellency shook his head. "No; no; it won't do! And now," again looking away, "leave me, my Lord, to consider." With which, the interview, as unsatisfactory to the one as the other, terminated.

Several days that passed were not calculated either to alleviate his Excellency's anxiety, or the Marquis' impatience; for during that period of waiting came no word of my lady, or news of her captors. Mysteriously as a phantom ship had the boat that had carried the Governor's daughter away appeared on the coast and vanished, and from none of the Governor's vessels, or any of the fishing craft could be gleaned information of its whereabouts. My lord, the Marquis, annoyed at what seemed but fruitless delay, was still for setting forth and inviting battle; but of this his Excellency would not hear, arguing, no doubt, to himself that in temporizing lay greater assurance of safety to his daughter than in precipitate action. So the situation grew hourly more trying, until—as if it already were not intolerable enough!—a new concern added ironical weight to present perplexities.

My young lord, between whom and the master of the Mount had been growing a more strained relationship, sought the Governor one day, and, in excited tones, announced he had just learned that the prisoner, the Black Seigneur, was ill and probably would survive but a short time longer in the dungeon where he was confined. As his Excellency knew, the fellow had been wounded, and now with scanty nourishment, want of air, and close quarters, was generally in a bad way.

His Excellency heard; moistened his lips and seemed about to speak, but was silent, while more anxiously the young man went on. Of course under different conditions, with care and attention—a well-lighted room and excellent food—they might hope to restore their prisoner's strength; at least, preserve for a time one so precious to themselves, upon the thread of whose life hung my lady's!

His Excellency still answered no word; only looked down, and, knitting his brows, the young nobleman restlessly waited. At length, with an expression on his face the Marquis had never before seen there, his Excellency rose, moved like an automaton to the bell, and called for the jailer.

"Monsieur le Marquis has a few instructions to give you." The Governor's voice, but a breath, told what the words cost him.

The man responded gravely, looking from one to the other.

"Use your own judgment in the matter, my Lord," went on his Excellency, and left them together.

After that, a change, subtle but deep-rooted, came over the Governor; a silent man always, now his taciturnity became most marked. Under stress of untoward circumstances, all the guests at the Mount, save the young noble, departed; but his Excellency appeared hardly to notice their going; drawing his cloak of reserve closer about him, seemed only to ask for that solitude, not difficult to find in his aërial kingdom. Sometimes for a long while he would stand in the cloister, gazing seaward; again wander in the church, look at the monuments, always to pass one of them quickly. Only on a single occasion, when the Marquis, who was daily becoming more nervous, sought him, with a favorable report of his prisoner-patient, did the Governor give sign that beneath this apparent apathy yet stirred malevolence and rancor.

"Yes, yes," he returned, a spark of ill-concealed venom in his glance; "he is doing well, no doubt! I am sure he will do well. But well or ill, I wish to hear no more of him! No more, Monsieur le Marquis!" His voice vibrated; surprised, the kinsman of the King stared, then stiffly turned away.

So matters stood, when one day, alone in the cloister, his Excellency was disturbed by a rough-looking fellow who brought a letter and said he would await the reply at the tavern in the town.

Deliberately the Governor took the missive, tore open the envelope, and surveyed the small bit of paper it contained. Whatever the brief message told him, his Excellency's face did not change, and he was still coldly, carefully studying sentences and words, after his fashion, when through the door my lord, the Marquis, stepped in some haste. Lifting his eyes, the Governor had no difficulty in reading the question on the young man's countenance. For a moment they looked at each other, and then the long, white fingers of his Excellency again sought the letter.

"They," his voice seemed to clip the words, "propose an exchange of prisoners, and give me three days to consent to it!"

CHAPTER XXX

A SOUND AFAR

About midway in the curve of one of the numerous bays, marking the coast-line, and several hours distant from the Mount, stands a stone cross erected by an English marauder to indicate the place of his landing. The symbol is visible on all sides from afar, for before it are the sands and the sea, and behind stretches the land barren of wood—low, level, covered only with marsh grass. Toward this monument of man's conquest—most prominent object in a prospect, dreary and monotonous—rode, late one afternoon, a band of horsemen. At their head galloped my lord, the Marquis; in the center could be seen a man with bound arms whose horse was led by one of the others. This person—a prisoner, thin, haggard, yet still muscular of frame—from time to time gazed about; a look of inquiry or calculation in the black undaunted eyes.

"What prison are you taking me to now?" once he asked the trooper who held the reins of his horse. "And why do you go in this direction? Is it you dare not ride along main highways on account of the people?"

"Never you mind!" came the gruff answer. "And as for the people, they'd better look out!"

"Bah!" laughed the prisoner. "You can put some of them in cells, but not all!"

"There may be something worse than a cell waiting for you!" was the malicious retort.

"No doubt!" said the other stoically.

But as his eyes again swept the horizon, from the opposite direction appeared another band of riders. At first the prisoner, regarding them, looked puzzled; then as the new-comers rode straight and rapidly on toward the cross, his countenance expressed a faint understanding. A fresh relay of men, he concluded; one his present guard would consign him to, and then themselves return to the Mount. Still was the meeting-place an odd one, and the demeanor of the two bodies of men not entirely consistent with his conclusions; for, as they drew nearer, both parties slackened their pace, suspiciously to scrutinize each other.

"Twenty—the number agreed upon!" muttered the Marquis, and spurring on fast, led his troops nearer the cross.

Not many paces distant the word was given to halt, and, as they obeyed, on the other side of the monument the strange men likewise drew rein. At the same moment, there flashed on the captive's mind a discovery. These faces, looking so grimly out over the marshy field at them, were not the wooden visages of paid soldiers, but of men he knew—his men! Across the space separating the two parties he could read their quick looks-their satisfaction—their complacency! He watched them with eyes in which pride and tenderness mingled. And then, for the first time, did he observe they had brought some one with them—a woman, or a girl—the Governor's daughter!

The bold black eyes of the prisoner regarded her fixedly. What did it mean? said his keen gaze. Colorless as marble, my lady held herself very erect on her horse; then while his glance yet probed her, the proud face slowly changed; on the cold cheek youth's bright banner flared high. The young man turned; following the direction of her gaze, looked at the Marquis; my lord's features radiated felicitations; his eyes shone with welcome. And a fuller understanding came over the prisoner; in some mysterious manner had the Lady Elise been made captive, and now had the nobleman come to escort his betrothed back to the palace.

My lady held herself very erect on her horse

My lady held herself very erect on her horse

Even as the Black Seigneur reached this conclusion, he become cognizant his bonds had been loosened; the reins placed in his hands. "You are free," said a voice and mechanically he rode toward his comrades.

Thus, near the crumbling and time-worn cross, was the exchange of prisoners effected; the girl whirled away by my lord, who seemed fearful of treachery, and the Black Seigneur left to the greetings of his men.

"Now, by the tuneful Nine,"—the poet, Gabriel Gabarie, pushing his burly form to the front, was the first to extend a hand—"but, from your looks, the Governor looks ill to the welfare of his lodgers!"

"And had we not captured my lady," spoke up another, gazing after the party of the Marquis, "he would have looked yet worse to the welfare of one of them, no doubt!"

"Drink this, Seigneur!" cried a third; "you must drink this—a special bottle we brought for the occasion!"

"Sent by old Pierre when he heard we were coming for you!" added the poet. "Your drinking-cups, lads! Unfasten the skin for yourselves! To mon capitaine!"—

Once, twice, deeply they drank—toast and vintage alike to their taste; then straightening, looked at the Black Seigneur whose eyes yet burned in the direction my lady had gone. With a start he seemed to recall himself to the demands of the moment; his first questions they expected; the ship—where did she lie? Snug and trim in a neighboring cove, ready to slip out, if occasion required and danger pressed—which contingency they did not just then expect, since at the moment was his Excellency more concerned with affairs on the land than matters pertaining to the sea. What these paramount interests were, the young man, on whose thin cheek now burned a little color, did not at once ask; only gazed inquiringly over the group, where one, whom he might have expected, was absent.

"Sanchez—he is not with you?"

A look of constraint appeared for an instant on the poet's face.

"No, he's with the people, I expect. You see," he went on, "things have been happening since you elected to enact the mountebank. The bees have been busy, and this little hive they call France is now full of bother and bustle. The bees that work have been buzzing about those that don't; they made a great noise at Versailles, but the King Drone only listened; did not try to stop it, fearing their sting. They hummed at the door of the Bastille, until the parasite bees, not liking the music, opened the doors, let them all in—"

"The Bastille has fallen?" The listener's voice rang out; his eyes, searching sharply the features of the bard, seemed to demand only the truth, plain, unadorned.

"It has," answered the other gravely. "And the tune sung in and around Paris has kept on spreading until now it is everywhere! You may hear it in the woods; along the marshes; out over the strand! The very Mount, immovable, seems to listen. When will the storm break? To-day? To-morrow? It needs but a word from Paris, and then—"

The poet broke off, and silently the Black Seigneur seemed to be weighing the purport of the news; for some moments stood as a man deep in thought; then, arousing himself, spoke a few words, and gave a brief order. Swiftly the riders swept away in the direction from which they had come, and only when they had gone some distance did the young man once more turn to the poet with a question. Whereupon the latter, spurring his horse nearer his chief, launched into eloquent explanation.

"And then," ended the bard, "the Governor's daughter walked into our ambush as unsuspectingly as a mouse into a trap!"

"The Governor's daughter cozened by Nanette!"

"That she was! A clever wench and a brave one, Nanette! Although," the poet's jovial eyes studied the dark face, "unless I am mistaken, she found the task to her liking!"

"You treated her, the Governor's daughter, well?" said the other abruptly.

"Gave her your cabin, mon capitaine, where," chuckling, "she ruled like a despot. Not once did she whimper, or beg favor—for herself! For the Marquis, it is true, she did plead—that day we took them!"

"He's her betrothed!" said the young man shortly.

"A marionette!" gibed the poet. "Some of the men were for making short shrift of him, and they might have—only for her!"

"They will soon be safe enough together now!" remarked the Black Seigneur.

Again a peculiar, half-questioning expression shaded the poet's eyes, while furtively he regarded the young man. "Yes, they ought to be!"

"The terms of exchange—what were they?"

"You for her! That was our demand. After the place had been agreed upon, his Excellency asked to name the hour, and further interjected a condition, binding both parties to secrecy in the matter, that the people might not know. They acted badly when the soldiers returned to the Mount without his daughter; they might behave worse, no doubt he thinks, when they come back with her."

"So will she be safely returned in the darkness! A wise provision!"

"That," murmured the poet, studying the horizon, "was evidently his thought. But," as the Black Seigneur, relaxing his pace, drew rein at a fork in the pathway, "yonder lies our cove, mon capitaine, and—"

"Do you and the men go there!" commanded the other, and gave a few further instructions.

"See that the ship is kept in readiness!" he ended. "As for me—" He made a vague gesture.

That evening found the Black Seigneur in the Desaurac forest; where, as a boy, he had fled for shelter, now some instinct, or desire he did not strive to analyze, drew him. As slowly he made his way through the wood, on every hand familiar outlines and details, seen vaguely in the last light of day, invited him to pause; but without stopping he moved on to the castle, and up to the chamber, where Sanchez, returning from America, had found him, a vagabond lad. Through the window the same unobstructed view of the Mount dimly unfolded itself in the dusk, and for some moments he regarded it—august, majestic; glossing its heart's black secrets with specious and well-composed bearing! As he looked, there suddenly came to him the remembrance of another impression; the same picture, seen through the eyes of a boy—standing where he was now! Then had the Mount seemed a marvelous series of structures, air-drawn, magical—home of a small and fairy-like creature, with hair of shining gold. Dusk turned to night; in the distance the Mount vanished, and through the break in the forest only the stars twinkled.

Then lighting his fire, the young man sat down at the side; with faculties alert, listened to the wind; looked at the flames. Demon-like they leaped before his eyes, as when he had waited and watched for the emissaries of his Excellency; and mechanically he placed his weapons on the same spot he had been wont to lay them in those days. There was little likelihood they would seek him now, however; the Governor was fully occupied elsewhere, looking to interests more important to himself and to—

Her ladyship! the fire leaped wildly, as laughing at fate's foolish prank. Her life for his! What irony! If she had betrayed him? "If?" His laugh crushed possibility for supposition; but almost at once itself died away! Indissolubly associated with the thought, a scene in a dungeon must needs recur; her denials; the touch of a hand; the appeal of light fingers thrust through the bars! Why? The questions he had asked then, were reiterated now; the hand that had gripped hers opened, closed; once more he seemed to see the steadfast, unswerving eyes; once more seemed to read in their depths, "Believe!"

The pine branches continued to crackle as with merriment; but his gaze was somber. How glad she must have been to see the end of her captivity! The sudden leaping of yonder flame was like the quick, bright flush that had mantled her cheek at sight of her liege lord to be! They should have arrived at the Mount ere now; about this time were entering the gates! He could see her, the Marquis at her side—

A sudden sharp detonation afar dissipated the picture. Other explosions followed, like volley of muskets; and, springing to the window, the Black

Seigneur looked toward the Mount; from it, flashes of light gleamed and glimmered. Then the loud report of a cannon reverberated in the distance.

CHAPTER XXXI

THE ATTACK ON THE MOUNT

The rock loomed black before them, as the troopers, escorting the Governor's daughter, rode up to the Mount. Entering the town, at its base, dark walls on either side of them shut out the broad map of the heavens and left but a narrow open space above; few lights were visible, so that many of the houses seemed tenantless; even at the tavern, unwonted stillness prevailed. Apparently was the return well-timed; in twisting street and tortuous byway, where hostile faces had been prone to frown upon the soldiers of his Excellency, emerging from, or ascending to, the stronghold of the summit, now only chill drafts of air swept down to greet them; passed on with shrill whisperings, and died away in the distance.

Nearing the massive portals that opened wide into his Excellency's realm, my lady suppressed a shiver; but the Marquis, in a low tone ventured to jest on the depressing and melancholy aspect of the Mount at that hour. To these light remarks she returned no answer, and he had just begun to rally her on a certain quietness of spirits, apparent on the beach and irreconcilable with the circumstances of the moment, when a sharp exclamation fell from the girl's lips.

In front of them, between the soldiers and the entrance to that upper part of the Mount, many dark forms had suddenly darted forth; at the same time from near-by houses came unmistakable sounds of life and activity; doors were thrown open and windows raised. The town they thought asleep had merely been watching; now showed its bright eyes in a multitude of menacing lights around them; below, where likewise a mysterious marshaling had occurred, from alleys, corners, and hovels, immediately after the passing of the Governor's party!

"What does it mean?" Again she heard the Marquis' tones, less confident now, as he turned to the commandant.

"Treachery!" The commandant's voice rang out. "They've broken faith with us!"

"Dogs!" My lord gazed uncertainly ahead; dubiously behind. "What are we going to do?"

"Do?" The commandant suppressed an imprecation. "Push on to the upper gates!"

"To the gates!" cried the Marquis; then wheeled quickly. "But you—Elise!"

"Never mind me!" she returned, with steady lips and eyes.

There was no time for further words; a sharp order from the commandant and the troopers spurred forward toward the entrance in the wall and those whose purpose it was to oppose them.

What happened thereafter the girl was but vaguely cognizant of; reports of guns, flashing of steel surrounded her; the clattering of hoofs mingled with the loud shouts of men.

"The Bastille of the North! Down with it!"

This was their battle-cry; on every side she heard it, though hardly realizing the purport of the words; confused, she listened to her father's name—her own—bandied about. She wondered why those on the wall, the soldiers within, did not fire and repel all these people.

Then almost at once came the answer. The troopers' comrades were mixed in the mêlée without; she and they, too—so adroitly had the moment for striking been planned—might be swept down in the volleys from the ramparts. A cannon boomed above; but its deafening reverberations were answered only with laughter and jeers— Mon dieu! Did his Excellency think to frighten them with sound, as if they were timid children fleeing from thunder? Was his Excellency aiming at stars?

And again that cry: "The Bastille of the North! We, too, will take our Bastille!"—dominated the clashing of arms and the tumult of strife.

For what seemed an interminable period, the Governor's daughter saw, through flashes of light, men struggling, striking; then launched suddenly forward, by an irresistible movement of the horses, found herself within the gates. The Marquis who had early been separated from her in the strife, was nowhere in sight. Behind now sounded the fray; a short distance from the wall, and she looked back; fiercer than ever, soldiers and people contended within the entrance; beneath the portals. As she strove to restrain her horse she heard the voice of her father.

"Mon père! Mon père!" she cried eagerly, divining his face in the light of lamps on that side of the wall. He answered only with a laconic command to go at once to the palace; and, regarding his features, tragically appealing to her at the moment—so strange and different they seemed!—she prepared to obey. But ere turning: "You think the soldiers can hold the gate?" she asked.

"Yes; yes!" he replied sharply, as if annoyed at the question.

"But if—"

"There is no 'if!" said the Governor, and as the girl rode away, his look, hard, steely, shifting to the soldiers, made quick mental note; they were holding the gates. Satisfied with the front his men presented, and, delivering a few brief orders to the commandant whose valor in rallying his forces had been commendable, his Excellency walked toward the great stairway leading up to the open space near the church. Arrived at this high point from which the town unfolded itself in the starlight and flicker of lamps, he sought, as best he might, to acquaint himself further with the situation; to judge the numbers of the assailants and the extent of their preparations.

The scene that met his eyes was not so reassuring as he had expected; that which until now he had considered but a spasmodic outbreak of a comparatively few townspeople, excited by the news of the Bastille and bent on any petty mischief, resolved itself into more than an orderless, desultory uprising. To his startled gaze the rock, like an ant-hill disturbed, seemed swarming with life. Even as he peered down, new relays of men poured upward from dark byways to the reinforcement of those already gathered at the portals, and, for the first time, his confidence, bred of contempt for the commonalty, became slightly shaken. Fate, which had struck him sharply in the capture of his daughter and the enforced negotiations leading to the release of one he would have dealt with after his own fashion, now gripped him closer. What did it portend? Whence came all these people?

Not all of them from the immediate neighborhood! Voices, among the assailants, had called out in what was surely the Parisian dialect of the rabble; here to propagate the revolution; extend the circle of flame! And they had seen that arms were not wanting! Muskets, pikes, swords, must have been kept concealed for some time in the town at the base of the Mount or on the shore. In his mind's eye, too late perhaps, his Excellency could see now how the assault had long been planned, how all these people had only been waiting. For what? The opportunity afforded by a treacherous word! Spoken by whom?

But a moment these reflections surged through his brain; an instant, and his gaze swung around, at towers—turrets—as a magician might apprehensively survey a fabulous architectural creation, handiwork of his dark craft, threatened, through an influence beyond his control, with destruction; then with a quick start, his Excellency wheeled; walked toward the stairway. About to descend, the sight of a figure coming up, caused him, however, to pause; in the flare of the light below, something in the manner of the man's advance impressed the governor as peculiar.

The movements of this person, who was under-sized, wiry, were agile and cat-like; first would he stop, look around him and listen; afterward spring forward a few steps as not quite sure of his course. But still he came on, keeping as closely as might be to the cover of shadows, until a growing impression he had seen the fellow before resolved itself into positiveness in his Excellency's mind. And with the conviction and a sudden remembrance of the place and the character of their previous meeting, a definite disinclination to encountering the figure on the stairs caused the Governor abruptly to draw into the entrance of the church. There, concealed, impatiently he waited for the man to pass on, thus affording him the opportunity to slip by and return to the gate.

Meanwhile, the Lady Elise had repaired to the palace; a prey to harassing doubts her father's words had failed to remove, she listened to those sounds of the strife she no longer saw. But that she wished to obey her father unquestioningly now—at, perhaps, a supreme moment for both of them!— she could not have remained where she was. Never had the palace looked so blank and deserted; she rang her bell; no one answered. The servants had apparently all left—gone, it might be, to look down on and behold this guerre à la mort waged near the gates. Or, perhaps, had they all, except the old nurse, fled from the palace, never to return?

As she asked herself these questions, in the distance the noise of the conflict grew louder; the shouts of the people more distinct, nearer! With a sudden premonition of disaster close at hand, the desire to see what was happening—to know the worst—seized her. No longer could she remain in her apartments; she must return to the ramparts—to her father; and then, if need be— The thought drove some of the color from her cheek, but in a moment her braver instincts spoke; there awoke within her the courage and the spirit of her Norman ancestry.

Pale, yet determined, she hastened down the long, dimly lighted corridor, and was nearing the door leading to the street when it suddenly opened and a man, tall and dark, showing in his appearance many signs of the fray, stepped in. At sight of her a quick exclamation fell from his lips; his bold, anxious eyes lighted. "My Lady!"

"You!" Her startled glance met his.

"I heard the firing; hastened to the Mount—here! I trust not too late!"

"Too late!" she repeated wildly. "Where else should the Black Seigneur be than here, at the Mount—at such a moment!"

"True!" he returned quietly. "Where else?"

She noted not the accent; behind him, through the open space a bright fork of flame, in the direction of the soldiers' barracks, shot into the air, and, at the same time, she saw that the officers' quarters and out-buildings glowed red. The knowledge of what it meant—that her apprehensions had been realized, sent a shudder through her, and quickly as the door closed, shutting out the sight, she ran toward the threshold, one thought in her mind—her father, and where she had last seen him! That she was seized, held, restrained, seemed but a natural, though terrible, incident of the moment.

"Pardon, my Lady! In a moment they will be here, and they will not spare you! Your father is not at the gate; he left before the soldiers gave way! Believe me, or not—it is the truth! As true as that, if you go out, they will kill you!"

And did he not want that; why else was he here? The young man's face darkened; he made an impatient gesture. They were but wasting time; already were the people close without; one of the assailants, a woman, had been shot in the assault; the others? Her Ladyship would understand; if she wished to save herself? His tones vibrated with strange eagerness. The palace had a rear entrance, of course? Then had they better flee upward to some place of concealment, and, later, when the people were concerned most in pillage, endeavor to find a way to leave the Mount. After that, it would be easy; his ship was waiting— Her wild words interrupted; her father—she would go only to him! She would never leave him now!

That which she proposed was impossible, quickly the young man answered. The mob—the terrible mob! Did she realize to what she would expose herself? Did she know the terrible danger? More plainly he told her. As for her going, it was not to be thought of; he must see she did not persist in her purpose.

"You?" My lady flashed him a glance. "You!" she repeated. "Whose men broke faith—"

"That may be!" His voice rang bitterly. "Yet," with stubborn resolution, "your Ladyship must not go!"

"Must not! And you presume—dare tell me that! You, the—"

"I would there were no need to cross you, my Lady," he returned, when behind him the door, leading from the street, suddenly opened; closed.

"Elise!" The voice of the Marquis, who had hurriedly entered, rang out; changed. "Mon dieu! What is this?" In the dim light, an instant my lord stared hard at the man before him; then with drawn blade threw himself upon him.

CHAPTER XXXII

NEAR THE ALTAR

"Morbleu! Here's a madman!" Ere the Black Seigneur could unsheathe his sword, that of the Marquis had pierced slightly his shoulder. "Put up your blade, my Lord!" As quickly springing back and drawing his own, he held himself in an attitude of defense. "In this matter are we, or should we be—of a mind!"

"We!" My lord's weapon played in fierce curves and flashes; he laughed derisively.

"I am here to serve her ladyship—if I can!"

"You!" A rapid coup de tierce was the Marquis' reply. "You! Whose outlaws carried her off before! You are pleased to jest, Monsieur Bandit!"

"No jest, my Lord!" coolly. "Moreover, it is you who serve her ladyship ill at such a moment in—"

"Mon dieu! You instruct!"

"I have no wish for this combat, Monsieur le Marquis!" As he spoke, the Black Seigneur retreated slowly toward the door. "But if you press too close—"

"Ma foi! You talk very brave, but I notice your legs take you backward. However, it will not serve; you shall not escape."

"No?" His back now against the door, the Black Seigneur defended himself with his right hand, the while his left felt behind for a bolt which it found; shot into place. "Then let us remove temptation by locking the door!"

"What! You did not, then, intend—"

A sudden fierce pounding from without on the door, interrupted.

"It was necessary to keep them out—but it will be only for the moment. So put up your blade!" peremptorily. "There is no time to lose."

"You are right!" The Marquis' face expressed scorn and unreasoning anger; his sword leaped to an accelerated tempo. "There is no time to lose. I shall honor you! The Marquis de Beauvillers will stoop to cheat the fourches pâtibulaires!" And my lord lunged, a dangerous and clever thrust that was met; answered. From the Marquis' hand the blade flew; struck the pavement; at the same time, a rending and tearing of wood came from the door.

The Black Seigneur leaped forward; but the stroke his adversary, now disarmed, expected, fell not on him; directed toward a lamp overhead, sole source of illumination of the corridor, the weapon struck hard. Shattered by the blow, the ornamental contrivance crashed to the floor; the place was plunged in darkness.

"Save yourself, my Lord!" said a calm voice, and my lady, standing now as it were, in the center of a vortex of wildly rushing figures, felt her waist suddenly clasped; herself swept on! Once or twice she struggled; resisted, hardly knowing what she did; but the sound of a low, determined voice, not unfamiliar to her, and the consciousness of a physical force—or was it all physical?—that seemed to beat down her will, left no choice but to obey.

Darkness gave way to waves of light; reflections of flame surrounded them; black trails of smoke coiled around. The girl's strength went; her breath came faster. A thick cloud choked her; she wished only to stop, when arms closed about her.

Upward! Still upward! By winding stairs, through passages and doorways, vaguely she felt herself borne, until a cold breath of air, blowing suddenly in her face, revived her; awoke her to a confused realization of the place they had at last reached—the upper platform at the head of the long, open stairway of granite. And with that consciousness, she again sought to free herself; but, for an instant the arms held her tighter, while a dark face bent close, scanning her features, then abruptly he released her.

"Your Ladyship is uninjured?"

"Yes: yes!"

"One moment!" Turning, he left her, and walking to the verge of that open space, searched quickly the waste of darkness below, far out to sea. The girl's glance followed him; wavered; her first apprehension awoke anew. Her father! Where was he? She clasped her hands despairingly as she gazed down the Mount; then around her. Suddenly, a bright patch of light—open doorway to the church—caught her eye and she started. At the picture, framed by the masonry, which the glow revealed, a low exclamation fell from her lips, and crossing the platform, and descending a few steps, she ran to the entrance of the sacred edifice.

"Eh, your Excellency; has your Excellency any orders?" sounded a voice.

There, before an altar, in the dim flicker of candles and the variegated gleaming from the ancient stained-glass windows, she saw at last him she sought; in one of the chapels, near the white marble monument to her mother, was his Excellency; but, not alone! Before him stood, or half crouched, the man Sanchez, who now was speaking.

"Shall I ring for your Excellency's servants and have the noise stopped?" Grotesquely he bowed, the while watching like an animal studying its prey. "Beppo! Where are you—fat rascal? Consign these swine to the gibbets! What! You can't obey because your ears have been cut off and your throat slit? That's too bad!" Fiercely the man laughed; then waved his arm toward the window, as if calling the Governor's attention to the sounds of demolition; the abrupt breaking of glass! "Patter! Patter! Merry little bullets, presents from the people, your Excellency! Métayage, your Highness!"

Still the other said no word; a figure, so motionless and white, it seemed but a wraith pausing at the side of its own "narrow house." A louder clamor without; a more vivid brightness of the red, yellow and purple hues, like a sudden wealth of strange flowers strewn on the marble floor, and again Sanchez laughed.

"Too bad! But 'tis I who must pay first! Who owe so much! Has your Excellency his strong box with him? Ah, he leans on it! Such a fine one, all of marble! Not easily broken into—or out of! Eh, your Excellency?" Swinging back something bright. "Full payment, this time! Not coppers, or round bits of lead, but steel, beautiful steel!"

Held to the spot by the abrupt terror and fascination of the scene, the Governor's daughter had made no sound, fearful of hastening the inevitable; but at the moment the man, with a last taunting word, launched forward, a cry, half articulate, burst from her lips. It was drowned by another voice, loud and commanding, which rang out from the entrance to the church.

"Sanchez!"

Perhaps the call disconcerted him; robbed the old servant's eye of its certitude; his arm of its sureness, for the blow aimed at his Excellency the latter was enabled to evade. At the same time, as with singular agility he moved aside to save himself, the hand the Governor had been holding to his breast, shot out like an adder. It struck viciously; stung deep—full in the side of his tormentor.

"That for your métayage!"

But a momentary expression of satisfaction was, however, permitted his Excellency; the petty tragedy became overshadowed by the greater!

"The Bastille! Our Bastille!"

And again a shower of bullets, directed in hatred, fell upon the church, because its windows were priceless; shone with saints of inestimable value! In the chapel, an aumbry and a piscina were struck; around the Governor, glass began to clatter and break into bits on the pavement, when suddenly he wavered; his hand sought his heart, then felt for and clung to the monument, as if abruptly seeking support.

"Why did you do it, Seigneur?" As my lady, exclaiming wildly, ran to her father, Sanchez, from where he lay, looked up to his master.

"Call out, I mean? Not that it matters much now!" His implacable glance, swerving to the Governor, lighted with satisfaction. "The people have paid. And 'twas I—showed them the way!"

"It was you, then—who broke faith in the negotiations for the exchange of prisoners?"

A smile came to the face of the old servant. "I had to," he said simply. "I alone am to blame. No one knew; except, perhaps, the poet, who may have surmised! It was treachery for treachery!" with sudden fierceness. "You could not have done it, nor your father, nor any of the seigneurs before him!" The young man seemed scarcely to hear; his glance had again sought my lady. "But I am only a servant—-and in dealing with a viper I used its own tricks! Did you think I had forgotten those stripes? Or the blow he gave your father—in the back?" A moment Sanchez's hand fumbled at his coat; drew out a bag of oilskin. "Here is something that belonged to your father. I took it from his breast the day he died, thinking some time—I can't tell what—only it contains a letter from the former lady of the Mount! When my master got it, he told me to pack a few belongings—that we were going— never to return!"

Sanchez's voice broke off; again he strove to speak; could not; put out his hand. Mechanically the Black Seigneur's closed on that of the old servant; even as it did so, the latter's fingers clutched suddenly; ceased to move. In the church now all was silent, but without arose discordant sounds, cries, harsh and vengeful, for the Governor!

Starting, the Black Seigneur gazed about, toward him they were clamoring for, now lying still, at the base of the monument. Then releasing the fingers, that seemed yet to hold him, the young man sprang forward, as my lady threw herself wildly, protectingly, over her father. At that touch, the Governor's eyes opened; met hers; the Black Seigneur's!

Nearer the door, now rang the shouts. His Excellency seemed to listen; to realize what they meant; to him—his daughter—

"The Governor! The Governor!"

"Trembles tyrans! Trembles!"

An ironical flash lit up, for an instant, the dying eyes. He, soon, would be beyond reach of these dogs—canaille! But she? His gaze again rested on the Black Seigneur; in that tense, fleeting second, seemed reading his very soul!

"Et la belle comtesse, sa fille!" cried the menacing voices.

A tremor crossed the Governor's face; his pale lips moved. "Forget! Save her!" An instant his eyes lingered persistently on the young man; then passed to his daughter; as they did so, slowly the light, more human and appealing than any that had ever shone there before, went out of them. My lady's fair head drooped until it lay on her father's breast; unconscious, she seemed yet to shield him with figure inert. But only for a moment!

"Et la belle comtesse!"

Stooping, the Black Seigneur snatched the slender form to his breast; ran back to the altar. There, looking around him, as one who made himself familiar with the place, his glance apparently found what it sought—a small stairway, entrance to the crypt. At the same time he started to descend, the people swept into the church.

CHAPTER XXXIII

ON THE SANDS

A man, bearing in his arms the motionless form of a woman, paused later that night in the shadow of a low stone hovel, near the lower gate of the Mount. As he crouched beneath the thatch projecting like the rim of an old hat above him his eyes, eager, fierce, studied the distance he had yet to traverse from the end of the narrow alley, where he had stopped, to the open entrance at the base of the rock to the sands. The goal was not far; but a few moments would have sufficed to reach it; only between him and the point he had so long been striving to attain, an obstacle, or group of obstacles, intervened. Before a bonfire of wreckage of stuff—furniture and household goods—several ragged, dissolute fellows sat with bottles before them, drinking hard and quarreling the while over a number of glittering gems, gold snuff-boxes and trinkets of all kinds.

"This bit of ivory for the white stone!"

"Add the brooch!"

"Not I! Look at the picture! Her ladyship, perhaps!"

"They have not found her?"

"No; for all the searching! But she is somewhere; can't have escaped from the Mount. And when the drabs and trulls lay hands on her!"

"Ay, when!" casting the dice.

The man, peering from the alley, hesitated no longer; behind sounded the footsteps of others, and gathering his burden more firmly, he strode boldly forth toward the group and the gate. At his approach, their talk—a jargon of "thieves' Latin" that smacked more of the cabarets of Paris than those of the coast—momentarily ceased; beneath lowering brows, they stared hard.

"What have you there, comrade?" said one.

"Look and see!" answered the man in a rough tone.

"Poor booty! A woman!" quoted another with a harsh laugh. "You're easily pleased. As if wenches were not plentiful enough on other occasions, without wasting time on a night like this, when diamonds and gold are to be had for the searching!"

"And silver plates and watches and rare liquors!" cried a third in knaves' argot. "Every one, however, to his taste! An you prefer a light-of-love to light such as these have," juggling with the gems, "you but stamp yourself a fool."

"You're welcome to your opinion, my friend!" The man with the burden spoke bruskly. "Good night!"

"Stay; why such haste? You seem not a bad fellow. Set the wench down. We'll have sight of her, and, perhaps," with coarse expletives, "if she's a pretty face, and a taste for this fiery liquor the old monks laid down, we'll find a gewgaw or two to her liking!"

But the man made no answer; was about to pass on, when the speaker noticed for the first time the woman's hand, white and small, hanging limply. "What's this? More jewels?" His exclamation was caught up by the others. "Not so fast, comrade! This puts a different face to the matter. Set down the booty, and," springing to his feet, "we'll see what it's worth."

"I'll not stop!" The man looked at him steadily. "On the Mount is, or should be, plenty for all! Go seek for yourself!"

"Pardi!" softly. "Here's one dares speak his mind!"

"I speak plainly," in a tone of authority, "and you would do well to heed!"

"Perhaps," interposing. "What say you, comrades?"

Evil smiles illumined evil faces; they, who had just been on the point of blows among themselves, now regarded one another with common understanding. One weighed tentatively that delicate weapon, a spontoon; a second stroked his halberd, as liking to feel the smoothness of the shaft, while a third reached for a gleaming "Folard's Partizan." And in the glare of the fire every implement showed sign it had been used that night. The point of the spontoon was as steel crusted o'er; the ax of the halberd might have come from a boucherie; the blade of the "Partizan" resembled a great leaf at autumn-time. This last wavered perilously near the unconscious burden; had the man made a movement to resist, would have struck; but the black eyes, only, combated—held the blood-shot ones. Though not for long; again the weapon seemed about to dart forth; the man about to hurl himself and his burden desperately aside, when, from above, came the sound of hoarse laughing and singing, and simultaneously a number of peasants, Bretons by their dress, burst into view.

"Eh, cockatoo, what now!"

Many of these new-comers were hurt; few free from cuts; but none thought of stanching their wounds. Their principal concern seemed for articles they carried—heavy, light; valuable, paltry—spoils from the high! Two staggered beneath a great chest stamped with the arms of the Mount and its motto, and appeared anxious to hurry—perchance toward the forest on the shore where they might bury their treasure. Others had in their arms imposing pieces of silver; vases and a massive surtout de table that had once belonged to the Cardinal Dubois. A woman, gaunt, toothless, wore a voluminous bonnet à l'Argus, left at the Mount by one of the ladies of the court; and waved before her a fan, set with jewels. She it was who called out:

"Eh, cockatoo!" shrilly. "Who would you be killing?"

"A selfish fellow that refuses to share!" answered he of the halberd, as if little pleased at the interruption.

"Refuses to share, does he?" she repeated, and, swaggering down, peered forward; only to start back. "The Black Seigneur!"

"The Black Seigneur!"

Those who accompanied her—a rough rabble from field and forest—gazed, not without surprise, or uncouth admiration, at one whose name and fame were well-known on that northern coast; but these evidences of rough approval were not shared by the alien rogues. On my lady's finger the gem still sparkled: held their eyes like a lure. Black Seigneur, or not, they muttered sullenly, what knew they of her he had with him; whose hand was not that of cinder-wench or scullery maid? Let them look at her face! She might be a great lady—she might even be the Governor's daughter herself!

"The Governor's daughter!" All, alike, caught at the word.

"An if she were!" fiercely the Black Seigneur confronted them.

While, hesitating, they sought for a reply, quickly he went on. Who had a better right to her? The Black Seigneur! The Lady Elise! Harshly he laughed. Was it not fair spoil? His Excellency's enemy; his Excellency's daughter. Did they think treasure sweeter than revenge? Let them try to rob him of it! As for the ring? Contemptuously he took it from my lady's hand; threw it among them.

A few scrambled, others were still for finishing the tragedy then. The people versus the lords and their spawn. "Kill at once!" the injunction had gone forth from Paris.

As he spoke, one of the fiercest put out his hand; touched my lady, when the fingers of the Black Seigneur gripped hard his throat; hurled him so violently back, he lay still. Companions sprang to his aid; certain of the peasants interfered.

"Let him alone!"

"He speaks fair!"

"Bah! To-night are all equal."

"Your Black Seigneur no better than others!"

"You lie!" In a high tone the woman with the great lady's hat broke in. "At them, my chickens! Beat well these Paris rogues, who come only for the picking!"

"Yes; beat them well!"

But the runagates of the great city were not of a kind to submit lightly; curses and blows were exchanged; knives gleamed and swords flashed. Amid a scene of confusion, the cause of it stayed not to witness the outcome; running down the sloping way, soon found himself on the sands; then keeping to the shadows, passed around the corner of the wall.

Here, for the time concealed was he safe; none followed, and, leaning against the damp blocks of masonry, breathing hard, as a man weak from fatigue, loss of blood, he sought to recover his strength. It returned only too slowly; the passing lassitude annoyed him; for the moment he forgot he had but recently come from the dungeon and the hardships that sap elasticity and vigor. He was impatient to move on; looked at my lady—and a sudden fear smote him! How white she appeared! Had she— His hand trembled at her heart; a blank dismay overcame him; then joy— At that instant he thought not of the gulf between them; was conscious only he held her—slender, beautiful—in his arms; that she seemed all his own, with her breath on his cheek, her soft lips so close. Above sounded the madness of the night; the crackling of flames; the intemperate voices! In the angle of the wall, with darkness a blanket around them, he pushed back the hair from her clear brow, bent over, closer—suddenly straightened.

"Pardi!" he muttered, a flush on his face. "Am I, then, like the others— pillagers, thieves?"

Several moments he yet stood, breathing deep; then, starting away, set himself to the task of crossing the vast stretch of beach between the Mount and the distant lights of a ship.

The sandy plain had never seemed so interminable; before him, his shadow and that of my lady danced ever illusively away; behind, the great rock gave forth a hundred shooting flames, while, as emblematic of the demolition of so much that was beautiful, higher than saint with helpless sword on cathedral top, a cloud of smoke belched up; waved sidewise like a monstrous funeral plume. A symbol, it seemed to fill the sky; to move and nod and flaunt its ominous blackness from this majestic outpost of the land. Walking in a vivid crimson glow, the Black Seigneur gazed only ahead, where now, on that monotonous desert, the rim of the sea on a sudden obtruded. As he advanced, sparkles red as rubies—laughing lights—leaped in the air; at the same time a seething murmur broke upon the stillness.

Toward those leaping bright points and the source of that deep-sounding cadence, the young man stumbled forward more rapidly, less cautiously, also, it may be; for while he was yet some distance from the water's rim, his feet fell on sand that gave way beneath them. He would have sprung back, but felt himself sinking; strove to get out, only to settle the deeper! The edge of the lise, with safety beyond, well he could see, where the satin-like smoothness of the treacherous slough! merged into a welcome silk-like shimmering of the trustworthy sands. That verge, however, was remote; out of reach of effort of his to attain; his very endeavors caused him to become the more firmly imbedded. Had he cast my lady aside, possibly could he have extricated himself; but with her, an additional weight, weighing him down—

Loudly he called out; only the sea answered. Now were the clinging particles at his waist; he lifted my lady higher; clear of them! Once more raised his voice—this time not in vain!

"Mon capitaine! Where are you?"

"Here!"

"We don't see you."

"You won't soon, unless—"

The end of a line struck the sand.

The night had almost passed; its last black hour, like a pall, lay over the sea, where, far from the Mount, a ship swayed and tossed. In the narrow confines of her master's cabin, the faint glimmering of a lamp revealed a man bending over a paper, yellow and worn; the lines so faint and delicate, they seemed almost to escape him!

"How strange, after all these years, the sight of your handwriting!—and now, to be writing you! Yet is it meet—to say farewell! For that which you have heard, mon ami, is true. I am going to die. You say, you heard I was not well; I answer what really you heard; the question, mon ami, beneath your words! ... And, dying, it is well with me. I have wronged no soul on earth—except you, my friend, and you forgive me.... I had hoped the years would efface that old memory. You say they have not.... It is wise you are going away."

The reader paused; listened to the sea; the moaning and sighing, like voices on the wings of the storm.

"You speak in your letter about 'trickery'—used to estrange us! Think no more of it, I beg you. What is past, is gone—as I, part of that past, when we were boy and girl together—soon shall be. And come not near the Mount. There can be no meeting for us on earth. I send you my adieu from afar.... It is only a shadow that speaks ... mon ami."

CHAPTER XXXIV

SOME TIME LATER

The little Norman isle, home of Pierre Laroche, so wild and bleak-looking many months of the year, resembles a flowering garden in the spring; then, its lap full of buds and blossoms, smiling, redolent, it lifts itself from the broad bosom of the deep. And all the light embellishments of the golden time it sets forth daintily; fringing the black cliffs with clusters of sea campion, white and frothy as the spray, trailing green ivy from precipitous heights to the verge of the wooing waters, whose waves seem to creep up timorously, peep into the many caves, bright with sea-anemones, and retreat quickly, as awed by a sudden glimpse of fairyland.

Near the entrance of one of these magical chambers, abloom with strange, scentless flowers, sat, a certain afternoon in April, a man and a woman, who, looking out over the blue sea, conversed in desultory fashion.

"From what your father tells me, Mistress Nanette," the man, an aged priest, was speaking, "the Seigneur Desaurac should be here to-day?"

"My father had a letter from him a few days ago to that effect," answered the young woman somewhat shortly.

"Let me see," apparently the old man did not notice the change in his companion's manner, "he has been away now about a year? It was in July he brought the Governor's daughter to the island one day and sailed the next!" Nanette made a movement. "How time flies!" he sighed. "Let us hope it assuages grief, as they say! You think she is contented here?"

"The Lady Elise? Why not? At least, she seems so; has with her, her old nurse, my aunt, who fortunately escaped from the Mount—"

"But the death of her father? It must have been a terrible blow—one not easy to forget!"

"Of course," said Nanette slowly, "she has felt his loss."

The old man gazed down. "I have sometimes wondered what she knows about the causes of the enmity that existed between his Excellency and the Black Seigneur?"

The other's eyes lifted keenly. "When last did you see her, Father?"

"She comes often to my cottage to walk and—"

"Talk?"

"Well, yes!" The fine spiritual face expressed a twinge of uneasiness.

"About the past?"

The priest shifted slightly. "Sometimes! An old man lives much in the past and it is natural to wander on a bit aimlessly at times, and—"

"Confess, Father, she has learned much from you?" Nanette laughed.

"No, no; I trust—"

"Surmised, then!" said the girl. "She is one not easily deceived. Clever is my lady! And you talk, she says nothing, but leads you on! If there's aught she wishes to learn that you know, be assured she's found out from your lips."

"Nay; I'll not believe—'tis true once or twice I've let a word slip. But she noticed not—"

"No doubt!" The island girl's voice expressed a fine scorn. "However, it matters little. Speaks she ever of the Black Seigneur?" suddenly.

"No. Why?"

"Why not?" Nanette's tone was enigmatic.

"I don't understand."

"At any rate, she is better off here than yonder in France, if tidings be true," said the other irrelevantly.

"Ah, ma belle France!" murmured the old man regretfully. "How she is torn within—threatened from without! But fortunately she has her defenders," his voice thrilled, "brave men who have thronged to her needs. I suppose," he continued abruptly, "it's to arrange about the new ship that brings the Seigneur once more to the island?"

"I suppose so," assented the other briefly.

"A true Frenchman, Pierre Laroche, your father, has shown himself, in giving one of his best ships to the cause! Although perhaps he would not have been so ready," thoughtfully, "had not the Paris Assembly seen fit to appoint André Desaurac in command of all the vessels to guard the coast against the intrigues of the French royalists with foreign powers and aliens! Well, well, he will find here many old friends!"

"Yourself, for example, Father, who helped him in the courts to establish his right to his name," said the young woman quickly.

"And you, Mistress Nanette," the kindly eyes lighting with a curious, indulgent look, "who went to the Mount alone, unaided, to—"

A frown gathered on the dark, handsome face of the girl. "Unaided?" she said, staring at the sparkles on the waves before her.

"Oh, the people never weary of talking about it! and how you—"

"Yon's a sail!" Abruptly the young woman rose; with skirts fluttering behind her, gazed out to sea.

Several hours later, just before dusk, a ship ran into the harbor, dropped anchor, and sent a boat to the shore. In the small craft sat a number of men, and the first of these to spring to the beach and mount the stone stairway to the inn, was met at the top; warmly greeted, by old Pierre himself! Mon dieu! To see the new-comer was like old times! Only now, the landlord observed jestingly, the profits would be small! But a fig to parsimony, in these days when men's patriotism should be large; do what he, the Black Seigneur, would with the new ship, even if he sunk her, provided it was in good company, and he went not down with her himself! To which protestations the other answered; presented his companions, and greeted the assembled company within.

Busy at a great board, laden with comestibles interspersed with flagons of wines, Nanette welcomed him briefly, and again his glance—keen and assured, that of a man the horizon of whose vision had widened, since last he stood there—swept the gathering. But apparently, one he looked for was not present, and he had again turned to the young woman, a question on his lips, when on the garden side of the house a door opened. It revealed a flowering background, a plateau, yellow in the last rays of the sun; it framed, also, the slender, black-clad figure of a girl, above whose white brow the waving hair shone like threads of gold.

"An old friend of yours, my Lady!" called out blunt Pierre.

A moment the clear, brown eyes seemed to waver; then became steady, as schooled to some purpose. She came forward composedly; gave the Black Seigneur her hand.

"I—am always glad to see old friends!" said my lady, with a lift of the head, over-conscious, perhaps, of the concentrated gaze of the company.

He looked at her; made perfunctory answer; she seemed about to speak again, when the hand he let fall was caught by another.

"Elise!" From among those who had come ashore, a man in fashionable attire sprang forward, a little thinner than when last she had seen him, and more cynical-looking, as slightly soured by world-contact and the new tendencies of society.

"My Lord!" Certainly was my lady taken unawares; a moment looked at the Marquis as if a little startled; then at the Black Seigneur:

"A pleasant surprise for you, my Lady!" said the latter. "But you owe me no thanks! An order from the chief of the Admiralty, properly signed and countersigned, directing me to transport the Marquis de Beauvillers hither, was not to be disregarded!"

"A somewhat singular dispensation of Providence, nevertheless!" observed the nobleman dryly. "After our—what shall we call it?—little passage of arms? You must acknowledge, however, that in truth the Lady Elise and myself had some reason to discredit your assurances that night—"

"Far be it from me to dispute it, my Lord," and the Black Seigneur turned, while the Marquis, slightly shrugging his shoulders, addressed my lady.

Half blithely, then half bitterly, relapsing occasionally from the old, debonair manner he had assumed, he spoke of his escape from the Mount; months of hiding in foul places, amid fields and forest, with no word of her; his success, at last, in reaching Paris, and, through rumor, learning where she was, and hastening to her—

A bluff voice interrupted further explanations and avowals; the steaming flesh-pots, it informed the company, awaited not soft words and honied phrases; monarch in his own dining-room, ostentatiously conscious, perhaps, of his own unwonted prodigality, Pierre Laroche waved them to their places—where they would!—so that they waited not!

Quizzically my lord lifted his brow; truly here was a Republican fellow who appreciated not an honor when it was bestowed upon him, nor saw anything unusual in a Marquis' presence beneath that humble roof. Something of this he murmured to my lady, in a tone others might have heard; but she answered not; took her place, with red lips the firmer, as if to conceal some weakness to which they sought to give way.

Not without constraint the meal passed; the host, desirous to learn the latest political news, looked at the Marquis and curbed a natural curiosity, until a more favorable moment when he and the Black Seigneur should be alone. My lady, although generally made to feel welcome and at home there, seemed now, perhaps, to herself, a little out of place, like a person that has wandered from a world of her own and strayed into another's. Cross-currents, long at strife in her breast, surged and flowed fast; the while she seemed to listen to my lord, who appeared now in lighter, more airy humor. And as she sat thus, with fair head bent a little, she could but hear, at times, above the medley of tones and the sound of servants' footsteps in clattering wooden shoes, the voice of the Black Seigneur—now pledging a toast to old Pierre; anon discussing winds, tides, or ships! A free reckless voice, that seemed to vibrate from the past—to stir anew bright, terrible flames.

Daylight slowly waned; lights were brought in, and, the meal over, old Pierre pushed back in his chair. My lady rose quickly; looked a little constrainedly at the company, at the Marquis, then toward the door. Anticipating her desire, attributing to it, perhaps, a significance flattering to his vanity, the young nobleman expressed a wish for a stroll; a sight of the garden. At once she assented; a slight tint now on her cheeks, she moved to the door, and my lord followed; as they disappeared, the Black Seigneur laughed—at one of Pierre's jokes!

"Have I not told it before?" said the host.

"Have you?" murmured the Black Seigneur. "Well, a good jest, like an excellent dish, may well be served twice."

"Humph!" observed thc landlord doubtfully.

After a pause: "I suppose he will be taking her away soon?"

"Her?" The young man rose.

"The Lady Elise!"

"I suppose so," shortly.

"We shall miss her!" grumbled the landlord as he, too, got up and walked over to the fireplace. "I, who never thought to care for any of the fine folk—I, bluff old Pierre Laroche!—say we shall miss her."

"Knows she how it fared with his Excellency's—her father's—estate? That little, or nothing, is left?"

"Aye."

"And she will agree to the promise I wrote you about?" quickly.

"That you—now that the right to your name has been vindicated—are content to accept half the lands in dispute; her ladyship to retain the other half?"

"Yes; in consideration of that which his Excellency expended in taxes—no small sum!—and what it would cost to carry on vexatious litigation!"

"You are strangely faint-hearted to pursue your advantage," said old Pierre shrewdly. "But," as the other made a gesture, "I put it to her ladyship as you desired me to, and—"

"She consented?" eagerly.

Pierre shook his head. "No, mon capitaine! She will have none of them. And you had heard her: 'A great wrong was unintentionally,' she accented the word, 'done the Seigneur Desaurac by my father, which has now been set right!' 'It has,' I assented, and would have urged further your proposal, when she stopped me. 'Speak no more of this matter!' 'Twas all she said; but—you should have seen her face, and how her eyes shone!"

The young man, looking down, made no answer. "An you are not satisfied," continued Pierre, "broach the question to my lady, yourself."

"I?" A look, half bitter, crossed the other's dark face. "Her father's enemy! Through whose servant, all her misfortunes came about! To revive anew what must so often pass in her mind?"

"Well, well; no doubt you know best, and, certes, now you remind me, she did turn cold and distant when I spoke of your coming. But let idle prejudices enter into practical concerns—it's on a par—of all improvidence! Why, 'twas not long ago, she brought me a jewel or two; Marie, it seems, had foresight enough to snatch them before fleeing from the Mount, and begged me to take them for our kindness, she said; which I did, seeing she would not have it otherwise—nor let herself be regarded as one who could not pay. But to business, mon capitaine!"

And thereafter, for some time, they, or rather, Pierre, talked; the others, save the Marquis, returned to the ship, and only Nanette, busy putting everything to rights, lingered in the room. At length, after papers had been signed and changed hands, the conversation of the host began to wane; frequently had he sipped from a bottle of liqueur at his elbow and now found himself nodding; leaned back more comfortably in the great chair and suffered his head to fall. The clock ticked out the seconds; the young man continued to sit motionless.

"'A mon beau'—" Nanette's voice, lightly humming, caused him to look up; with the old mocking expression on her face, the inn-keeper's daughter paused near his chair.

"It was kind of you, mon capitaine, to bring to my lady her Marquis!" As she spoke, she looked toward the garden.

"Why not?" he asked steadily. "The passport and orders were correct."

"Were they, indeed?" she said, tapping the floor with her foot. "You remain with us a few days; or, as of old, must we be content with a brief visit?" she went on.

"We leave to-morrow."

"To-morrow?" The girl's eyes wore a tentative expression. "Late?"

"Early!"

"Oh! In that case, perhaps I shan't have time," Nanette paused; looked at her father; old Pierre's slumbers were not to be broken.

"For what?" asked the Black Seigneur shortly.

"To tell you something!"

"Why not—now?"

"You—are inquisitive?"

"No!"

"Even if it were about—" she looked toward the door that led to the garden.

"The Lady Elise?" he said quickly.

"Oh, you are interested? 'A mon beau'—" a moment she hummed. "You do not urge me?"

"Wherefore," laconically, although his eyes flashed, "when you have made up your mind to tell!"

"You are right!" She threw back her head. "I have made up my mind! How well you understand women! Almost as well," she laughed mockingly, "as a ship!" He made no response. "When you thanked me once, mon capitaine, for all it pleased you to say I did for you, you may remember," her voice was defiant, "I did not once gainsay you!" More curiously he regarded her. "Perhaps it pleased me," her hand on her hip, "to be thought such a fine heroine. But now," her tone grew a little fierce, "I am tired of hearing people say: 'Nanette risked so much!' 'Nanette did this!—did that!'—when it was she who risked—did it all, one might say."

"She? What do you mean?" The black eyes probed hers now with sudden, fierce questioning.

"That 'twas the Lady Elise saved you. Went knowingly—willingly—as hostage—"

"The Lady Elise!" he cried, an abrupt glow on the dark face.

Nanette's eyes noted and fell, but she went on hurriedly: "She knew of the ambush in the forest; saw part of the note I dropped on the beach—it was brought to her by my aunt who warned her." And in a quick rush of words, as if desirous to be done with it, Nanette told all that had transpired at the Mount.

Incredulously, eagerly, he listened; when, however, she had finished, he said nothing; sat like a man bewildered.

"Well?" said the girl impatiently. Still he looked down. "Well?" she repeated, so sharply old Pierre stirred; lifted his head.

"Eh, my dear?"

She went to the mantel; took from it a candle.

"The Seigneur finds you such poor company," she said, "he desires a light to retire!"

The dawn smote the heavens with fiery lashes of red; from the east the wind began to blow harder, and on the sea the waves responded with a more forcible sweep. At a window in the inn, the Black Seigneur a moment looked out on the gay flowers and the sea and the worn grim face of the cliff; then left his room and made his way downstairs. No one was yet, apparently, astir; an hour or so must elapse ere the time set for departure, and, pending the turn of the tide and adieu to old Pierre, the young man stepped into the garden, through the gate, and, turning into a rocky path, strode out over the cliffs. The island was small; its walks limited, and soon, despite a number of difficulties in the way he had chosen, he found himself at its end—the verge of a great rock that projected out over the blue, sullen sea. For some moments he stood there, listening to the sounds in caverns below, watching the snow-capped waves, the ever-shifting spots on a vast map, and then, shaking off his reverie, started to return.

"A brisk wind to take us back to France," he said to himself; but his thoughts were not of possible April storms, or of his ship. His eyes, bright, yet perplexed, as if from some problem whose solution he had not yet found, were bent downward, only to be raised where the path demanded his closer attention. As he looked up, he became suddenly aware of the figure of a girl, who approached from the opposite direction.

A quick glint sprang to the young man's eyes, and, pausing, he waited; watched. At that point, the way ran over a neck of rock, almost eaten through by the hungry sea, and she had already started to cross when he first saw her. The path was not dangerous; nor was it easy; only it called for certainty and assurance on the part of the one that elected to take it. My lady's light footstep was sure; although the wind swept rather sharply there, she held herself with confident poise, while from the brown eyes shone a clear, steady light.

"I saw you leave the inn," she said, drawing near the comparatively sheltered spot, where he stood, "and knowing you would soon sail, followed. There is something I wanted to say, and—and felt I should have no other chance to tell you!"

Had she read what was passing in his brain, she would not have faced him, so confident; but, ignorant of what he had learned, the cause of varying lights in his dark eyes, the tender play of emotion on his strong features, she broached her subject with steadfastness of purpose.

"You went away so suddenly the last time, I had no opportunity, then, to thank you for all that you did; and so, I do now—thank you, I mean! Also," a touch of prouder constraint in her tone, "I appreciate your over-generous proposal through Pierre Laroche; although, of course," her figure very straight, "I could not—it was impossible—to entertain it. But I am glad you were able to prove. You will understand—and," my lady ended quickly, "I thank you!"

He looked at her long. "It is I who am in your debt!"

"You?" Her brows lifted.

"Yes."

"I—don't think I quite understand." In spite of herself and her resolution, the proud eyes seemed to shrink from a nameless something in his gaze.

"Nor I! Nanette was talking with me last night!"

"Nanette!"

In words, direct, unequivocal, he told her what he had learned; and although my lady laughed, as at something absurd, and strove to maintain an unvarying mien, his eyes challenged evasion; demanded truth! At that moment the space where they stood seemed, perhaps, too small; to hem her very closely in—too closely—as, drawing back, she touched the hard rocky wall!

"Why?" Still endeavoring to regard him as if the charge could only be preposterous, too unreasonable to answer, she was, nevertheless, conscious of the flame on her face—tacit refutation of the denials in her eyes! "Why?" she repeated.

"That is just what I was asking myself when I saw you, my Lady."

"And, of course, knowing there could be no—that it was too senseless—" The words she was searching for failed her; she looked toward the path over the neck of rock, but he continued to stand between it and her.

"I have heard the story in all its details; all that passed at the Mount, while Nanette was there. And," instead of having undermined his belief, she felt she had only strengthened it, "I am sure you went to the Monastery St. Ranulphe, knowing—"

"You are sure!" she interrupted quickly. "It wasn't long ago you were sure it was I who betrayed you, and—"

"I was wrong, then; but," his eyes continued to meet hers, "I am not wrong now."

Behind her, my lady's hand closed hard on the rock.

"Deny it!" his voice went on. "In so many words!"

"Why should I?" She caught her breath quickly. "I denied something to you once, and you did not believe."

"I'll believe you now!"

"I should feel very much flattered, I am sure; but after—" A spark of defiance began to gleam in her eyes. "You are sure one moment, and not, the next! You are ready to believe, or not to believe!" More certain now, she lifted her head; she, whose assurance and wit had never failed her at court, would not be put to confusion by him!

His answer was unexpected; to her; to himself. Perhaps it was the peasant— the untamed half-peasant—in his blood that caused it; that made a sudden, unceremonious act, his reply! He caught both her hands; drew her to him. He knew she could never care for him—she, the beautiful lady! But he forgot himself for the moment; thought only of what she had done; her courage, her fineness, her delicate loveliness! Her life for his. To pay a fancied debt, perhaps? And all the while he had thought— Self-reproaches fell from his lips; were followed by bolder, more daring words. All he would have said the night on the beach, when he had borne her from the fiery rock to the ship, now burst from him; all he had felt when he had held her in his arms— motionless, unresisting, the still, white face upturned, offering itself freely to his gaze!

At the neck of the rock, beneath his feet, the waves thundered; near them, wild birds circled, wheeled and were borne on by the strong breath of the wind. Had he spoken; what had he said? A gradual consciousness of the beating of the sea smote his senses, as with rhythmical regularity it arose. He listened; slowly in his eyes that light that demanded—claimed, as it were, its own—was replaced by another; his hands released hers. My lady made no sound; her proud lips trembled. Very pale, she leaned back.

So silence lengthened. "Pardon, my Lady!" he said at last, very humbly. "It had not occurred to me my secret was not safe; that I, master of ships and men, should not be master of myself! But I had not expected to be alone with your Ladyship, and," a shadow of a smile crossed the strong, reckless face, "your Ladyship can weigh the provocation! If the excuse will not serve, I have none other to offer. Certainly, will I retract nothing. What's said, is said, and—no lies will unsay it!"

He looked at the water; the tide was nearly in; he turned. She would never see him again, for which she would be very glad, since the sight of him must always have been hateful to her. Had not fate decreed—bitterly—she should look upon him only as an enemy? It might be, in time, she would condone his presumption, when his presence would no longer vex her! He was going one way; she, another, soon, with—

"You—you are mistaken, Monsieur!" My lady's tone was tremulous.

"Mistaken?"

"The—Marquis de Beauvillers left last night, on a fishing bark."

"Left!" abruptly he wheeled. "Why?" She did not answer. "You mean?" Before the sudden swift question that shone from his eyes, hers fell.

"Speak!" He seized her hand; his dark, eager face was near hers now. "You have sent him away? He will never return?" She lifted her head; answered not in words; but a new light in her eyes met the flash of his. "My Lady!" he cried, bewildered for the moment at what that glance revealed. An instant she seemed once more striving to combat him, when, drawing her gently toward him, he bent lower; kissed softly her lips.

 His dark, eager face was near hers now

His dark, eager face was near hers now

"Is it, then, true—"

"You find it so hard to believe?"

"That you love me? That I seem no longer your enemy?"

"My enemy? You? Who risked so much—saved my life! Ah, no, no! Do you not remember," softly, "he, too, said—'Forget!'"

"I only remember I have long loved you! For me have you ever been the princess—who dwelt in the clouds—in a palace, enchanted—" Her face changed. "That saddens you! Forgive me!"

"It seems like a dream—that life, then! All made up of lightness and gaiety; courtiers and fine masques, until—" Beneath the bright gold of her hair, my lady's brow knit.

"Until?"

"Nay; I know not until—just when! Only, for long, I seem to have lived in a world, unreal and false. Last night, when in the garden, I felt stifled. This marriage! Arranged—for what?" She made a quick gesture. "The words came—had to come—though they hurt my lord's pride; touched his vanity! Nothing deeper! It was gone. Besides—"

My lady stopped. "Go on!" he urged, his voice eager.

"That is all. At least, all I would acknowledge to myself, then."

"And now?" His arm tightened; he held my lady close. "Now?"

Her lips lifted; though silent, made answer in the abandonment of the moment, the past and all its vicissitudes vanished; only the present held them—the present and the future, beautiful as the horizon, now rosy and glowing beneath the warm touch of the dawn.

The tide came in and the tide went out.

"Mon capitaine must have changed his mind," said old Pierre at the inn. And he gazed toward a ship, stranded on the sands of the harbor.

THE END